TITANS

"FROM THE STARS"
SERIES

BOOK ONE

A NOVEL BY C. M. STEPHENS

All vectors and all fonts are royalty-free and free for commercial use: Vectors from All-Silhouettes and by VEDI; Typeface: Libre Baskerville by Pablo Impallari; CINZEL by Natanael Gama; Cardo by David Perry; Bilbo, Ruthie, by TypeSETit; Leafy Glade by West Wind Fonts; Angelina by Anja Denali; Victorian Designs One, and Deco Dividers, by Sassy Graphics; Cover and Map by LMR.

Summary: Adara learns about her family's secret legacy and has to choose between her husband and the man from her distant past, all while preparing for a fight against an ancient evil that has been spreading across Earth for countless generations.

ISBN-13: 978-0-9994475-0-5

ISBN-10: 0-9994475-0-5

For more information visit:

www.livingmyrhapsody.com

To my husband:
Thank you for sharing the adventure
with me.

A note from the author:

Time is a thief – so live to the
fullest, be good to yourself and
others, and have no regrets.
Find ways to explore, feed your
curiosity, and learn from both good
and bad.

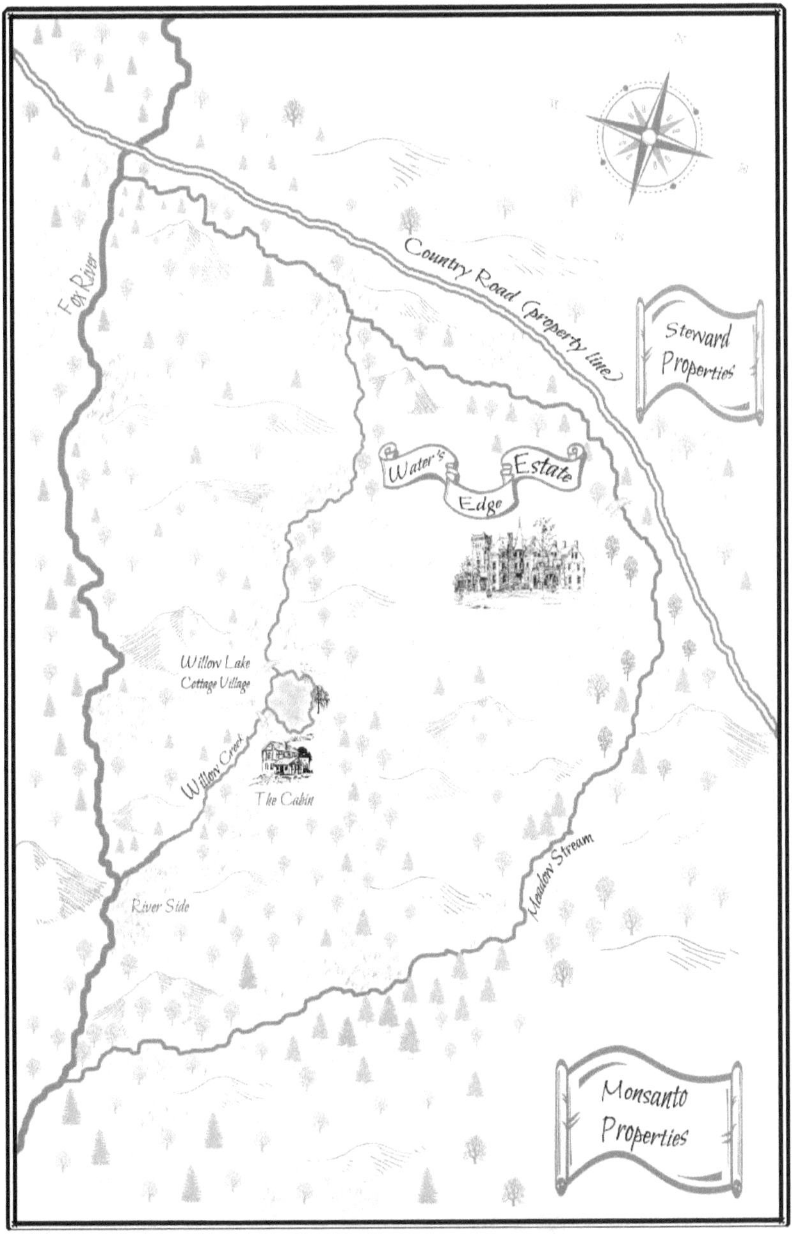

N

Fox River

Country Road (property line)

Steward Properties

Water's Edge Estate

Willow Lake Cottage Village

Willow Crest

The Cabin

Maulov Stream

River Side

Monsanto Properties

CONTENTS

Prologue

"The portal will be closing soon. The Alignment is almost over," the woman reminded.

"No matter now. All four of them have crossed the barrier safely," the tall man answered. He looked through the portal at the couple sleeping in the massive bed that took up a great portion of the room. Moonlight was peeking through the opened curtains, casting shadows across the mangled blankets covering the bed.

"So now we wait," the woman said.

"Like we have been for centuries," added the tall man, lifting his hand and sweeping the images in front of them in a smooth motion.

As he shifted images between the bedrooms, few more sleeping couples filled the view before them, one after the other. He stopped on the fourth and last couple sleeping in another bedroom. The window was opened, and they could hear water splashing in the fountain outside.

With a soft, sweeping motion of his hand, the tall man zoomed-out, changing the images.

Now they were standing outside the mansion on the brick terrace. The sky was dark and clear, but the stars appeared dimmed, as the moon dominated heavens and Earth that night. Cool moonlight, casting long, dark shadows, illuminated the grounds.

The tall man stepped out across the iridescent portal with numerous dimensions outlining the passage; he approached the lighted fountain. He ran his fingers across the water. *Fascinating. So simple, yet so beautiful. So much sensation.* The cool water dripped down his hand, splattering on the bricks.

After a moment, as he stepped back through the immense portal, the woman said to him, "How could things have gone so bad, so quickly? The Earth is crying."

The short stature man answered with regret, "We have not been paying close enough attention, and the time goes by so quickly there. Unfortunately, time rules this planet."

"Yes, but we are here now," the tall man answered and swept his hand across the portal, zooming-in on one of the sleeping couples.

The naked bodies were partially covered with white, silk sheets. The man and a woman slept, embracing each other.

Looking at them, the tall man added, "However, I don't think we can assume that all will go well just because all four of them are finally there. We cannot take that chance."

"That is true. We need to make sure the mission will be successful; we should not wait until the four of them are born," the woman added, swept her hand across the portal, and zoomed-in on the massive waterfall, thousands of miles away from where the couples were sleeping.

"What if we..." the short stature man started.

The water was rushing violently down the boulders, splashing on the rocks below, drowning all other sounds around the three figures standing in the portal.

The tall man shifted the images and again zoomed-in on the mansion where the four couples were fast asleep.

He smiled and said, "That could work."

"Should we tell them?" the woman asked, looking towards the bedrooms and shifting images to show the sleeping couple on the large bed.

"No. Maybe later. Let's first see what happens. We still have a long time before they will be ready," the tall man decided.

"But who will go?" the sort stature man asked.

"I got this," Nerissa answered and approached from the darkness behind them. As she came towards the portal, the light illuminated her perfect face.

"And I will help her," Rainer stepped forward and put his hand on Nerissa's shoulder.

The woman asked, shifting the images with her hand, "What about the beast? Who will—"

"I will take care of that," Kayla interrupted and stepped towards the light.

Now all they had to do was watch and wait for a perfect time to cross.

CHAPTER ONE

Watch

GENTLE BREEZE DANCED between the trees that surrounded the vast estate. Stars shone brightly against the black velvet sky; everything was quiet and serene, with only an occasional hooting of an owl in the distance—the calm before the storm. An aura of tension lingered all around the grounds, and despite the light breeze, there was a sensation of ominous stillness that filled the air.

The estate was outlined by a mixture of oak and pine trees that stretched practically as far as the eye could see in all directions, forming a barrier and keeping all the secrets that filled the grounds.

From high above, the mansion resembled an indistinct, alien-looking object, illuminated from within and submerged beneath dark waters. Inside the great stone structure, almost all the lights were off, with the exception of few dim nightlights illuminating some rooms on the upper floors.

In the back of the building, shadows of people moving inside the kitchen shifted on the brick terrace.

Adara was sitting in the bedroom on the second floor. Looking around the spacious room, she was trying to push away the awareness that the night was not yet over.

She reclined in the comfortable, oversized chair and ran her fingers across the soft blanket that covered her legs; it made her feel warm and relaxed.

As she sat there, she suddenly felt her phone buzzing and relentlessly vibrating in her pocket. She took it out and looked at the screen. Bright light filled the area and shone at her tired, yet beautiful face.

After staring at the phone for a moment, she silenced the vibrations and put it back in her pocket.

She did not want to go yet.

Here and now was so peaceful. On the one hand, she wanted to go and do what needed to be done—what she waited so long to do. On the other, it would change everything. Everything.

I will go. I want to go. I just need few more minutes, she thought.

Next to Adara, in the large bed, her daughter was stretching comfortably under the pink and white covers.

The spacious room had high ceilings, white half-wall paneling, and dark wooden floors. The area above the paneling was painted creamy yellow; but now, in this dim light coming from the table lamp, the color of the walls and the paneling looked almost identical. White furniture in the room contrasted high-gloss, dark floors. It looked as if bottomless, dark waters had filled the room, and the furniture was floating on the surface.

Adara took a deep breath in as she again pulled her phone out. After a moment of hesitation, she sent a quick message, put the phone back in her pocket, looked around the room, and smiled with an amused grin.

The bedroom looked as if it were taken from one of those decorating magazines, and the only thing indicating that an actual child lived there was a pile of clothes and a pair of shoes on the enormous, soft, cream-colored rug in the middle of the room.

Long, white shelves displayed unique and quite unusual decorations. Various statues and different-colored stones from all parts of the world were neatly arranged in rows; definitely not the trinkets that would belonged to a pre-teen.

Adara looked at her daughter who was still squirming under the soft covers. Her daughter's emerald-green eyes were fixed on her.

A loud hoot of an owl made Adara shift her eyes up and above her daughter's bed, and look out the window.

From inside the room, you could hear crickets chirping in the garden, and other sounds that carried from the nearby forest. The quiet noises flew softly through the opened window. With each gentle breeze, the white silk curtain lifted slightly, creating soft shadows on the wall and on the floor.

"Mom. Can you tell me that story?" the little girl asked. Her intense-green eyes seemed to shine brightly in the faint light. With her back to the window wall, she was lying on her side, facing Adara. Her long, dark, slightly messed up hair was loosely braided to one side. Few strands fell on her perfect, tanned, porcelain-smooth face. She swept them away impatiently and covered herself tighter with the silk comforter.

The girl appeared to be around eleven years old, but something in her expression made her look much older.

"Which one do you want to hear tonight?" Adara asked, and, smiling brightly, gazed at her daughter.

Without hesitation, the little girl whispered with excitement, "I want to hear *all* of them."

"Nerissa." Adara sighed. She turned around slightly and glanced at the heavy, white bedroom door. "We don't have time for *all* of them. And besides, you are half asleep sweetie."

"Fine." The little girl yawned and rubbed her eyes.

Nerissa truly did not mind, as she knew that the best adventures awaited her while she was asleep; her dreams could take her anywhere she wanted.

"Then start with the one about when you were born," Nerissa pleaded sleepily as she curled up under her covers.

The only thing Adara could now see, when looking at the bed, was a porcelain-smooth face and a pair of intense-green eyes staring at her.

"I want to hear it again before I leave; I want to remember *all* your stories," Nerissa mumbled and yawned again.

A muffled knock on the heavy, wooden door interrupted their conversation.

The door opened slowly without a sound.

Adara turned around to see who it was.

"We're ready in the kitchen," a woman whispered through the cracked door and smiled at both of them. Her sapphire-blue eyes sparkled intensely despite the soft lighting.

"I'll be there shortly. Nerissa negotiated one story; and how can anyone say *no* to those eyes." Adara chuckled. "I'll join you soon," she added with a distant gaze.

Nerissa peeked from under her silk covers and muttered, "Goodnight Charlotte."

"Goodnight. Sleep tight princess," Charlotte whispered to Nerissa, then looked at Adara with a mournful smile and slowly closed the door.

After she left, Adara turned to look at her daughter.

Nerissa yawned again and urged groggily, "Well? What about the story you promised?"

"You know all the stories by heart, but alright, one story, and then off to sleep. You have a big day ahead of you tomorrow," Adara reminded her and shifted her eyes to the stack of suitcases by the door—all packed and ready to go.

She then stood up and slowly went around the bed towards the opened window. After looking outside for a moment, she grabbed both glass panes and closed them tightly.

When she returned to her chair, Nerissa had finally settled down; her dark, braided hair lay softly against the white, silk pillows.

Adara tucked her daughter back in, gently smoothed her soft, dark hair and swept few runaway strands from Nerissa's face.

After kissing the top of Nerissa's head, she sat back in the chair and covered herself with a blanket.

She started her story, but shortly after, realized that Nerissa was slowly drifting away.

The deeper into the story she got, the clearer the memories became.

Nerissa was asleep.

Sitting there, in her cozy chair, Adara did not want to leave. *Little bit more time.*

Her thoughts went back to the story, to the events of that night long ago, and to everything that followed...

Twenty-four years earlier...

It was already dark. The rain just started pouring. Streets and sidewalks in front of the hospital looked deserted. All the lights in the front of the building shone brightly, reflecting on the wet pavement. Few cars rolled along the main street.

Eva stood by the hospital room window, gazing down at the parking lot by the main entrance. Even though it was dark, looking from the third floor, gave her a good view of the surroundings.

Closing her bright, amber-brown eyes, she slowly took a deep breath. After few moments, she opened them again and looked at the window; the rain drops were running down the smooth, cold glass.

With a slight hesitation in her voice, she asked, "Is she going to be different? Do you think she's going to know?"

He did not answer right away.

Eva kept looking at the raindrops racing down the window pane.

After few moments, she looked up and realized it was taking him a while to answer—too long for her comfort.

Eva could see the reflection of the room in the glass pane. She turned around and, with a heavy sigh, stepped away from the window. Going past the table, she noticed her shimmering, charcoal black gown resting over the chair. Her face lit up as she remembered wearing it just a couple of hours ago. She ran her fingers across the fabric and let it fall back down over the chair.

After few more steps, she approached the crib, where her newborn baby girl was sleeping peacefully. *So beautiful and fragile.* Eva stood there for a moment and marveled at the miracle before her.

Standing there, Eva looked out of place. Her pale-blue hospital gown that ended by the knees, her hair pinned up, her neatly pedicured feet standing on the cold, glossy floor—it painted an odd picture.

She did not want to be there, but nonetheless, there she was.

"Michael," she asked him again, "what do you think. Will she know?" She looked at him, waiting for his answer.

He was sitting leisurely in the big, brown, leather chair, holding a magazine.

"No. Of course not. They never do. You know that." He took a slow breath in, and let it out. He looked up at her with his bright, amber-brown eyes and continued slowly, but it sounded more like a well-rehearsed answer, as if he was prepared for her question or was trying to convince himself instead, "We already talked about it. They never do; not until after their eighteenth birthday, when they blow the candles out—with their new breath, they *awake* and get *infused* with the knowledge of our people."

Trying to keep herself calm, she looked at him hesitantly.

Michael sat up and stretched his arms, placing them on the back of his head. The muscles under his white shirt tensed as he moved. Shifting his arms down, he rested them on top of his head for a moment, and then slid them to the back of his neck.

He noticed his shoulders were tense. Slowly, he rubbed his neck and shoulders, and, with a soft groan, stretched again. *It's been a long day.*

Eva went around the bed to approach his chair. She stood behind him and placed her slender hands on his shoulders.

Michael took her hand and kissed it.

After he let her hand go, she slowly massaged his shoulders. Few moments later, she stepped away from him and walked towards her bed and sat down on the side of it, her hands firmly holding the edge.

Thoughts kept rushing through her head. *What have we done?*

Now that their daughter was here, everything became so real.

Michael looked at the baby sleeping in the crib and calmly asserted his wife, "That's how it has always been."

Eva turned her head to look back at her daughter. "Yes... but you know that this time was... not the same. This time... it was different," she repeated nervously.

After a moment, she sat up straight, looked at him, and continued, "It was the night of the Alignment—"

"We agreed not to talk about that anymore. We must make sure no one else knows or even suspects anything." His bright, amber-brown eyes seemed to shine even brighter. Now he sounded uneasy and worried. "You know that it's forbidden to conceive a child during the Alignment," he added, looking at the crib; but again, it seemed like he was talking to himself, attempting to convince himself more than trying to calm her down.

"Yes, we knew that, and we still did it," Eva replied, staring at their daughter.

The baby was sleeping, snuggly wrapped in the blankets.

"She is so pretty," Eva whispered.

Looking at his wife, he smiled and stated, "Every parent says that about their child; but you're right, she's... breathtaking." He took a deep breath. "Whatever comes of this situation, I don't regret our decision," he assured his wife and glanced at their daughter.

His face showed the severity of the situation as he emphasized slowly, "But I still think that we took a great risk. I don't want her to suffer because of what we had done." Puzzled, he added, "I don't know what came over us—"

"But no one has to know about *when* she came to be."

Michael turned his head and stared out the window. He kept looking out even though he could not see any details from where he was sitting.

Quietly, he declared, "Just like all our people, we made a vow to not conceive a child during the Alignment... that is one of the rules... and we broke it. I still don't understand why; what possessed us to do so; to take such a risk."

"But what puzzles me more... is that we got her."

"What do you mean?" He looked at her, for a moment not following what she meant.

Eva stared back at him surprised. "We know that when both people want to conceive a child, after the act, within a short time, the woman knows when the soul is inside her and what name it has chosen."

"It's always been like that for us; what are you getting at?"

She was surprised that they had never noticed that before. "Haven't you ever wondered why we were given our daughter that night? I mean... I have heard rumors of couples trying to conceive during Alignments in the past, just to see if it can be done, but no one has ever succeeded."

She stood up and slowly paced around the room as she spoke to him, "I don't know how it's possible that we actually were given a child that night."

She continued pacing around the room as she talked to herself, thinking about that night, "We want and we get; that's been the motto of our people. However, that has never worked for conceiving during the Alignment... I wonder what was different that time."

She stopped by the window and rested her back against the glass. She stared at him.

Michael grinned and, still looking at her, said, "Don't get me wrong, I do remember that night, but there are parts of it that are... not so clear to me."

He got up slowly and walked towards Eva as he spoke, "I still am wondering what effect it may have on her. " He stopped by Eva and gazed towards the crib.

Eva pushed herself away from the window wall and went towards the bed. When she got there, she sat down and confessed to him, "I don't know, but I think we could *not* have done it any other way. It was beyond our control; it was meant to be."

"What do you mean? There is no such a thing as *meant to be* and *beyond our control*... that doesn't exist for us. We make our own destinies and our own choices." Then he continued slowly, trying to make his point, "We get what we want. This is *who* we are. We want, and we get."

"I know. But those circumstances were beyond us. And with that, I hope she won't be harmed because of how she came to be."

After a while, she added, "As we agreed, what's done is done; let's not spend any more time dwelling on it. What's more important is the question of what do we do now. She came so quickly; I thought we had more time."

Eva noticed he got quiet.

She approached the window, stood next to him, and said, "I know you're worried, but the more we talk about it, the more I think everything will be alright."

Her mind traveled back to the Water's Edge Estate—the mansion where Michael's parents settled after leaving Europe.

It was there that Michael and Eva, along with few more stranded travelers, spend that unusual night. She still recalled the exquisite mansion, and spacious rooms filled with antique furniture that belonged in the museum.

Being here, in the hospital room, made the memories appear so distant. With a sigh, she placed her head on his chest, put her arms around his torso, and held on to him tightly; she could feel his steady heartbeat.

Holding her close, he inhaled the sweet, indulgent sent of her hair.

Eva felt his heartbeat increasing and his muscles tensing up.

She closed her eyes, and thinking about that night, a while back, she remembered the room with tall ceilings and flowy, dark curtains in arching windows. The room was dark and the air seemed to stand still; intoxicating and oddly stimulating scent filled the air; it was so fresh and energizing, like flowers and some spices she could not recognize. The sound of splashing water coming from the fountain outside the window was very soothing.

Opening her eyes slowly, and with a soft sigh, Eva realized where she was now. She lifted her head and looked into his eyes.

Michael noticed her gaze and, after few seconds, he felt it too; a familiar sensation was surrounding him.

Smiling at her, he replied, "Of course I remember that night. I will never forget it. It was magical, you may say." His hand was slowly running up through her hair.

"You can say that again," she answered and turned her head towards the hospital crib. "And here is our little miracle."

Michael grinned and whispered while not taking his eyes off his wife, "You know what I mean."

He thought about that night, from almost nine months ago. "I always get lost in the moment when I get close to you, but that night was something different altogether," Michael murmured, breathing in her sweet sent as he kissed her neck.

She chuckled and pressed herself against him.

"With you, it's always some kind of excuse to change the subject. But I guess, any excuse is a good excuse... to be close to you," she whispered as he showered her neck with soft kisses, his lips making contact with her warm skin.

He held her close and studied her amber eyes. "I can never get enough of you," he confessed, embracing her body and kissing her gently, his lips slowly moving down as he slid the hospital gown off her shoulder. "I love you so much. The more time passes, ...the deeper... I fall for you...," he whispered between each kiss.

He put his arms around her again, and his embrace, like his kisses, became more intense.

As he tasted the skin on her neck, a familiar wave spread through Eva's body. After few seconds, she gently pushed his shoulders away.

Michael looked at her, his eyes still dazed, not wanting to stop. "What's wrong?"

"We actually have more important things to take care of at this moment." Eva tried to catch her breath. She could not hide the fact that his closeness also had an effect on her body. Her knees got weak, so she was glad he held her tightly, supporting her weight.

Michael joked when she rested her back on the window wall next to him, "You mean more important than this." He turned and kissed her again but then gave her some space as she walked towards the bed.

She sat down and said, "I wish you would take it more seriously. There are so many issues we have to discuss; we have things to plan in case someone starts asking questions. Plus, we need to discuss this with Nicola, —"

There was a loud knock on the door.

Eva sighed with frustration and took a deep breath, as the nurse was coming into the room.

"How are you feeling Mrs. Monsanto? Any pain or discomfort?" Despite the late hour, the night shift nurse looked rested and energized.

"We're fine," Eva answered.

The nurse looked up from above her notes, adjusted her black-framed glasses, and stated, "It's only been few hours since you gave birth in the back of the limousine and were admitted here, but you're saying that you don't need any pain medication?"

Fighting the urge to tell the nurse to leave, Eva answered, "Yes. I 'm doing just fine; thank you."

Michael interrupted and turned to Eva, "Well actually... honey," he kept looking at his wife but then turned to the nurse and said, "Eva is just trying to be brave, or it must be the adrenaline still running through her veins." He looked back at Eva and smiled.

The nurse tilted her head and smiled as she said, "Mrs. Monsanto, you should know that nowadays, it's silly not to use modern medicine to ease the pain and discomfort; we don't live in the Dark Ages, and women don't have to suffer anymore. There are medications to help patients deal with pain." She took a breath and continued, "I'm sorry you didn't get here in time. You must have been so scared in the back of that car."

Eva shifted her eyes at Michael, then turned to the nurse and said, "It wasn't that bad. Really. It was an easy labor. I was lucky."

Then she looked back at her husband but directed her answer to the nurse, "And since you mention it, yes, I would appreciate something for the pain; I didn't want to be a bother."

"Oh, no bother at all. That's one of the reasons I am here. I'll be right back with the medicine." She walked out with the clipboard under her arm.

When the door closed behind her, Michael joked, "Honey, what's next, an appendix surgery without anesthesia?"

He laughed and stretched in the chair but then got serious and reminded her, "We need to keep pretenses. We're required not to draw attention to ourselves. Humans feel pain, we need to fit in and make them think we're the same. We cannot come across like some alien creatures. It will cause fear and confusion for them. Plus, it's against the rules."

"Are you done?" she interrupted bluntly. With each word she uttered, her amber eyes turned darker. Still looking cross and gloomy, she continued, "You know I hate when you say we're not human; you make us sound like some sort of... freaks!" she raised her voice, but she knew he was right. They needed to fit in; they could not break the rule. Not another one.

Michael approached her after realizing he truly did upset her.

He quickly apologized, "I'm sorry sweetie. Of course we're not freaks. I forget how it upsets you when I talk about us like that. Our people were not the first ones here, but it's still our home." He paused for a moment, "And besides, what does it mean to be human anyway.

We are almost like them; body, brain, soul, plus we have few extra abilities, and we live longer, right?"

Eva smirked at him. "Is that what you call it—living longer and few extra abilities?" She sighed with a slight grin and looked at their daughter.

Again, there was a knock.

The nurse came in. She shut the door and said, "I've got the medicine." She handed Eva the pills, along with a small cup of water. She watched her swallow the tablets.

"Have you decided on the name?" she asked, taking the empty cup from Eva.

"We..." Michael started, but Eva answered first.

"As a matter of fact, we have."

Surprised, he looked at her and sat back in his chair, observing her carefully.

"Her name is going to be Adara Destiny," Eva declared with determination in her voice, then looked at Michael.

"What a unique name, Adara—so pretty," the nurse said as she was filling out the name card, which she then placed on the crib.

On her way out the door, she stopped and exclaimed, "Oh my, where is my head. I almost forgot. We are so busy today. The lady, who came to the hospital after your arrival, brought over a change of clothes for you Mrs. Monsanto."

The nurse paused for a moment. "She wasn't happy when I told her we didn't allow any visitors at this time of night; plus I know that you said that you did not want any visitors either; well that I didn't tell her of course. But either way, she really wanted to see you and your baby. But then she got a phone call and had to leave. She wanted me to let you know that she will get everything ready for your arrival back at your house tomorrow. I understand you still want to leave first thing in the morning, yes? Your personal family physician has already signed your discharge papers."

Michael and Eva just sat there, listening to the nurse's winded explanation, trying to gather their thought. They imagined the commotion that Jennifer must have caused in the reception area. Trying not to smile with tired amusement, they felt sorry for the nurse having to deal with Jennifer's overwhelming personality.

The nurse continued after flipping through papers in her clipboard, "She also said that your family has been attempting to reach you, but your phones appeared to be turned off. She wanted me to inform you that your cousins, Nicola and Paulette, have delivered healthy baby boys." She studied her notes. "Just before leaving the hospital, she received a phone call from your mother, Charlotte." The nurse looked at Michael.

She smiled apologetically. "As per your previous instructions, no one was allowed to visit, so I had to take the message from that lady, even though she wanted to give it to you personally."

Holding one hand on the door, the nurse said, "Isn't that an odd coincidence that the three of you went into labor on the same night?"

Still holding the magazine on his lap, Michael answered, "I guess the full moon could do that to anyone. But just a note, Nicola and Paulette are not our cousins; we have the same last name, but there is no relation. Our last name is quite common in the region we come from."

"How interesting. And yes, I heard about those things happening from time to time, full moon and all. But speaking of the lady in the waiting room, she had been so persistent, especially being very worried over the early labor. I mean, you had given birth on the way to the hospital. As a hostess, she must have been terrified; about your safety that is. She seemed quite concerned; but exactly like you instructed, we informed her that all was good with you and the baby."

Michael chuckled. "I bet Jennifer was quite... loud in the waiting room. She's a friend of the family," he added quickly.

The nurse was getting intrigued and listened attentively.

Seeing how engrossed she was, Michael continued, "We were celebrating her son's fifth birthday at their estate and, as it culminated with the firework display, Eva went into labor."

The nurse looked interested, so he proceeded, "Jennifer is our neighbor. She is also a close friend of the family, my parents to be exact. Jennifer's property is across from our, and my parents', property. Jennifer has always been quite protective of her guests, so she insisted on meeting us here after our driver took us to the hospital. But as it happens, the hospital is over an hour away, and unfortunately, we didn't make it in time."

Quickly glancing at the crib, he thought about what happened on the way to the hospital. Their baby had not been due for few more weeks, and now, finding out that two more babies were born, shortly after their daughter arrived, got him curious as to why Eva, Paulette, and Nicola went into labor that same night.

He suspected it had something to do with that night when the children were conceived. All on the same night, it looks like. The sudden realization made him feel uneasy.

His thoughts were racing, *There were four couples at the house that night. Three babies born. So what about Maureen and her husband? They were with us that night, several months ago. Maybe they didn't experience it like the rest of us.*

His thoughts traveled to the past, and he wondered if that night, at the Water's Edge, would forever link them in some way. Then, sudden fear closed around his heart when he realized Eva and he were not the only ones who would need to keep the secret. It also involved Nicola, Paulette, Maureen, and their spouses. They have not kept contact since then, so it was all news to him to suddenly find out about the pregnancies the births. *Why would Charlotte tell us that? Did she know something?*

Michael noticed that Eva was getting uncomfortable with this conversation. He realized she must have heard his thoughts. After seeing her gaze, he decided not to go into any more details even though the nurse was quite captivated at that point.

The nurse turned to Eva and admitted, "I don't know Ms. Jennifer, but she seems truly concerned about all of you. And no wonder, since your little girl came early, or at least that's what we all thought at first." She added with a hint of authority, "It happens sometimes that doctors, and parents-to-be, miscalculate the due date." She smiled faintly and continued, "Well, anyway, I'm glad I remembered what Ms. Jennifer wanted me to tell you." The nurse hesitated for a moment. "Jennifer..., I keep thinking that I know her from somewhere."

Eva looked at Michael, and then at the nurse as she answered, "She is Jennifer Steward, wife of David Steward, the founder of this hospital."

"Oh my goodness gracious," the nurse exhaled the words. It looked like she lost all the color in her face. Then she whispered slowly, "And I was on the verge of being rude to her when she kept giving us directions and was constantly asking for updates."

"I am sure you were just doing your job. You're following all the policies set in place, and that's what matters. Right?" Michael reassured her but realized that the nurse found little comfort in those words.

She left the room, slowly closing the door behind herself.

Eva was emotionally exhausted.

She rubbed her temples with both hands and mumbled quietly, "I can only imagine how busy the next few days are going to be. Multiple babies born to our Family House. And then Jennifer, an outsider, on top of it all, interfering." Then she added more audibly and with more annoyance, "Jennifer is going to love all the commotion that will come with all this."

"Whatever her personality, I know she really and truly cares about our wellbeing; we have to give her that."

He looked at Eva and chuckled. "Now going back to the name," he changed the topic, "you said *Destiny*. I thought we both knew her name is Adara. We don't chose the names; the children come with their own names. And her name is Adara." Michael sounded curious when he continued, "So what gave you the idea to call her Adara *Destiny*?"

Eva glanced at their daughter and answered, "Because she was *destined* to be here. Her being here... it looks like it was out of our control; so what better name than Destiny." Before he could interrupt, she added, "And to tell the truth, I really like that name, *Destiny;* it gives her a little... mystery, don't you think. You must admit, it's a beautiful name." She argued with a beaming smile as she observed his reaction.

"It is a beautiful name, but couldn't we just call her Adara. I mean that *is* her name."

"I guess we could, but I wanted her to have a special name because she is... unique," Eva emphasized, not taking her eyes off her daughter.

"What, to remind us of how she came to be," he said with a grimace, but she could hear pride in his voice. "Fine; it will be *our little* secret. Our little *Destiny*."

After some time, the nurse knocked on the door again. She opened it wide and came in, slowly rolling in a cart with an enormous bouquet of flowers on top of it.

She set the flowers on the table and spoke to Eva, "These are from Mrs. Steward and her family. She brought them before she left; I apologize, but I couldn't bring them sooner. We are swamped tonight. It must be that full moon; this floor hasn't been this full in a long while. Where are all these babies coming from?" The nurse laughed. She moved the cart and took out a bag with neatly folded baby clothes. On the bottom of the cart, there was a small suitcase with the change of clothes for Eva.

"Mrs. Steward left a message at the nurses' station and said that she took care of all the arrangements for your return home."

Eva smiled, genuinely surprised. "That is so nice of her."

"When she brought these over before she left, she seemed to truly enjoy herself. It's amazing. I mean that woman is so full of energy; it's already after midnight."

"Yes; she's extremely dedicated," Michael replied.

"Would you be needing anything else?" the nurse asked. She did not know how to behave around them, now that she was aware of who they were. She knew that people who were friends with the Stewards were from a completely different circle than she was used to. She had never met anyone more important than these people here. But they looked so normal.

Michael sensed that the nurse was quite upset after finding out who Jennifer was.

Both Eva and Michael knew that Jennifer made sure everyone treated her with, as she called it, *respect she deserved.*

In general, Jennifer was a good person, but when it came to her status and her family, she made sure everyone knew whom she was and how important she and her family were; and god help anyone who got in her way, or who said anything to tarnish her family's name.

As the nurse was getting ready to leave, she looked at the crib and asked them, "Is she your first one?"

Caught off guard, Eva looked at Michael and realized they were not ready for that question.

"Yes," they both answered.

Michael continued, "She's our first."

"She's extra special then. Again, congratulations." Then she added, "If you need anything else, just let me know." After that, she left and closed the door.

Eva and Michael stared at each other for a moment.

Then Eva said, "It feels so weird saying that."

"She's our first child; and our last one."

"The Rule of One," Eva added, melancholy resonating in her words. She knew that only Lords could have multiple children if they chose to do so. However, those children were limited to only one. It was not possible to break that rule; many had tried, but none had succeeded. Neither Eva, nor Michael were the Lords; therefore, they were governed by the Rule of One.

"We are never given more than one," he recited and kissed Eva, surrounding her in a loving embrace. He realized that even though they knew about it, vocalizing it, and having an outsider raise the subject, made it more real and brought that perspective to light.

After a moment, as he relaxed his shoulders, she said, "That reminds me. Marie, after I told her our news, said that she will be visiting us soon."

Michael grinned. "Your mother has been waiting a long time for a grandchild. She never missed a chance to bring up that topic, each time she visited. Now we finally can have some relief from that endless... from those endless questions."

Reluctantly, Eva looked at the crib and asked, "I wonder when the other Lords will find out about

Adara... and about her being different." She continued looking at the crib as if she was expecting her daughter to just disappear.

Michael replied, "No one will know she's different. It's not as if she has a mark on her face stating when she came to be. Adara is safe; no one could ask for more powerful godparents; they will keep a watch over her."

"Yes, your parents are not the people anyone would want to mess with. But we haven't ask, and they haven't agreed yet," she grinned.

Michael's parents were one of the Lords themselves, and heads of their entire Family House—one of the most respected Houses amongst their people.

She pondered out loud, "I wonder what they will say; when they see her, I mean. But I guess no one will know her powers, not until she gets them; and that will take years."

Michael was thinking about other children who were conceived that night. *Now, we all need to keep the secret. We are in it together.*

Eva said, "We'll figure it out." But she was not sure how to go about it yet. Wanting to get her mind away from those thoughts she sat down comfortably on the bed and arched her head back, resting it on the plastic headboard. "I can still remember my eighteenth birthday and getting my powers, like it was yesterday. Do you remember yours?"

"Yes. After you blow those candles out, nothing is ever the same." He grinned, letting his mind go back to that day. "I still am surprised by how well you took it. It took me hours to pull myself together after mine. I thought there was something wrong with me. You, on the other hand, went on as if nothing happened. Just like it's supposed to be." He laughed.

She came over, stood next to him, and gently hugged his back from behind, sliding her arms under his, and embracing his chest. His back and his arms were hard as rocks; she could feel them through his shirt as he embraced her.

Slowly standing up on her toes, Eva arched her head up and kissed him on the side of his neck. They stood there in a silent embrace, holding each other tightly.

After a while, he sat down in the chair and watched her take few steps towards the bed.

She changed the topic. "I know it's silly, but I could eat something right about now. Would you do me a favor and get me something from the cafeteria. I am dying for a Chef's Salad," she pleaded with a smile as she went around him.

Michael looked at her in disbelief just as she was coming from behind the chair.

She stopped in front of him.

Tilting his head slightly, he muttered, "Are you serious? You want a salad? Now? The fact that we don't need to eat could be useful at this moment, you know. It's the hospital food we're talking about here sweetie."

"Yes, I know that, but I really feel like having that salad," she said, surprised at her own cravings. "When we walked the hospital with Jennifer, before it officially opened, she said that the Chef's Salad was her favorite thing in this place. I didn't try it then, but now, for some reason, I can't stop thinking about it. I want to see what she was talking about."

Michael peeked at his watch and smiled.

Eva looked back at him and said, "You don't keep your thoughts to yourself, I see. Yes, I realize the cafeteria is closed, but we both know that it won't pose a problem for you. Be my hero. I don't think it would look nice if I wandered the hallways in this silly hospital gown," she ended with a theatrical gesture, laughing quietly.

"Alright, I'll get you that salad. I'll be back soon," he announced and, with a groan, slowly pushed himself up from his comfortable chair.

Michael stretched his arms and fixed his white shirt.

Eva stepped behind him and embraced his back as he took a step towards the door. Her cheek rested on his broad shoulders. She stood there for a moment, enjoying the warmth of his skin, radiating through the smooth, white shirt. She did not want to let him go. Being close to him felt so amazing.

He chuckled and said, "I enjoyed it too, but the thoughts of your food cravings are getting too loud in my head." He turned around, smiling, and kissed her forehead.

Few moments later, when he walked out of the room, he felt relieved that the conversation took a more casual turn. Then he wondered if it was Eva's plan all along— to relieve the tension.

No. He chuckled.

He could feel her craving for that ridiculous salad.

Nonetheless, he welcomed the opportunity to take a walk.

After Michael left the room, Eva stood up to go to the window. Her bare feet touched the cold floor; she looked around for the slippers, which were somewhere by the bed.

Here they are. She put them on and made her way towards the window.

It was still raining outside.

The lights were shining brightly. Someone walked briskly on the sidewalk, trying to make it to the car before being completely drenched.

Eva thought it would be wonderful to feel the drops of rain on her face right about now; and some fresh air would do wonders for her mood as well.

She touched the window.

It was cold.

She moved her fingers down the glass and finally placed the entire palm on the window surface. For some reason, she felt trapped and wanted to turn around and run.

Something did not feel right.

Eva took a deep breath and closed her eyes as she exhaled slowly.

Calm down.

Keeping her eyes closed, she took another deep breath in. Slowly, she exhaled, opened her eyes, and looked out the window at the sidewalk below. Her mind seemed to calm down; she felt her muscles relaxing with each slow breath she took.

Then she noticed a strange sensation creeping up in her mind.

It was as if someone was watching her—not from the outside, but from inside the room.

CHAPTER TWO

The Eyes

WITH THE WINDOW completely uncovered, Eva felt exposed, so she quickly closed the curtains, which stretched wall to wall.

Hesitating, she kept facing the curtains; she held the thick fabric with both hands and peaked outside. Streets and parking lot were deserted. Eva knew she and her daughter were alone in the room, but it felt like someone was watching her.

The sensation increased, so she instinctively turned around and looked around the room.

No one was there.

Slowly, she scanned the room again as she walked towards the bed.

I must be imagining things.

She tried to make sense of what she was feeling, but to no avail; the strange sensation that someone else was in the room was overwhelming.

In order to distract herself, she decided to tidy up the messy hospital bed.

Covers and blankets lay mangled and draping on the side. She bent over the bed, when something caught her attention.

With the corner of her eye, she saw something bright by the crib.

When she turned her head to look at it, the light was gone.

The idea of a faulty light bulb over the crib crossed her mind.

She looked up at the ceiling above—*nothing*.

But as she was looking up, she noticed that the light was actually coming from the crib. Without blinking, she slowly shifted her eyes at the crib to get a better look.

When she looked inside, she froze.

In the crib, there was her baby girl lying calmly, looking around the room with her sparkling blue eyes. The inside of the crib was glowing.

It was hard to tell where the warm light was coming from, but it filled the entire crib. There was an atmosphere of goodness and peace surrounding her daughter.

Eva saw that her baby's face was perfectly calm, but the mesmerizing, intense sapphire-blue eyes were fixed on Eva.

Our babies, no, our people have amber eyes. Lords are the only ones with blue eyes, as a sign of their status. But intense-blue... that's unheard of. What's happening here? And that glow?

Slowly, she approached the crib and, without blinking, kept staring at her daughter's face. As she walked closer, the eyes seemed to follow her; when she stopped by the crib, it looked like the baby was watching her.

Eva blinked.

At that moment, the glow disappeared. Adara blinked as well, and after that, her face looked like a face of any other baby.

Where did the light go?

After the initial shock, Eva wanted to try something. She looked away and, with the corner of her eye, gazed in the direction of the crib, but not directly at it.

Again, there was the glow. *So it's only in the corner of my vision.*

She blinked and looked straight at where the light was coming from. The light was gone. She tried again, but this time slowly, without blinking, she shifted her eyes in the direction of the light.

There it was. Her baby. Her baby girl was glowing.

This is not happening; it is not possible. She's only a baby.

She kept staring at her daughter, who was now peacefully dozing off.

"This is amazing," she stated out loud, her thoughts racing through her head. She realized she was sitting on the side of her bed, frantically twisting a corner of the blanket, all while staring at her baby girl.

What if I'm imagining it? I am overwhelmed and confused. It must be my mind playing tricks on me. "We are *different*, but this is insane," she murmured. "That glow."

She stared at the crib.

The baby was lying still. All Eva could see was Adara's little chest rising and falling rhythmically with each breath; calm and peaceful, now with her eyes closed. She looked comfortable and warm, wrapped in soft blankets, looking like any other baby.

I wonder if she has anything unusual on her body that would explain this.

She began unwrapping the blankets to take a closer look.

I didn't notice anything when she was born. But... I wasn't looking for anything then. "Who wrapped her up so tight," she murmured. Her hands were trembling.

She was nervously trying to undo the blankets. Thoughts started rushing in again; she pushed them away.

Eva tugged at the blanket a bit too hard, and as it moved, it slightly jerked the baby's body.

Adara awoke and started fussing.

Finally, Eva undid all the blankets and started working on the little snap-on shirt. She took it off gently, trying not to upset her baby even more. But at that time, Adara was already upset, opening and closing her eyes, looking agitated.

As her daughter was fussing and looking around the room, Eva realized that her daughter's bright-blue eyes were getting darker. Eva tried not to look at the eyes, and she continued searching for any marking on Adara's body.

Nothing on her arms, tummy, or legs. Maybe her back? "No, nothing there either; good," she whispered, puzzled.

She stopped and thought, *What am I looking for anyway?*

The baby, fully awake, was now crying fiercely.

Eva felt so bad for waking her, so she carefully bundled her up.

She did not know what to do next.

Adara's dark-blue eyes were wide open; she looked at Eva through the tears.

Those blue eyes. Weren't they bright-blue before? Maybe it's the lighting, but the tears? Babies don't have tears yet, do they? But at least the eyes didn't... she stopped.

And then it happened.

Adara cried fiercely, her eyes opening and closing. Then her eyes started changing color again. The irises went from, now, dark-blue to completely black.

Looking at her baby in the crib, Eva covered her mouth with both hands but could not hide the gasp. She felt tears running down her face; it was too much for her.

She wailed quietly, "Oh, no; no, no. That only happens after the Awakening. It's *not* real. She's just a baby. It's just a dream." *I will wake up any moment.*

Eva knew it was not a dream, but the reality was too hard to handle.

"My poor baby; my poor little baby. I'm so very sorry sweetheart," she whispered as she slowly picked her up.

She was gently rocking her baby as she spoke to her, "I'm so sorry. What have we done to you? I hope you can forgive us one day." Warm, salty tears ran down Eva's face again. Her voice broke at the last words, "My little girl."

Adara was calming down and, by now, was just making quiet gasping sounds.

Eva held her daughter, gently rocking her. Then she remembered something—something that happened several months ago.

It was that day, when Michael's mother, Charlotte, the patron of their Family House, said something to Eva; it did not make any sense at that time, but now, the meaning was perfectly clear.

The message that Eva had forgotten; it was something she was supposed to forget:

"...the tears will open your mind, and you will know what to do."

After that, Charlotte had put her hands over Eva's ears and held them there for few seconds. Eva saw Charlotte's lips moving, but she could not make out the words. Then everything became blurry.

But that was such a long time ago.

Now, Eva was in the hospital room with her baby girl cradled in her arms. She remembered that strange message and, now, she knew.

She looked at her baby and whispered, "It will be alright. Everything will be fine; you'll see."

She knew what to do, but it did not make things easier at all. Now she realized that the life ahead would be full of sacrifices. She knew they will have to be ready to protect their daughter at all cost; it brought her great heartache knowing that Adara was different.

Eva knew she loved this little person even more than life itself, and there was no limit to what she would do to protect her baby girl.

CHAPTER THREE

Control

MICHAEL WAS WALKING down the empty hallway, trying to locate the cafeteria. His thoughts kept circling around his daughter.

After a while, he realized it was a second time he went down that corridor.

He groaned with frustration.

"Who the hell designed this place," he muttered to himself.

He was distracted and was not paying attention to where he was going.

Annoyed with his aimless wandering, he stopped. With his eyes closed, he took a deep breath in. He slowly exhaled.

It felt good.

The calming movement of his chest rising and falling helped him relax. One more breath—and everything became quiet. A different kind of quiet—no humming, no distant voices of people moving along the hallway. It was as if someone hit the mute button, and the only sounds he heard where the ones he was trying to find.

"I'll just do it my way," he muttered as he opened his eyes.

Michael looked to the right and listened—the sound of x-ray buzzing, other machines clicking, endless voices and conversations, laughter, crying...

No; not there, he thought and looked to the left. Buzzing of the vending machines. He slowly inhaled, letting the air pass through his nose and into his lungs. Breathing in, he thought, *Cleaning agents, spilled soda, milk...*

He sighed.

A hint of disgust spread across his face. "And we've got the cafeteria."

Now he knew where to go.

He walked through the beige colored hallways that lead to the cafeteria entrance.

No wonder I avoid doing it my way; too much information, too much to filter. He added out loud, "But I guess it beats walking aimlessly up and down the hallway."

Getting closer to the entrance, he slowed down a bit. He did not crave anything, and in fact, the search for this place made him feel queasy, his stomach churning at the mere thought of getting something for himself.

It's for Eva. Then he uttered with distaste, "I seriously don't know what she was thinking, wanting food from here?"

For a moment, he felt bad for being so judgmental about this place. It was a great hospital after all. Best staff, latest technology; everything was done to the highest standard—as with everything the Stewards owned.

This hospital was the newest of their 'babies'. Both Jennifer and her husband were quite passionate about investing into the community. Having almost unlimited resources made it possible for their passion to become a reality; generations of friendship with the Monsanto family had its perks.

Michael knew that the Stewards were proud but good people; they always invested in projects that were beneficial not only to themselves, but also to the community. Both David and Jennifer were attorneys, working at one of the Monsanto branches. However, Jennifer stepped away from the firm few years back after having problems during her pregnancy. She decided to concentrate on her family and on raising their only son, Kyle.

Michael's thoughts were interrupted when he stopped in front of the entryway.

Holding his hand pressed against the frosted-glass door leading to the spacious cafeteria, Michael chuckled when he thought about Eva. He remembered that she could get cranky and seriously annoyed if she did not get what she wanted, or if things did not go her way.

Then he admitted to himself that he *did* like pleasing her; he enjoyed doing whatever it took.

He knew that to someone who did not know them that well, she could appear demanding and stubborn. But he also knew it was not exactly like that. In their relationship, it evened out; and as a matter of fact, he could not remember Eva ever refusing him anything he asked for either.

Just before stepping through the glass door, a sudden wave of longing came over him.

He was missing her.

It felt as if Eva needed him. Now. Or was it he who needed her. He was not sure.

No, that's silly. He paused and made a slight move as though to turn around, but then he continued through the door. "She really wants that salad," he grumbled.

The place was empty, or almost empty, as there was one person behind the counter, cleaning the glass refrigerator door.

The chairs were flipped on top of tables, and floors were freshly mopped.

The room was nicely decorated with pleasing artwork, now bathed in the dim lighting.

Michael got closer to the counter and noticed that the salad Eva wanted was behind the glass.

The man cleaning the fridge door turned around and said, "I am sorry sir, but the cafeteria is closed for the night. We will reopen at six." Then he added, "But there are vending machines right by the door, on the left."

Michael gave him an apologetic look.

Great. Just great. In the hospital with all the cameras; just what I need.

Then he explained to the man behind the counter, "My wife has her mind set on the salad, just like the one behind you."

The man turned to look in the direction Michael was pointing.

Michael continued, "She had a rather difficult day and a long labor; she really, really wants that salad. And as you can see, the fridge is not locked."

Michael took out a ten dollar bill and placed it on the counter.

"You can put the ten behind the door of the fridge with a note for the morning staff."

The man stared at him. After a moment, he started to say, "But I—"

"I need that salad," Michael demanded and stared in his eyes, slowly uttering the words.

The man kept staring at Michael and, without breaking eye contact, reached under the counter to get a paper bag. He looked down and wrote a note on the bag, reached for the masking tape, and placed the note with the money on the inside of the glass door.

He handed Michael the salad. Then he just stood still, looking at Michael with a blank expression on his face.

Michael continued in a calm voice, "I don't want you to get in trouble, so at the end of your shift, go to your supervisor and say that some weird guy came here and started talking all crazy. Also, say that you were not sure what to do, so you did what I asked."

The man blinked slowly.

Michael turned around and walked to the glass exit door. With the salad in one hand, he pushed the swinging door with the other. As he stepped into the hallway, he glanced at the man behind the counter.

The man stood there, confused and disoriented. Michael sighed and continued walking, letting the door swing close behind him.

Swooshing sound of the door swinging back and forth resonated in his ears as he made his way to the elevator.

I don't think I'll ever get used to this.

He always felt like some twisted puppeteer when he made people do what he wanted—bending them to his will.

It was a hard habit to break. The guilt always surfaced; eventually.

Some of his kind, and actually majority of them, enjoyed controlling humans. They thought of it as a natural and normal part of who they were. Some loved it and felt it was their right since that was how things had always been.

Michael and Eva were part of the Family House that was against using their powers to oppress humankind. But he knew that suppressing the control was against their nature.

As he made his way to Eva's room, he realized how tired he was—not physically, but emotionally. In his head, he was debating the morality of their actions; trying to justify the reason for using their powers.

Are we really better than the Dark Lords?

He was close to the main elevators when he stopped by the massive, round fountain in the middle of the main entryway inside the hospital.

The water was shimmering and splashing as it cascaded down the marble steps and stones. He gazed at the glistening drops and got lost in his thoughts, *We are born different and are given this ability on our Awakening; it's who we are. It's not as if we are hurting anyone; physically at least.*

But he knew the irony behind it since those arguments had been used to explain almost everything his people have been doing for millennia. So many of them abused their powers to the point of nearly breaking the rules that were set by the Sentinels—the mysterious ones who granted his people refuge on Earth.

All his people knew what the rules were. The Lords received them when they made the pact, and the descendants got them during the Awakening. There were not many rules, but the Sentinels were extremely strict when it came to everyone following them. The three most important rules included: not getting discovered, not mixing with humans, and not killing. Seemed simple and easy for most, but as always, there was someone who rebelled.

Not getting discovered was usually the hardest rule to keep, since after being given all the powers, during the Awakening on their eighteenth birthday, most everyone was tempted to use those powers any chance they got. It had been especially hard to uphold that rule in the past, but nowadays, people were used to unbelievable things happening, as they were dismissed at hoaxes—everything that used to be unusual became not so strange anymore. But still, the complete knowledge of what has ever happened here on Earth, along with the ability to control humans, and, to top it off, the awareness that since the *initiation,* they could consider themselves immortal—it was all quite overwhelming. The idea of total power, control, and unending strength was a lot to take in all at once.

After being born to their Family House, the children were exactly like human children, vulnerable and fragile. That was also the reason for having powerful godparents, who were always there to protect the child from any harm and danger.

The eighteen birthday, referred to as the Awakening, was the time when all the knowledge was transferred. At that time, when the candles were blown out, endless knowledge of everything their people lived through was *infused* into the person's mind. The fascinating part was that the body did not change during all that; it was the mind that changed; allowing the realization that the body was safe from everything—the so called, mind-over-matter. The idea that nothing can hurt me because I will not allow it to hurt me in any way, was the main point that a person got when realizing he or she was immortal.

The other rule that prohibited taking lives of others, strangely, was not an issue they had to worry about; it was, as Michael referred to it, a no-brainer. You take a life, and your life is taken from you; no matter if you killed a human or one of your own.

For Michael, at first, it was strange to know that he could not be killed by anyone, and that he was not allowed to kill anyone either.

It was as if nature balanced itself.

Michael knew they could not interfere with human lives that way. He had heard stories about those who had tried, and few that actually broke the rule and had killed. He had heard that those who did, had disappeared, vanished into thin air; they stopped being, and all trace after their bodies was gone. Life for life, everyone proclaimed.

Michael recalled other rules from his Awakening.

Not mixing, nor mating, with humans. That rule did not make sense to him, but he realized that his people never felt the urge to join with mortals. He suspected that, even if they had tried, they would not have been able to have children together—another rule enforced by the Sentinels.

As he was thinking about the time of his Awakening, he remembered how images flooded his mind that night. Exactly like a movie on fast forward, only million times faster but still as clear as real life, with all the details and all the channels turned on all at once—so he would not miss a single thing as his mind was recording everything. When it was all over, in only few seconds, he had memories of the times since the Lords settled on Earth. It was the time when their lives had started here.

"If people knew their real history," he voiced out loud. Then he thought, *We have a hard time keeping our society in line even though there are just several hundreds of us and considering that we are more rational and have so many things to give us advantage. I wonder how humans would do with the true knowledge of their past.*

Standing by the water, he observed the orange Koi fish swimming in the fountain pond and hiding behind green leafs. *We are calculative, and we follow our reason; some of us too much; especially some Lords. They really should loosen up a bit.*

Thinking about it some more, he knew that some Lords appeared stiff and emotionless, but most were energetic and full of passion for life. The Dark Lords, who separated themselves from other Lords, including Michael's Family, were colder, not showing too much warmth. *We are like a big happy family. Big and formal family. Well, at least some of us.*

Because his Family House, and many others like them, believed in equality for all kind, it created separation between different Houses. The Dark Lords thought of humans as the lesser kind that should be made to serve. The Dark Lords, heads of those Houses, got their name because they believed in spreading oppression over humans—all happening from behind the scenes, by manipulating humans into submission, subtly enough for humans not to suspect anything.

To Michael, the idea of treating humans as inferior was disturbing, to say the least. He knew that his people were different, but he also knew that humans were fascinating and special in their own way.

Eva and Michael were raised during the times of slavery uproars in Europe and Asia. As a result of that, Eva's family members were big proponents of the freedom movement. That still resonated within her on a deeper level.

For Michael, blending in came easily, but for his wife, even though she also was one of the freedom fighters, it was a different story—she wanted to fit in, but it was a struggle for her to do so. The perspective of centuries she has spent on Earth was sometimes visible in how she reacted to everyday life. Michael tried explaining to her that there was nothing wrong with them being who they were.

At one point, he tried a different tactic to get his message across. He told her that humans could not become them, and that they could not become human no matter what—so there was no use trying.

Eva understood it, but her need to coexist with humans remained. She never gave up the efforts. That was one of the reasons they always had human friends, like the Stewards.

As Michael's mind wondered, he started thinking about their daughter, Adara—the new life they had created.

His thoughts went back to the night when they had deliberately broken one of the sacred rules.

He couldn't remember whose idea it was, but that night, several months ago, he did not care about the rules at all. It felt good to do something that gave both of them so much pleasure.

He recalled that evening when they met with their friends at the Water's Edge—his parents' current residence. He smiled, remembering everyone having such a great time and being so... irrational, so human. It felt strange remembering it from a perspective of time. His memories were getting clearer, now as he thought about the events of that evening.

Michael sat down on the edge of the fountain; the marble was cold to the touch. He ran his fingers across the water. The events of the night became so vivid.

It turned out to be a very strange evening...

...Eva and he had been on their way to the annual Family Gathering, held few hours up north. They usually took the expressway and traveled north on it, but there was news of an oil spill caused by a jackknifed tanker. They were informed that the road would reopen the next day, at best. Faced with that fact and dreading the delay, they had no choice but to take a long way round through the countryside road, which lead past their neighbors, the Stewards, and later by his parents' residence—Water's Edge.

Hills, meadows, and forests stretched as far as the eye could see in all directions. Clear, blue sky in the south was in contrast to the cloudy gray veil that was still visible in the north. The storms had been gone for a while, but the road was still wet in some areas.

They were driving through what seemed like never-ending hills covered by thick forest, separated by patches of tall-grass meadows.

Michael knew that soon they would be passing by his parents' estate. The thought of seeing Charlotte and Marcel brought a smile to Michael's face; they were always welcoming and supportive.

Their properties, on the west side of the road, were next to each other, and the Stewards were their neighbors from across the road on the east side. Michael and his parents lived so close to each other but, surprisingly, had not been spending that much time together, as each of them enjoyed extensive travels.

When they passed by the impressive mansion that belonged to the Stewards, Michael knew that the Water's Edge was not far away on the left. They did not have time to stop at his parents' house though. And besides, he knew that no one was home, as Charlotte and Marcel had most likely already left for the Gathering.

They were just past the Stewards, and about a mile away from the Water's Edge, when the car trouble started. The engine began making strange noises. They slowly drove through the winding road that was surrounded by tall pines on both sides.

"I can't believe this; it's a new car. What the hell is wrong with it?" Michael snapped, annoyed by the situation.

"We can stop at the Water's Edge and have it checked out," Eva suggested, as she looked ahead to see how far they were from the side road leading to the entrance.

Michael turned left onto the driveway. They crossed the bridge that went over a rapidly flowing stream, still muddy and raised from the heavy rainfall.

As they approached the gate to the grounds, the gas pedal started giving them trouble, so Michael carefully maneuvered the car and managed to steer it through the gate that was slowly opening. The car drove few more yards and then stopped. Michael tried to re-start the engine, but as he turned the key in the ignition, there was only a rattling sound, which also stopped after few attempts.

"Great. Just great," frustrated, Michael grumbled and hit the steering wheel.

"Well, at least we got in the driveway," Eva announced and stepped out of the car.

She looked in the direction of the house and sighed, as she realized the house was still quite a distance away. She didn't mind walking, but still, the thought of going up the sloping hill in her high heels annoyed her. Aggravated, she took off her shoes and walked barefoot on a gravel-lined road leading to the house.

Michael got out of the car, went around to the back, and started pulling out their luggage.

Surprised, Eva stopped and turned around on the gravel road, the white stones crunching beneath her feet.

She asked, "What are you doing? We only need to call and wait for the mechanic. Why are you taking the bags out?"

Michael grabbed the second bag, closed the trunk, and concluded, "There is no mechanic close to this area. The closest one is past the exit we were going to take, which now is blocked off. It's late Saturday afternoon and chances of us getting out of here are slim. We won't be able to leave here sooner than Sunday afternoon." He stopped next to her and looked at the house. After a short pause, he continued up the road.

Eva exhaled and followed Michael up the slight hill that lead to the mansion. The gravel crunched softly under her feet. The stones did not bother her at all. Cold, hard rocks massaged her feet as she was stepping steadily.

When they got closer, and passed some trees that surrounded front of the property, the rest of the house became visible.

It was a gorgeous beige brick, three-story mansion with a wide staircase leading to the main door that had tall columns on each side. It was enormous, and as one got closer, it was apparent that the house was build out on both sides and was much larger than it seemed initially. From the distance, the sides were obscured by the tall pine trees, which made the house look not as wide; but while close, the angled additions on both sides became visible.

When they got close enough to see the main entrance and the garage on the far right side, they saw that there were three cars parked on the far right end of the building.

Eva and Michael looked at each other in confusion.

"It's possible that Charlotte and Marcel could still be home," said Eva, "but what about these cars?" she pondered, recognizing them all.

The two vehicles belonged to their friends within their Family House who lived about an hour south from here; but the third one belonged to their distant friends from another House; they lived in a different area, much further south—their House has separated a while ago, but Michael and Eva still were close with them. Nonetheless, Eva was even more surprised seeing all of them here, together.

After walking up the wide steps leading to the main entrance, Eva was the first one at the door, so she rang the doorbell. Few moments later, the door opened, and they saw Jason, one of *their family* friends who lived nearby, south of here.

He opened the door and greeted them with a big smile. His sparkling white teeth were in contrast to his dark, tanned skin and short, dark hair.

"So I see we are not the only ones who got stranded here for the night," Jason proclaimed with a chuckle. "Nicola, guess who's at the door," he yelled as he looked behind. "It's Eva and Michael," still smiling, he shook his head and let them in.

Eva let Michael go in first, so he could get the luggage inside.

Jason gave him a friendly punch in the shoulder and helped him with the bags while he said, "It looks like we're all going to spend the night here."

Jason set their bags near the stairs and said to them, "The only road leading to the expressway north of here is blocked by the river that flooded the area earlier. We are all stuck here. Just our luck; I was actually looking forward to this year's Family Reunion; I was told that this one is the *special one*," his voice faded as he lead them to the family room down the hall.

Eva and Michael put their coats on the bench and followed Jason.

Both Michael and Eva felt at home here—this was Michael's Family House. He enjoyed the peaceful countryside atmosphere. Moving here from Europe was a nice change of scenery; they felt right at home in the North America. The vastness of space and greenery that surrounded the estate was a welcomed change.

The house was always full of life, as Charlotte enjoyed entertaining her guests.

She was a cheerful and energetic woman, frequently welcoming and inviting her family and friends to dinner parties or charity events.

Even though the Lords lived here for millennia, most of them did not look a day over thirty. Their people aged at the same rate as humans did, but they stopped *aging* at around thirty. Some, however, looked like they were in their sixties; it all depended on their preferences and circumstances.

Those who preferred to be seen as older, did so to keep pretenses and to blend with whomever they lived around at that time. Only in certain cases, a member of their family would temporarily age him or herself to look elderly. That was only done to blend in with their human friends and close neighbors. But if they wanted, they could return to the desired adult age at any time;

however, they could never look younger than they did at the time of their Awakening.

In Charlotte's case, the late thirties look was meant to fit in with the human friends.

Charlotte was of medium height and had a graceful, slim figure, and a very smooth, cat-like way of moving around. She usually wore her chocolate-brown hair pinned-up in some elaborate braid that twisted in different directions—that day, it lay softly on the side of her neck, and come down in front on her shoulder.

Eva smiled when she saw her friends sitting in front of the fireplace. They waved at her and pointed to an empty spot on the sofa.

Charlotte got up and gave Eva a big hug. Then she approached Michael and embraced him, holding her son for a bit longer.

"Charlotte. So nice to see you," Michael said. It had been a long time since he stopped calling her *mom*. They were more like good old friends at this point. The lines between generations faded after few centuries.

Confused, Eva asked, "So what are you all doing here? Are we doing our own Gathering tonight." She chuckled and sat down on an oversized sofa.

"It looks like it," Nicola chirped, looking over the book she had on her lap.

Michael looked at his mother. "No, but seriously, what are we going to do. We have never missed a Family Gathering before. No one is allowed to miss it."

Michael looked at Eva, and together, they noticed that everyone else was relaxed and not making a big deal about the fact that they were all apparently stranded here.

Charlotte assured them calmly, "It's fine; everything has been taken care of... the rest of the Family has been informed about the special circumstances we are all in. We can have the Gathering here. We need at least one Lord to be present, and since I am here, we're set."

"Where is Marcel? Isn't he here?" Eva asked about Michael's father.

Marcel, as Charlotte's husband, was also one of the Lords. In fact, each Lords was married to another Lord; after they came here together in pairs, they were joined in the bonding ceremony of marriage. With their kind, when they bonded, they did it for life, or in their case, considering they were practically immortal, for eternity.

"Actually, he left yesterday to be early for the Family Gathering and to take care of some issues that came up. He made it just in time to avoid the floods. He left on a short notice, but I stayed behind to take care of some things; I don't like traveling in a rush," Charlotte explained.

Eva asked, looking at her friends, "So what happened to you? What are *you* all doing here?"

"For them," Paulette said and pointed to the others, "it was probably the same thing as for you—a detour gone wrong with the oil spill blocking the road, and then the river flooding after the heavy downpour over the past few weeks here. For us, I guess the river did it. We were in this area on a business matter at the Stewards. And now, we are all stuck here because of the flooding."

Jason chuckled and added, "Tell them about the car."

Paulette rolled her eyes and sighed. "When we turned back from the river, the car trouble started and we had to pull over. That is the reason you are here, isn't it?" Paulette asked. After a pause she looked at her other friends sitting around her.

She continued, "Filipe already took a look at the cars and has no idea what's wrong. They should all be working just fine, but they are not." She chuckled. "He wasn't happy to have to admit that he couldn't fix them... because he knows all about cars."

Filipe only smirked at her without adding anything else.

Then he added reluctantly, "It must be all that rain water. It's messing with the cars."

It did not make any sense to Michael because the roads were mostly dry where they were driving. But before he said anything, Eva interrupted.

"But where is Andrew? He came with you, didn't he?" she asked.

"He is outside getting things ready for the Gathering," Paulette answered as she stood up and headed for the kitchen to bring some fresh tea.

Andrew and Maurine were considered newlyweds, being married only a decade. They rarely spent time apart.

When it came to Paulette and her husband Filipe, they celebrated their seventieth anniversary few years back.

Nicola and her husband Jason were married for almost as long as Eva and Michael, which was getting closer to ninety.

Michael looked around and saw that everyone was relaxed, and enjoying their time together. Paulette was in the kitchen preparing more tea.

In the living room, the conversation continued.

Michael sat comfortably on the spacious sofa, and Eva leaned on him slightly, her legs curled up and covered by few pillows.

Michael asked, "What was Paulette talking about, when she mentioned tonight's Gathering. I didn't realize it needed special preparation."

Nicola put the book down and answered, "I'm actually reading about the ceremony right now. There is a whole book written about different rituals the Lords were performing after they came here." She marveled and was almost out of breath when she said, "These rituals are extremely old; as old as they are, or older." She pointed to Charlotte.

Charlotte chuckled and chocked on the tea she was drinking. She coughed few times to clear her throat and said, smiling comically, "Excuse me. I am here and I can hear you very well, for my old age."

They all laughed but knew that Nicola was right. Charlotte and other Lords were old. Very old.

Michael looked at the book Nicola was holding.

He noted, "This book doesn't look that old to me."

Charlotte answered, "Oh, this is merely a replica. The original book, or should I say, the scroll, is too fragile to be handled."

Nicola said, catching her breath, "This book right here contains most treasured and secret rituals."

"What? Like some witchcraft?" Maurine chuckled nervously.

"Oh, please. I'm not talking about magic; I am talking about our history," Nicola announced. Then she opened it where she had previously placed a bookmark.

Still excited, she explained the contents, "See, this ceremony is about unlocking the knowledge and powers, asking for life and fruitfulness. It is simply... beautiful. Imagine, all of us have everything we could ever want, and we still find time for such humble things, like these ceremonies."

Michael smiled, thinking how poetic it sounded. *Nicola always likes to add at least a little bit of drama to keep things interesting.*

Nicola continued as she turned towards Charlotte, "I wonder who the Lords were communicating with during those ceremonies."

Charlotte simply sat there, smiling at her. She did not answer, and Nicola did not ask again.

Nicola continued, "We don't have such a thing as religion that we practice. It's amazing that our people believed in something greater than themselves; or were they talking to the Sentinels?" she looked down at the book and sighed.

Maureen laughed. "You and your questions. We could sit here all night and talk about the possibilities. Charlotte already told us earlier that tonight is going to be a special night. It's a night of the Alignment; that doesn't happen often. We should concentrate on what we need to do before the evening starts."

Eva looked up from her pillow, "What? We need to do something? Do we have to read that book by tonight?"

Just then, Paulette came in with the tea and was joined by Andrew. She assured the group, "Oh, heck no. Nicola only wanted to read about it. There is nothing more we need to do."

She placed the tray with the tea and pie on the coffee table. She continued, "Everything is prepared; we simply need to clear our minds a little so that we're ready for a time of meditation. This is a ceremony for wisdom and power after all; we need room for that," she giggled and kept sipping on the tea she poured for herself.

Michael looked at Eva and chuckled, "I'm all for not driving; and a little knowledge never hurt anyone." He handed Eva a cup of tea, took one himself, and they both took a sip. The hint of herbs tasted refreshing; the sweet tea seemed to hit the spot.

They sat there talking for a while when Charlotte got up and gestured for everyone to follow her. She announced with excitement as she walked through the door towards the back terrace, "It is time."

What happened that evening, and the memory of events that took place later that night, send a pulse down Michael's spine. It turned out to be one of most intense, passionate, and bizarre nights he had ever experienced throughout his life.

Everything started as always during the Family Gathering, with Charlotte retelling the story of their arrival on Earth. She began with stating the rules that were put in place, and ended with ceremonial acknowledgment of gratitude to the Sentinels for granting their people permission to make Earth their new home. But what happened after was far from ordinary.

Charlotte mentioned the Alignment, followed by other things that, now, Michael could not recall for the life of him.

Somehow, after that, he found himself with Eva in one of the downstairs sitting rooms on the oversized sofa. He could not explain why, but he was filled with the urge to be with her. He felt the longing intensify each time he met Eva's eyes.

The lust overpowered him.

What pushed him over the edge was that she wanted it with the same, if not with more, urgency.

They did not make it to their bedroom. He had never lost control of himself like he did that night. He remembered Eva, on the sofa, leaning against the tall, leather arm of the massive piece as he pushed against her. Her warm breath close to his ear as she was gasping for air. Somewhere in the distance he heard another couple. Listening to someone else enjoying the night, as they had, excited him and sent his body into a frenzy.

Eva held his face in her hands and moistened her lips, slowly moving her tongue across them. Her knees were far apart and close to her body as he moved up on her, faster and faster. She arched her back and relaxed her hips as he thrusted himself into her. At that moment, when he felt her relaxing her body a bit more and taking him deeper inside as she spread her legs wide, he knew he could not hold on any longer. Michael heard her asking him to go harder and faster. The wave of pleasure crashed over him as he came while thrusting himself insider her. Right before his orgasm, he heard her scream in ecstasy as she moved one of her hands between her legs, and with the other, clenched the back of his neck.

It was still a blur for most parts when he recalled bits and pieces of it. At some point, he knew they had ended up in one of the bedrooms upstairs. And all he heard when falling asleep, their bodies covered by cool, silk sheets, was the shimmering water of the fountain outside an opened window.

In the hospital, Michael's thoughts were interrupted when he realized he was already in the elevator, and he somehow had gotten to the right floor. He did not remember leaving the fountain by the hospital lobby.

As he got out, the door closed behind him with a soft swoosh. He followed the brightly lit corridor to Eva's room and passed the nurse's station. He was trying to concentrate on where he was going.

The door opened without a sound when he gently pressed down on the handle and pushed. He stepped in quietly, as to not disturb Eva and their baby.

"I got it," he announced, holding the salad.

Eva was facing the window, holding their baby in her arms. When he got closer to her, she slowly turned around.

Michael sensed that something was not right; Eva seemed somewhat disturbed, yet strangely calm.

"What's wrong? Is the baby alright?" he asked nervously, trying to suppress the panic that was slowly creeping into his voice.

"Well, it depends..."

Michael put the salad on the table and approached her. He looked down at the baby to check for himself.

"Well what!? What the hell is it Eva; stop scaring me like that," as he raised his voice, his eyes were turning dark, until they become a shade of ebony-brown.

He had forgotten what fear felt like, but now, he was remembering it, with all intensity.

Even though Eva looked calm, he could sense the tension in the air. She was blocking her thoughts.

She said slowly, "She is fine..."

Michael was confused. He demanded, "I know something is not right, so just tell me what it is."

"I'm afraid we'll have a problem keeping our secret. Look at her eyes."

"What? What are you taking about?" Uneasy, he looked at Adara.

Eva took few steps towards the crib and placed her baby inside. "Have a look," she directed.

As she gently touched the baby on the cheek, the little girl opened her eyes and looked around the room. They both saw a pair of mesmerizing, sapphire-blue eyes looking around and trying to focus on something.

Michael could not believe what he was seeing. "What in the world? What an unusual color."

After a moment, he added, "She is beautiful."

Surprised, Eva looked at him and said, "Is that the first thing that came to your mind? Don't you see the problem here?" She raised her voice.

He kept looking at Adara when he answered, "This is unusual, but I don't see the problem—"

"Then, take a look at that," Eva interrupted and slightly pinched Adara's foot.

"What the hell are you doing!?"

"Shhh! Just look."

At that moment, the baby made a grin, and before her eyes closed shut from crying, her irises turned completely black.

Michel froze in disbelief.

Eva picked their baby up and cradled her, rocking her side to side. She noted curiously, "The same thing happens when she gets upset or is simply uncomfortable; her eyes get dark, and when she's really upset they turn black."

"Just like ours," Michael whispered. He sat down on the chair and murmured quietly as he arched his head back, looking at the ceiling, "And I thought she was safe."

"We have to do everything possible to guard the secret and keep her from harm," Eva said with a determination.

"When I spoke with Charlotte and Marcel, right after Adara was born, they were still traveling but said they would be back home by the time we got back. I wondered if they suspected anything. They were not surprised, and actually, now that I think about it, they seemed extremely thrilled by the news. At first I didn't think much of it, but now, I suspect they knew all along."

As different thoughts rushed through his head, Michael knew that his parents would always keep Adara safe.

No one can find out. She has to remain our secret.

CHAPTER FOUR

The Prophecy

EVA WAS PACING up and down the hallway of their two-story house located just a few miles south of the Water's Edge.

It had been two days since they left the hospital. That gave them enough time to settle in with their baby girl and to have the Stewards over for a visit just the other day.

Even though the Stewards had been friends with the Monsantos for generations, the rule of keeping the secret still remained. Throughout generations, Monsantos had kept their true identities a secret, knowing that mind control and passage of time can erase everything.

Stepping out of the kitchen, Michael said to Eva, who was pacing up and down the hallway, "It's not even seven in the morning." He went back in to finish making his coffee.

Eva was glad that Jennifer visited them the day before and helped set up all the things for the new baby.

She answered, projecting her voice to reach Michael, "I think they will be here early, I can feel it." Right after she said that, a loud knock at the door startled her and made her turn. She approached the door and opened it without hesitation.

"Good morning Eva." Marcel embraced her as he walked through the door. "It is so good to see you again. And no better occasion than under such joyous circumstances."

"So, I see that congratulations are in order," Charlotte raved and hugged her daughter in-law.

Marcel, standing next to Charlotte, looked strong and distinguished as always. His olive complexion and dark brown hair with few strands of gray made him look both energized and distinguished. He had to age himself a bit to fit the role of the father to Michael—but still, he looked more like an older brother than a father.

For Eva, sometimes, it was strange, thinking of Charlotte and Marcel as Michael's parents. Time had made family lines quite blurry.

Michael knew that his parents had been on Earth for thousands of years. Looking at them, it was unreal to think that they had been here all this time and had lived through so much over the centuries.

Looking outside the door, Charlotte announced, "Nicola and Jason, along with Paulette and Filipe, are not far behind." As she said it, two cars pulled up, and Eva saw her friends get out of their cars, each couple carrying a baby carrier.

With a smile on her face, Charlotte continued, "Their first official meeting."

Eva was not sure what to make of that, but Charlotte did not elaborate.

Everyone walked inside and, after greeting one another, followed Eva to the family room.

Marcel's strong voice broke the silence, "Eva, I see that Michael is still in the kitchen, perfecting his morning brew." He took a whiff of the air and smiled. "I find it interesting that he drinks it, but it must be for the taste. Did he get yet another variety from your travels abroad? And I guess we all like our routines." He chuckled, walking behind Charlotte.

Eva answered him as they walked towards the family room, "There are some things we get attached to and are not willing to give up, no matter the logic."

They sat down in front of the fireplace and felt the subtle warmth radiating from the flames. Soft crackling of the firewood intensified after Eva added few more logs and moved the cinders with an iron spike.

Charlotte said, looking around the room, "I have always loved the way you decorated. So welcoming and cozy. I see that you spent some time here," she pointed to the few blankets and cups on the table. Then she looked to the far side of the room and noticed a wooden bassinet.

"We have already met the boys," Charlotte said and pointed to the babies, now in the arms of their parents. The two couples were sitting comfortably on the sofa.

"May we see our granddaughter?" Charlotte asked and took Marcel's hand.

Michael came out of the kitchen with a coffee mug in his hand and looked at them as they approached the bassinet.

He greeted everyone quickly and then turned to Charlotte and Marcel as he said, "I realize you already know what we're going to ask you." He then looked at the bassinet.

Charlotte said, approaching the baby, "So this is Adara. It has been such a long time since—" After a moment, she added, "Yes. We would be honored to be her godparents. To protect her and ensure her safety until she gets her powers and reveals herself," Charlotte proclaimed, still looking at the sleeping baby.

Eva and Michael looked at each other, not sure what to make of that.

Then Eva asked, "What do you mean about revealing herself. We realize that she is different, but..." She was unable to hide the uneasiness in her voice.

Charlotte and Marcel looked at each other; Marcel explained, and when he spoke, everyone heard pride in his voice, "She is more special than you think. She is one of the chosen ones we had been waiting for... for centuries. She is part of the prophecy." He marveled and pointed to the babies.

The other parents were calm and at ease; it was apparent that they already knew what Marcel was talking about.

"These three," he pointed to the babies, "are going to save our people and will unify humankind by bringing equality to the world. They have the power to stand up to the Dark Lords and give the world a chance at peace."

Michael put down his coffee and approached them as he looked at Adara sleeping in her bassinet, "Yeah, sure. I think you got the wrong children. Don't you think you demand little bit too much from such small babies?"

There was an uncomfortable silence.

Noticing that no one said anything, Michael continued, "Our Family has been advocating equality for centuries. But no one is able to come to any kind of understanding. And besides, how do you know she will be willing to fight for that cause."

Charlotte explained, "They will not start until they grow up. And anyway, the cause was her idea. She was the one who organized the plan in the first place."

Eva could not believe what she was hearing. "You mean they have to stand up to the Dark Lords? But these children are so... fragile."

Charlotte stressed, "Eva, you know there is nothing fragile about your daughter and the boys. You saw Adara's eyes. Brayden and Ethan's are the same."

Marcel added, "You see, each one of these babies has a free soul. Their blue eyes are the sign of freedom. We had been promised warriors, marked by blue eyes, signifying they were Lords reborn. These children are those Lords. But they are not like any other Lords. They are not limited by the rules, or chains, that were put upon our people."

Charlotte said, "Those children are a gift from the Sentinels. When their time comes, they will fight the evil that has been spreading on Earth for countless generations. They will stand up to the Dark Lords and stop the oppression. We were warned that if the evil is not stopped soon, there will be no going back. These children are the answer, and our greatest secret."

"They are our salvation," Marcel added bluntly.

Later that morning, Eva was standing by the bay window with Adara sleeping in her arms.

She was thinking about the events of the night when Adara was conceived. Eva remembered the dream she had late that night, long ago, when she was sleeping next to Michael. She could swear she had heard voices in their room; and when, in her dream, she looked around, she saw a couple of silhouettes standing by the bed, holding hands. The dream faded as quickly as it appeared. Now, she wondered if it had been a dream at all.

She turned around and noticed that Nicola and Paulette came into the room and sat down on the sofa behind her.

Eva joined them after placing Adara in the wooded bassinet by the window. She said, "I didn't know what that night was going to bring, but I don't regret it." She looked at the crib.

Nicola added, "In a way, I am not surprised. Now that we know, I feel reassured that it was supposed to happen this way."

Paulette agreed, "It does feel right. As if we are being lead through this. Like we are not alone."

Eva smiled.

Adara started fussing, so Eva approached the bassinet and picked her up. Adara's sapphire-blue eyes glimmered and shined as if being illuminated from within.

Both Filipe and Jason quietly walked into the room, each holding their son. The boys were wide awake and comfortably cuddled in soft blankets. Their intense sapphire-blue eyes shone brightly.

Eva turned around and laughed, looking at the two babies. "All three of them look like siblings. Because of their eyes, they look like they are related."

They all chuckled and agreed, seeing the similarity between the children. For their people, it was normal for a child not to bare any resemblance to the parents. Each generation went through a complete genetic mutation, and no one was surprised when children had an *unexpected* skin or hair color. Therefore, to see three children with the same, previously unseen, eye color was truly an extraordinary sight.

In the hallway, Charlotte and Marcel stood by the doorway and looked at the three couples by the bay window.

Unsure, Charlotte whispered to Marcel, "Should we tell Michael about his... heritage?"

Her husband looked at her but did not answer.

After a moment he said quietly, "Because of that, Adara is... unique; more fragile. We will have to keep her safe; she is different from the others. I will talk with Eva and Michael. She will need to be closer to Water's Edge so we can ensure her safety."

Then he added, taking Charlotte's hand, "It was necessary. Because of that, Adara is very special. That's what gives her the advantage over us. Over everyone."

"It was a great sacrifice for our cause. It was one of the most difficult choices we had made." Charlotte took a pause before saying, "We understood the significance of that blood relation."

Marcel looked at the people in the room and said quietly to Charlotte, "Those babies are the fulfillment of the prophecy we were given. Everything was carefully planned. The evening of the Gathering. All of them at the Water's Edge. The ceremony. But was it enough?"

Both Charlotte and Marcel thought back to the events of that night. *It was meant to be,* they both thought.

After a moment, Marcel said, "It's a tragedy what happened to Maureen and Andrew."

They looked towards the babies.

Charlotte said with resolve, "They may see Adara and the boys as being quite helpless, but that will change when the children become of age and get their powers."

"So what do we do now?"

"Now we wait and see… we keep them safe and wait for their time to come." Charlotte sounded determined but Marcel could hear a faint note of fear in her voice.

CHAPTER FIVE

Hold

SIXTEEN YEARS LATER...

Adara grew up to be a quite energetic and fun-seeking young girl. Eva and Michael moved to the Water's Edge to ensure protection for their daughter. Even though their house was not that far away, the protection barrier that had been embedded into the grounds around the Water's Edge was unsurpassed. That was the safest place for their daughter.

Adara loved exploring the grounds, and usually spent a lot of time in the nearby woods, or by the river on the southwest side of the property.

Since her birth, the mansion had always been full of people, including children who were invited, along with their families, to stay over weekends, winter breaks, and summer vacations.

Charlotte and Marcel watched over Adara and the boys as their parents spent most of the time traveling, forming alliances, and strengthening friendships across various Family Houses. They wanted to ensure that when the time came, those families would join their side.

Adara was always surrounded by friends, but there was one boy in particular who spend a lot of time with her, practically never leaving her side.

His name was Kyle.

He was the only son of Jennifer and David Steward, who were the closest neighbors of Water's Edge and remained good friends with Eva and Michael.

The Stewards had been living in this area for generations and the events of the night when Adara had been born bonded the neighboring families even more.

After the three Monsanto children were born, the estate flourished. The extensive southwest fields of the enormous property near the Willow Lake were transformed into guest houses for those visiting. The cottages were encircling the Willow Lake, located on the southwest side of the estate. The entire southwest area along the river, stretching to a lake, was transformed into something resembling a small village of cottages with driveways and open backyards.

Despite all the changes, the grounds closest to the mansion remained untouched with the exception of a large gravel area designated for the cars that could be parked along the northwest side of the building. Now that the family gatherings or charity events were held almost every month, Charlotte and Marcel found it necessary to make the appropriate alterations to their home and to the surrounding grounds. The estate blossomed.

One day, Charlotte said to Marcel while they sat on the vast terrace near the rose garden, "I don't know if it's such a good idea to let Adara spend so much time with that boy. He's not one of us. This will make everything much more difficult later on. When the time comes, they will both get hurt if we let this go any further."

Marcel looked over the flowers by the stone patio and kept sipping his wine. "I think we should let her make her own decisions; she will turn eighteen in two years, so the time is almost here."

As he uttered the words, he could sense Charlotte building an argument, so he smiled and quickly added, "But I will have a talk with Kyle; he's a few years older than Adara, so I guess this would be a good time for me to talk to him about some things."

Charlotte stirred her tea while looking at Adara and Kyle walking towards the rose garden; they were still quite a distance away.

She added, "I am surprised she's not interested in Ethan; it would make things lot easier when the time comes. No more heartbreaks."

"And not for the lack of effort on Ethan's part. He's already drawn to her. I do not understand why she doesn't show any interest in him."

"It must be because they were raised too close together, almost under the same roof."

"But that did not stop her from falling head over heels for Kyle. That boy spends more time here than he does in his own home," Marcel pointed out.

He knew what Charlotte was going to say, so he added quickly, "We know she will end her relationship with Kyle after her Awakening."

He kept looking in the distance. "It was so unfortunate that the other couple perished in that incident. Now everything is so uncertain. Ethan will have Adara while Brayden will have to fight without the support."

Marcel added on a more positive note, "But it will be alright. It has to be. We have waited so long for everything to fall into place. Some of the puzzle pieces are still missing, but we're getting closer for certain. And who knows, maybe the forth one was born somewhere already, we just don't know it yet."

With a feeling of regret, Charlotte said, "She was not born during the Alignment, and the next one will not be here for many more years. In addition, she wasn't born in any of our Families; I know that for sure. If anything, she was born into one of the rival Houses, and I for one, will not be visiting other Lords asking for the update on their family status. They are the ones we are rebelling against."

Marcel pointed out calmly, "We are not fighting them yet. There has been no open revolt in a long time. We have to keep the peace until we are ready to act."

Charlotte whispered, "Everything is getting so close now. I'm feeling impatient, as if something is urging me to act."

"I feel it too. We have been waiting for a long time, and the battle is almost upon us. It is difficult to just sit and wait for things to start. But I know that any false move could undo all the hard work. We need to remain patient."

After a moment of silence, Charlotte added, "What puzzles me in this situation is that Kyle is being blocked. I don't understand why we are not able to influence him."

Marcel nodded, "Like I told you before, I suspect it has something to do with Adara; she must be blocking him from us, somehow."

Charlotte wondered out loud, "Just like the others, she doesn't know about her heritage, so I don't understand how she could be doing what she's doing."

Marcel sighed, "Sentinels are silent about that too."

Charlotte looked at the rose garden. "They are coming back. No better time for the talk than now." She looked at Marcel and smiled.

He got up with a groan and headed towards the young people who were getting closer to the patio.

He knew the conversation was necessary, but he was not thrilled about being the one to initiate it.

Adara's hair was visible from a distance as it reflected the bright sunlight in her fiery, chestnut locks.

With his arm raised high, Marcel shielded his eyes from the bright sun and said, "Beautiful day, isn't it?" Then he added quickly, "Adara dear, Charlotte wanted to ask you something about your party. There are still some details she wasn't sure about. Would you be a dear and humor her? You know how particular she gets when it comes to party planning."

Adara nodded.

But before she started towards Charlotte, Marcel added, "Kyle and I will be there soon. I also need a word with him before the party."

She looked puzzled, so he quickly added, "It's a guy thing. We'll meet you in the house shortly."

They watched her walk towards Charlotte, who was by the kitchen door.

Kyle saw her leaving and suddenly started missing her. They had just spent an entire morning together, but he was already missed her. He gazed at the terrace that stretched across the back part of the mansion. Alongside it, multiple entryways lead to different parts of the house; from where he was standing, the kitchen was on the far right of the building.

As the door closed behind Adara, Kyle turned to the man next to him.

Marcel was still looking at the kitchen door when he heard Kyle's voice. "So what did you want to talk to me about Mr. Monsanto? Something about Adara's upcoming birthday party?" he inquired in a grave voice, as if he knew what was coming.

Marcel turned to Kyle, regretful grimace spreading across his face. "Well, not exactly."

Kyle looked at Marcel and started feeling uneasy.

Marcel could sense that it would not be the most enjoyable conversation.

He never paid much attention to Kyle's appearance, but now, he noticed that this young man was not a boy anymore. He was as tall as Marcel, and just like him, had broad shoulders, dark hair, and olive complexion that seemed to catch all the sunrays.

After a short pause, Marcel stated, "I've heard that you are following in your father's footsteps and are planning to join our firm. It will be great to have you in our company when your internship is up. You will be the youngest attorney our firm has ever had." Then he added, "But then again, you are truly talented and...

please, do not tell anyone I said so, the most visionary and passionate one there."

Kyle felt a bit embarrassed, but he truly loved what he was doing there as an intern. The home schooling and graduating early from the university fast-tracked his career. He worked hard, but the knowledge and success came surprisingly easy to him. That is how he was able to achieve so much in such a short time.

Kyle answered, "I enjoy what I do. It feels like second nature to me."

Marcel patted him on the back. "Well, I'm pleased with your choices. You will be very successful at what you do; I know it. But as you know, this type of career does not allow for much spare time."

Looking at the kitchen door, Kyle asked, "Is that what you wanted to talk to me about? My career choices? Or is there something else?" He was trying to be polite but did not like where the conversation was heading. Especially with the last thing Marcel said. He could sense there was more, and he did not feel like playing games. Not on that topic.

Marcel answered, "There is one more thing. I will try to make it as short and to the point as possible," he said as he made few steps towards the stone patio.

Kyle walked with him.

Marcel continued, "As you know, Adara's parents entrusted us with her safety. I know that you and Adara are very close. I am fine with that. However, I also know that things between the two of you are moving little too fast for my comfort."

Marcel could not read Kyle's mind, but he could imagine that the young man's heart was sinking. He felt sorry for him, as Kyle's family had been close to his for generations.

He continued, "You should remember she will be sixteen this weekend, but that does not make her an adult. I also realize that Adara is different from other girls her age, but again, that still doesn't change anything. There are things she wants from you, and there are things you want from her. I realize it is normal even though it may be embarrassing for you to admit to that."

Kyle felt like someone punched him in the stomach. He suspected this conversation was coming sooner or later, but it did not make things any easier, now that it had started.

Marcel continued relentlessly, "Adara usually gets what she wants... but not this time. I am going to be strict about that."

Kyle stood there like a statue, with a resignation on his face, unable to move.

Marcel continued, "I think you are a wonderful young man. You are what, twenty?"

Kyle answered in a broken voice, "I just turned twenty-one."

Marcel realized that he and Charlotte have missed the party the Steward held the other week. They had to attend a family meeting that was held with the new allies they secured. He raised his brow and concluded, "Five years can make a big difference. I want you to make sure that Adara waits until she is old enough to make her own decisions. And by *old enough*, I mean turning eighteen. Then she will be free to do as she pleases, but until then, it is up to the adults to make sure she is safe and doesn't make choices that she will regret later in her life... choices like intimate contact."

Marcel could see that Kyle felt uncomfortable, so he continued slowly, "And again, when I say adults, I mean us, which also includes you."

Even though Kyle tried to keep a calm and collected composure, he still looked miserable, standing there like a man who just lost his most precious possession. He tried keeping his face as emotionless as possible, but the pain was still visible.

Kyle asked, "So, do you want me to leave Adara? To break up with her?"

Marcel answered as they were making their way towards the kitchen door, "No, I am not asking you to do that. I am asking you to make sure Adara doesn't get what she will soon ask of you. Do not do things that cannot be taken back. In other words, no sex. Charlotte and I... we want her to be happy, but some things have to wait until she's an adult."

Marcel slowed down his steps and eventually stopped.

Facing the house, he looked at Kyle and said, "This is the only time I will talk to you about this because I know that you are going to take this conversation seriously. Our families have been friends for years now, and I know that you would not want to do anything to upset that friendship." Marcel was trying to sound as friendly as possible, but it was hard to dismiss the gravity of his words.

He added, "Now let's go to the kitchen and see what they came up with for the additional entertainment Charlotte wanted. Come on... smile, it's not the end of the world; we both know that. And as an adult, I am sure you realize it is for Adara's own good."

So many thoughts raced through Kyle's mind. He was embarrassed, angry, and heartbroken—all at once.

He loved Adara. He had been by her side for as long as he could remember.

She was his first love. His only love.

This conversation felt like a nightmare. Having someone bring him to the ground like that felt devastating. He knew how young Adara was; and some of those things Marcel talked about still remained unsaid between Adara and him.

Now hearing Marcel voice what both Kyle and Adara had been thinking about felt brutal and intrusive.

But as an adult, he knew that Marcel was right. Adara was young. Too young.

And yes, she always got what she wanted.

Earlier that day she almost got exactly that. It nearly got out of hand this morning by the river bend.

There, in the cool water, touching her warm body, he had stopped himself and he stopped her, but barely. He realized that the only reason they were able to not go any further was because things happened unexpectedly.

They were caught off guard and wanted to do what felt right at that moment. Luckily, they had realized it was wrong and stopped before reaching the point of no return, as Adara called it later.

Now thinking about it, Kyle was not as upset about the conversation with Marcel. It helped him see things from a different perspective. It was so easy to get lost in the moment with Adara.

The flashback rushed through his head—he was holding Adara's soft hips as he lifted her up in the crystal clear water, so she could climb on his shoulders and dive into the river.

It all started so innocently.

Next thing he knew, her lips were on his, her arms wrapped around his neck as he held her hips against his waist. They were chest-high in the river as she moved her body closer to his, swooshing of the water between their torsos sent an intense sensation down his back.

He had caught himself forgetting where he was when he kissed and tasted the skin on the side of her neck, feeling her warm breasts on his chest, his burning skin cooled by the water rushing between them as Adara moved impatiently, trying to move her bikini to the side.

He stopped suddenly realizing what was happening.

She did not want to stop. Reaching down, she was trying to lower his trunks. She tightened her legs around his waist.

He could not hide it. He was ready to take her; but he gently pushed her away and calmly looked at her.

"Not here. And not now," surrounded by the clear, brisk water, he had whispered in her ear.

The guilt of what he had almost done sent shivers down his spine. *I cannot lose control like that ever again.*

Adara and he talked about it later as they rested on the grassy shore.

He apologized to her, and she admitted that she too acted on impulse.

That was a close call. It cannot happen again.

Trying to shake the images from that morning, Kyle looked at Marcel with determination, and concurred, "Yes sir. It is about Adara. We have to protect her. You can trust me. I would never do anything to hurt her. I love her and I respect her," Kyle confirmed with resolve, his face stern and stoic.

Marcel smiled and patted Kyle on his shoulder as they entered through the kitchen door. He saw Kyle stepping through the threshold and felt a sting of sadness. Marcel stopped for a moment, as he was struck with a sudden, deep sensation of heartache that was yet to come; he felt the impending pain—of the day when Adara turns eighteen and no longer is the same.

The moment she blows the candles out, gets *infused* with the knowledge of the life she had before this one, she will remember what she shared with Ethan. She will also remember the purpose in her life and will no longer have feelings for Kyle.

She will cease being Adara that Kyle knew, and will resume her previous life. The memories of her love for Kyle will float away as quickly as the flames leaving the candles.

CHAPTER SIX

The Birthdays

TWO YEARS LATER...

It was the middle of the week and the house was getting ready to celebrate three important birthdays. The Water's Edge was steaming with excitement as people were rushing from room to room.

Adara was in the kitchen, finalizing the seating arrangements; Kyle was helping her sort the cards, placing them in the small box she had on the table.

Adara sighed, "Mom and Charlotte always go overboard with those preparations. They said it's the tradition in our family; to celebrate like that, that is. And apparently, this particular birthday is especially important to them."

She looked at all the cards on the table; there were a lot of people attending. Too many for her comfort.

With a soft sigh she continued, "I remember the family and friends turning eighteen; those were the most exquisite parties I have ever seen. And I guess they will not make this one any less grand. I still think it's too much."

Kyle smiled and suggested, "We should humor them. They enjoy it. Plus, it's not just for you. Your cousins are celebrating their birthdays too. All on the same day," he added with a comedic gesture of grandeur.

Adara scoffed, "They are not my cousins. We have the same last names, but that's only because our families originate from the same place. As far as I know, there is no relation. But I guess growing up together, in the same house, for most of the time, makes them kind of like family."

She placed few more cards on the pile to sort, and then she continued, "It's their birthday, but they are nowhere to be found."

Kyle was curious. "I always wondered why you had never noticed Ethan or Brayden. You never seemed even a bit interested in either of them... ever."

He looked at the box on the table and then slightly raised his eyes to see her reaction.

Adara looked at him with a question in her eyes and asked, "What are you talking about?"

Then she opened her eyes wider, realizing what he meant. "Are you serious? We were raised in the same house." After a pause, she added, "But for your information, I did notice them." She could see how his face changed for a split second.

Adara laughed. *Is he jealous?* With a beaming smile, she threw one of the empty cards at him and said, "Sure I noticed them, but my heart beats for you." Then she added with frustration, "But, I guess I'm doing something wrong since you're still resisting me and my attempts at seducing you. Not even romantic Spain can break the wall you put up. " She giggled, but her smile faded quickly.

She continued in a gravel voice, "I was sure they sent me away for that semester abroad on purpose. They said it was to show me more of the world; to go visit our distant family. Don't get me wrong; getting away from Water's Edge was a welcomed change, but it also meant being away from you. I missed your smile and your energy."

He laughed. "What do you mean my energy?"

Adara' eyes got serious when she said, "You have this goodness in you and such hunger for life. It's difficult to describe. Being there, away from you, with my distant family, felt so odd. It was as it they were bored. Like nothing impressed them anymore. It felt strange. I missed your sense of adventure."

"But you have that within you already. You are plenty adventurous." He chuckled.

"It feels better when I can share it with someone who appreciates it. I wanted to share it with you. Thank you for visiting me there…"

Kyle thought about his visit to Spain. Back then, he had decided to surprise her, knowing it would make her happy to see him after being separated for so long. But he subconsciously knew that the visit was for him even though he said it was for her; he had not been able to be away from Adara any longer.

She said she missed him. But it was he who was hurting each day they were apart. Seeing her smile, and listening to her talk, always brightened his day. Adara was so thirsty for knowledge and open to different perspectives. There was never a dull moment when she was near. There was always something to talk about.

His busy days at the law firm seemed to be set up like that on purpose. He loved what he did, but being separated from her dulled everything.

His sudden decision to fly to her had hit him hard; he was on the jet that same hour. He did not stop until he saw her bright smile and felt her arms around him.

Kyle had known she would be back to Water's Edge soon, but he could not resist the unexpected visit.

He showed up during the party at the villa she was staying at while in Spain.

When he got there that evening, not long ago, he pulled her to the side. The music was blasting across the granite hallways. Looking down at the people dancing in the main room, they stood in the unlit corridor balcony that stretched around the perimeter of the room with the dance floor below them.

His hands caressed the outside of her thighs as he moved his fingers up, towards her waist, under her short skirt. He embraced her from behind and kissed her neck. The scent of her hair was intoxicating.

He tasted her skin, the tip of his tongue slowly making its way from her neck to her shoulder.

Adara sighed and pressed herself against his hips and moved her hand between their bodies, touching him. That move sent a pulse throughout his body. At that moment, he did not care about what he had promised before. All he wanted then was to have her.

The combination of alcohol, music, being close to her, and how she touched him, made him lose control.

Standing behind her, he reached underneath her skirt, and slipped his hand between her lace panties and her skin, touching her soft, warm stomach, and moving his hand lower.

She let out a soft moan and pressed herself against him even harder, slowly moving her hips side to side, teasing him.

Kyle knew she felt how hard he was.

She asked him to lift her short skirt, rip her panties off, and take her from behind.

When he hesitated, she whispered, out of breath, as he kissed her shoulder and moved his hand lower, down her panties and between her legs, "Please. I need you. I do not want to wait anymore. You always stop. Not today, please. I don't want to do it myself anymore."

He knew exactly what she meant. He knew that touching himself, while he thought about her, brought some relief each time he came, but it only made being near her so much more painful. He wanted her so badly.

But he promised.

"We can't," he uttered breathlessly, trying to convince himself.

It did not work.

He kept moving his fingers between her panties and he realized he could not stop. His fingers slid effortlessly back and forth and he felt how wet she had become under his touch. *What am I doing?* "We can't," he repeated.

They had never done anything like that before. He had never touched her that way. "We can't," he repeated, hoping to believe it himself.

"Why? I love you, and I know that you love me. I need you. I want you in me. I want to feel you inside," she pleaded and moaned softly as his fingers moved faster and faster. She parted her legs wider and lifted her skirt.

"I promised. No sex until you are old enough. Until you are eighteen." He gasped for air. *So what the hell is this? No. I don't care.*

The thin fabric of his pants was the only thing keeping him from ripping into her from behind, as he realized that she somehow lowered her panties.

"That is not fair," she said, panting, and reached to the back looking for a button of his pants.

He grabbed her hand to stop her. "No. I promised."

"I want to feel your skin on mine. I just want to feel you. I am so close. I don't want to do it alone again. Make me come. Please." She begged, gasping for air. "Don't enter. Just let me feel you on my skin." Her breaths became shallower as his fingers moved skillfully around her moist entrance, without slipping in.

Kyle unzipped and lowered his pants slightly. Moments later he was pressing his penis against her buttocks. Her warm skin felt so soft against him.

Adara let out a gasp and moved his hands onto her hips, as she herself started moving her finger in and out and around her vagina. Her senses were overflowing; she could not keep herself upright; her knees were weakening, so she leaned against a console behind a massive square column next to where they were standing.

She moved her fingers faster and faster; she clenched her thighs tightly.

Right before she came, she felt Kyle slid his hard penis between her thighs just outside her vagina.

The place where he wanted to enter was so close; he felt her pulsating opening so tight and wet, ready for him to enter her. The softness of her skin, her wetness, and her heat radiating all around and against his penis made him climax with her as he thrusted himself in and out between her clenched thighs, all while trying to remind himself not to rip into her.

The memory of that night, not long ago, haunted him, as he was not sure if what he did that evening meant that he actually broke the promise he had made. He did not enter her. But did it mean they had no sex? He was not sure how to classify that. She was still a virgin. But she was not untouched. Did he violate the promise? He chose to think, no. He did not. *It was all on the outside. I merely touched her on the outside.* That thought brought some solace to his conscience, but not enough to leave his thoughts.

Kyle put away the card he was holding, got up, and walked around the table. He pulled up a chair next to Adara and sat down on it. He took her hand and pulled her to sit on his lap.

With her cheeks flushed, she put her arms around his neck.

Kyle whispered softly, looking into her eyes, "I love you so much it hurts. The thought of losing you makes me feel dead inside." The words seemed to choke him as he uttered them with cracking voice.

Looking at the window behind Adara, he paused for a moment and then confessed, "There is not a day that goes by when I don't think about you, and how much you mean to me."

Holding her tight, he kissed her softly, gently touching her lips with his. Each move he made showed the pain of having to control himself. He wanted to embrace her and hold her tightly; and never let go.

After taking a deep breath, he said, "Do you remember the night when I told you I loved you?"

He took her hand and kissed her wrist.

Adara remembered it vividly. That cold autumn night was burnt in her memory; she recalled how he held her and told her how much he loved her, flooding her with kisses.

Kyle continued, "There was something I haven't told you about what happened that evening. That night was when I felt fear for the first time in a long time. Right there, on that pier, I felt terrified because I finally had something I cherished so much; the mere thought of losing it made me cringe in pain and fear."

He softly touched her cheek with the back of his hand and gently swept few locks that fell out of place. "I don't think I had actually told you about the time when I first realized that I was in love with you. It happened when we got stranded in the storm one afternoon, coming back home from our swim at the river."

Kyle continued while holding her tight, "You know how I always had that irrational fear of storms ever since I was a child. However, that afternoon, being caught in the bad weather, all I could think about was your safety. You told me that you were scared, and that you couldn't move. At that moment, I felt so much strength awaken in me; I felt as if I could actually fight that storm and face anything, just to keep you safe. I embraced you and held you in my arms."

Adara recalled the images from that afternoon, as if they had happened yesterday. She smiled and said, "And you told me you would never let me go and would always be there to protect me. Then you told me that together we were stronger than anything else on this Earth." She kissed him softly. Then she continued, "That afternoon in the pouring rain, with lightning all around us, I stole my first real kiss from you. I was fifteen back then. Seems like ages ago."

Holding her tightly, Kyle whispered, "I know it feels weird, but I cannot remember the time when I had not loved you. But that night, I had realized how empty my heart would be without you in my life. The only fear I had felt since then was the fear of losing you."

Adara smiled and contemplated on the past. "I have always been surrounded by so many people and never had a reason to feel alone. But it felt to me that people, who surrounded me, were like flickering lights—there, but not actually there. It's hard to explain, but it felt like the only steady and real thing was your presence. Everybody has always been there for me, but it was as if they were observing me, waiting for my next move. I felt, and still feel, loved by them, but I think they are waiting for something; like things are not real at all."

She placed her head on his shoulder and continued, "Whenever I felt lost and couldn't find a place in the world, I knew I could count on you to let me know what was real. It is scary to admit, but I feel that if I will not have you in my life, I will simply fade away; that I will become someone I don't know. I will lose myself. You help me... be me." She ended with a whisper.

Kyle noticed she had tears in her eyes even though her voice did not break. He kissed her salty tears away and embraced her tightly.

She pulled away for a moment and gazed at him.

He said, "All that aside, I told you before that I made a promise to wait. Until you were old enough. I couldn't take our relationship to the next level... until now."

Adara smiled, her bright-blue eyes beaming playfully. She leaned over and kissed him slowly, tasting his lips. "Did I hear it correctly? Did I hear you say, you couldn't until *now*? So in your opinion, you think that you can *now*?" She kept giggling and kissing him.

Trying to gasp for air, he kissed her and softly spoke between the kisses, "After you blow those candles out and officially become a consenting adult, I will make you mine... if you will still have me. I will not stop at anything then."

He was drowning her in kisses, and gasped for air himself. He said, trying to catch a breath between his words, "The memory of what happened in Spain makes me wanna take you right here, right now. The only thing stopping me is the thought of what would happen if someone walked in on us. I would not stop even then.

They would have to leave, or watch. And that would not go well with our families."

She knew he meant it.

Kyle's kisses did not stop.

Her lips felt heavy and wet. Her body was pulsating with every heartbeat. It felt so good to be so close to him. She could feel his lips on her shoulder; his hot breath on her skin, each time he exhaled between his kisses. As he held her waist with one arm, and her neck with the other, she felt like she was floating. The only thing holding her still and in place was Kyle. She was gravitating towards him; it felt so right.

Adara had forgotten where she was for a moment until she heard an excited voice coming from the hallway.

It was her mother.

Eva was quite excited about something and was making her way to the kitchen. "They are here. They are parking their car by the west entrance." The closer she got to them, the clearer and louder her voice became. "Would you be a dear and help them get their bags into the guest rooms."

Kyle and Adara stood up and looked at Eva as she stepped into the kitchen.

When she saw them, she smiled and stopped by the counter. She tried hiding the sadness. Seeing them so happy together, brought to mind the fact that it would soon all be over. Eva knew that today was the day when everything would change for the four young people, Adara, Ethan, Brayden, and Kyle. Nothing would ever be the same after tonight.

Eva pushed her thoughts aside and said, "They are unpacking, and I'm sure they could use some help with that."

Adara answered, "I'm still not done with the cards. Can you finish that for us mom." She pointed to the box.

Eva offered, "I'll take care of this; you two go and say *hi* to Ethan and Brayden." She sat down and looked at Kyle, "Thank you for helping out with the party arrangements."

"It's my pleasure Mrs. Monsanto."

Eva chuckled and reminded him, "It's Eva, remember? Eva and Michael."

Kyle smiled, looking at her unusually youthful face. "Yes of course. Eva. I will learn someday." He smiled and quickly left the kitchen to catch up to Adara.

Eva sat down and looked in the direction they left, trying to push away all the depressing thoughts from her mind.

The party was going as planned. Charlotte and Eva truly outdid themselves. The food was delicious; the waiters were making rounds, ensuring guests had everything they wanted, including a full glass of champagne or wine. The music was playing in the background.

The table on the side of the room had an array of sweets and three enormous birthday cakes. The middle of each cake read: *Happy Eighteenth Birthday. May the Doors to the World Open for You.*

Each one was inscribed with the name of the birthday person; one for Adara, one for Brayden, and one for Ethan.

On the left side of the table was a small round cake with pink and red roses, and a small inscription woven into the ornate details that read:

We Remember

But the letters were so inconspicuous that no one paid any attention to the design, nor to the writing.

It came time for Adara to blow out her candles first. Ethan would go next, followed by Brayden.

Kyle was standing next to Adara as she got ready. The guests started to sing the birthday song for her.

Kyle asked her quietly, "Do you know what you're going to wish for?"

"I sure do." Her eyes fixed on him, she whispered with a smile, "I will wish for us to be happy and to spend our lives together."

Kyle smiled at her and warned, "You shouldn't say what you wish for out loud, or it won't come true."

Adara smiled mysteriously as the guests finished the song.

With one breath, she blew out the flames.

CHAPTER SEVEN

Together

THE SOUND OF clapping and ovation spread across the room, and the music started playing louder.

Kyle moved closer to Adara and kissed her on the lips.

After few seconds, she slowly pulled away. She opened her eyes gradually and looked at him.

Kyle did not know what to think.

He asked, "Is something wrong. What is it?"

He saw her serious face so close to him.

After a moment of silence she said, "I would prefer if you would stop kissing me in public and... continue it somewhere more private if you don't mind. And do it properly. Just the way I like it."

His eyes brightened when she added mischievously, "Also, I believe there was something I have been asking for... but never got."

Kyle gazed at her and asked, "And what would that be?" He chuckled quietly.

Adara stepped closer to him and touched his chest, then embraced him as she leaned towards his face and kissed him slowly, with her lips slightly parted.

He could feel her breath on his tongue and her wet lips on his. He pulled away and smiled, feeling so happy just being near her.

Kyle teased, "I think I may know exactly what you mean. And if I'm right, it's something I had wished for even before I could admit it to myself." He whispered in her ear as he saw people approaching them, "Now there is nothing stopping me from getting what I want and what is mine."

Before she could respond, she noticed her friends getting closer, extending the wishes from a distance.

She quickly addressed the crowd near her. "Let's not forget that there are two more cakes with candles on them, waiting to be blown out. Let's make room for Ethan and Brayden," she shouted and clapped as she waved at them to approach the table.

The staff were already lighting the candles on Brayden's birthday cake.

As people were gathering around the two remaining guests of honor, Adara took Kyle's hand, pulled him to the side, and said, "I don't think they'll miss us whatsoever. What do you say we skip the rest of the party, sneak out, and go somewhere where we can be alone."

They smiled at each other as they left the house through the north entrance.

In the grand family room, the crowd was gathering around Ethan and Brayden, as they decided to make the formalities short and blow out the candles simultaneously.

At the back of the room, Charlotte, Marcel, and other Lords from partnering Family Houses were standing in shock, still not believing what just took place few moments ago.

Charlotte said it first. "What just happened? What in the hell happened?"

Paulette clarified, "Or rather what did not happen."

"Something must have gone wrong," Marcel wondered. "But what? It's not as if we have to do anything to make it happen when they turn eighteen. It's automatic when they blow out the candles. That's when they *awake*."

Someone added, "Well, in Adara's case nothing happened. She obviously did not get her powers. She's still *asleep*."

Marcel interrupted, "Let's see what happens with Ethan and Brayden; now it's their time," he said as they were about to blowing out the candles.

Lords looked in the direction where Brayden and Ethan stood. Everyone held their breath in anticipation as the two young men were taking their first breath after the flames were blown out.

Next, the Lords noticed that both men were looking in their direction.

After that, Ethan and Brayden smiled briefly to the crowd and started receiving wishes and getting handshakes.

Marcel exhaled. "At least Ethan and Brayden *awoke* like they were supposed to. That's a relief," he muttered.

Ethan was making his way towards the Lords, but Brayden got stuck behind, talking to some guests.

Paulette smiled with hesitation and came closer to greet her son, "Congratulations on rejoining us. And happy birthday of course."

Ethan hugged his mother gently, then he turned to the rest of the Lords. "Where is she? Where is Adara? I don't see her. I cannot sense her presence at all."

Scanning the crowds in the room, Charlotte realized it too. She could not sense her either. As if Adara was deliberately blocking them. *But she doesn't have her powers yet. How is it possible that she's hiding from us?*

Loud music spreading across the room; guests were talking in groups. Everyone was busy enjoying the party. Only a small group of people was aware of what had happened. They needed to make sure to not cause a scene, so Charlotte led them to a sitting room adjacent to the grand family room.

Charlotte's voice seemed to break a little when she spoke, "She must have left the room just a few minutes ago; with Kyle. She is still *asleep*."

Even though Ethan was trying to hide it, everyone could see the intense agony on his face.

Ethan said, "Yes, I know. But where did she go? I can't sense her anywhere." He looked through the opened door, as if hoping to spot her somewhere in the crowd.

Everyone near him was silent.

After a moment, Ethan continued, "During my Awakening, the Sentinels told me she's not ready yet, and that she will *awaken* when it's her time. Brayden suspects it has something to do with the fact that his Emma is not here. Now I know whose cake it is in the corner."

Then he added, "Brayden is devastated. He almost gave up on the fight, even before it began. The Sentinels had to convince him to come back here from the Void and to wait for her. He agreed and decided to look for Emma—to see if she was reborn."

Everyone looked at him in silence. No one wanted to state the obvious.

Ethan looked at the door leading to the hallway and continued, "But I need to find Adara. Now that our cards are on the table, the Dark Lords may try to attack us. And she is not ready; she is still vulnerable. I need to protect her."

As he tried to step towards the door, Marcel stopped him. "I'm afraid it's not a good idea for you to go after her now. To her, you are simply Ethan, a friend she knows; but that's all you are to her, a friend. And you know that you can't force her to stay under your protection. She is eighteen now; we cannot even see her in our minds anymore; and neither can you. Am I right?"

Marcel could see the devastation in Ethan's eyes, but he continued talking. "She's blocking us. She did not *awake*, but she's already powerful in her own way."

Charlotte added, "The best thing we can do for her now is to make sure that no one knows where she is. We have to hide her somewhere safe until she's ready."

Ethan turned around and looked at them, "Are you serious? Do you mean to tell me that you're allowing her to stay with Kyle? Do you realize you are talking about my wife!?"

They saw fire in his eyes.

He continued, "We belong together; we had been together ever since we all came here; and that includes all of you," Ethan pointed to the Lords standing in front of him.

Their faces were solemn and full of pain.

He added bluntly, "Don't forget, we all made this pact together. But it was Adara and I, along with Brayden and Emma, who made the sacrifice and left Earth to be reborn stronger and during the time when we had the greatest chance at victory. This time is now, and I am not planning on fighting alone. Do not forget who you are talking to; I am not simply just a boy who turned eighteen; I am one of you; I am ageless, reborn in this body by my own choice, with your approval and support."

Ethan felt anger rising within him. He was inconsolable. "Adara is my mate, my wife, my love. How can you ask me to let her leave with this mortal man? I can't watch her leave. I will not let her leave!"

They stood there, helplessly watching Ethan's heartbreak and fury.

Brayden came around from behind. "Ethan, you have no choice. She doesn't remember you yet. You need to let her live her life until she's ready to join us."

Eva was almost on a verge of panic at the thought of Adara being out there in the world, vulnerable.

She urged, "We have to get her out of here. We cannot risk her being discovered."

It was too much for Ethan; he stormed out of the room.

Brayden reassured Eva, "I will find her and bring her back home safely."

As Brayden was leaving to find Adara, he heard the Lords talking about how to find a place for Adara to hide and wait until she is ready. Until she *awakes* and gets her powers.

❖

Driving through the narrow road, Adara and Kyle were making their way towards the cabin. The road was gently sloping down towards the vast lake in the valley. The sky was completely clear, with stars shining brightly over the estate.

They were passing other guest cabins that were spread around the lake, along the winding dark road, lit with ornate-looking, sparsely set street lights.

The air was slightly cool and fresh, with gentle breeze blowing through the trees.

Kyle pulled up to the driveway and parked the car.

The sounds of the nearby forest were making their way towards where they were standing; the sounds became more audible when Kyle turned off the engine.

He approached the cabin and opened the door.

It was a spacious, two-story, stone and wood cottage, with a heavy wooden front door, and a large porch in the front and back of the building, overlooking a nearby forest.

They went inside and turned on a dim light in the foyer.

Adara could feel the tension in the air, as if the room were filled with electricity. Her skin was tingling and her body was pulsating, overflowing with anticipation.

They did not speak when they drove here. Now, being inside the cabin, they were simply looking at each other, knowing why they were here.

So many things had already been spoken before.

They wanted to be close, and yet, now that they were here, they seemed to prolong the separation.

Adara watched as Kyle bent over the fireplace, and was adjusting few logs before building the fire.

The warmth slowly started spreading around the room. Crackling sounds filled the air and softly resonated around them.

Adara slid off her shoes and shoved them next to the dark leather sofa. She then walked barefoot to the windows and pulled all the curtains, shutting them tightly.

Now Kyle was watching her reach the curtains and gently stretching her arms as she pulled the fabric.

He broke the silence and embraced her tightly from behind, "I finally have you alone."

Adara let out a sigh, feeling the tension leaving her body when he pressed himself against her.

He turned her around to face him. He saw that her lips were parted slightly.

Kyle held her close, as she placed her cheek on his chest.

He inhaled the scent of her hair and slowly slid off the strap of her gown.

Stepping behind her, he whispered in her ear, "I have promised to wait until you were eighteen. I don't have to wait anymore. If you want me to stop, I need you to tell me. And if you do, please say it loud and clear."

She looked back at him and felt her heart beating faster; the warmth was spreading across her body.

Kyle declared, "You were always mine, and I was always yours. My heart beats for your heart."

Adara leaned her head back as he kissed her neck. "Always and forever." She exhaled. Each heartbeat pulsating and centering around her belly.

They stood in front of the fireplace; the flames were growing stronger.

Adara turned around and gently pushed Kyle to sit on the dark leather sofa.

She stood in front of him, took his hands, and slowly placed them on her thighs, helping him lift her long gown up and away from her knees.

He moved his hand under the fabric and pulled down her panties as she held the long dress.

With her bare foot, she slowly moved her white panties to the side.

Still sitting on the sofa, he got closer to the edge and moved his hands up her thighs; first on the outside, then again, with top of his hand, on the inside. When he touched her with his fingertips, he noticed how soft and warm she felt.

Still standing, Adara let out a sigh, feeling her legs getting heavy. A pulsating warmth spread across her back and hips, through her lower stomach, and centered between her legs. She ran her hands across his hair and glanced down at him. When he looked up, she noticed he was breathing heavier, and his eyes were dazed.

Kyle froze mid-move, as if asking for permission to proceed.

She took his hand and moved it higher up her thighs. Slowly, she led his fingers where she wanted him to go.

She let out a moan, feeling his hand move rhythmically between her legs with her hand on top of his.

Adara gasped for air enjoying his warm and wet fingertips moving down there.

Kyle could sense her thighs parting ever so slightly with each move he made. He sat up even closer on the edge of the sofa and placed his hand on Adara's hip, pulling her closer to himself.

His face by her stomach, he took a breath in. The scent of her perfume filled his lungs. He took another deep breath in.

She unbuttoned his white shirt and loosened his belt.

All you could hear was ruffling of clothes and heavy breathing.

The buckle on his pants made a clear, clanking sound when Adara removed it with a steady grip.

There were no words, just breathing.

She gently pushed him, so his back was against the couch.

Kyle lifted her gown up, which kept slipping, and shifted Adara on top of his lap with her thighs spread far apart. He pulled the top of her dress down, exposing her breasts. Marveling at the sight before him, he touched them and kissed her hardening nipples, sucking on them gently, his tongue sliding on her skin. As he kissed her, he noticed she was trying to catch her breath.

With her hand, she lifted his face; she kissed him passionately, tip of her tongue teasing his.

Her lips were soft and moist.

Kyle unzipped his pants. He was struggling with her dress, trying to lift it up higher.

Adara felt like she was floating on a cloud, but at the same time, was heavy as a stone. She wanted him inside her; the ache that spread across her abdomen was only topped by the need to feel him inside.

She looked down and saw his white shirt and his gray pants completely opened. She reached towards his face and ran her fingers across his hair, moving her hand down to his cheek, his lips, down his neck, his chest, going lower and lower. His skin was warm and smooth... she moved her hand down on his stomach... she slid it lower... inside his opened pants... she stopped... she felt he was ready... more than ready.

The front of her gown kept slipping. She let out an impatient sigh.

Adara looked into Kyle's eyes and slowly raised her hips as he was still moving his fingers inside and around her opening, massaging her gently. Each move sent pulses across her abdomen and hips.

After few minutes, she could not control herself; she felt like he would make her come right then. She felt the tension rising inside her; she moved impatiently wanting him in her; now.

Still sitting on the sofa, he impatiently tugged his pants down, exposing his erected penis.

He placed his hands on her hips and grabbed her buttocks as she slowly, but steadily, lowered herself onto him, still touching herself, on the verge of orgasm.

That moment... She felt him inside, sliding in effortlessly through her wet opening. The pleasure and sweet pain spread throughout her body, but she did not have time to dwell on the pain, her body overtaken by intense ecstasy.

Adara kept stimulating herself, and she moved herself back and forth slowly. She felt how Kyle filled her deep inside. She felt his fingers join hers between her legs.

Sigh... Was it her or was it Kyle? She couldn't tell.

Everything was blending together. Her heavy breaths... his heavy breaths...

As he moved his finger in her rhythm, she touched his stomach and noticed red streaks her fingers made where she placed her hand.

He looked down as well... They both let out a gasp... another sigh. Sweet pain turned to dense ecstatic agony, looking for a release.

He kept pushing up on her as she kept pushing down on him. He moved his hands to the sides of her buttocks, grasping tightly each time he thrusted.

With one hand on his chest, and the other still touching herself, she felt as if she were melting inside. She let out a sigh, feeling the approaching release. She felt him move inside, rhythmically up and down, up and down... faster.... and faster. She was moving her fingers around her bud, sliding them where he was entering her. Soon, all she could feel was a rhythmic up and down, pushing harder, faster, deeper... and ...and... she heard herself scream...

The orgasm hit her hard, with a wave of pleasure spreading in all directions, coming from where her fingers moved rhythmically... She stiffened briefly, losing herself in the moment.

His movements got even more intense; she was melting... sweet agony...

She was floating down, but he did not stop... he started moving faster and harder.

Adara, started to play with herself again and let out a loud moan as she climaxed for a second time. She knew that *one* was never enough, so why would it be different now. She smiled at the thought.

Did she hear Kyle join her? Yes... It was both of them; each in a sweet explosion of pleasure.

He slowed down. His body still trembling.

Their hearts were pounding; all they could hear was their breaths.

Exhausted, she collapsed on his shoulder and clang to him.

After a moment she sat up, looked at him, and smiled, feeling happiness surrounding her.

He took her hand and placed it on his cheek; he kissed the inside of her palm.

Adara placed her other hand on his face, caressing him gently.

In a smooth motion, Kyle laid her down next to him on the oversized sofa.

Adara felt a warm and pulsating sensation where he entered her body, just moments ago. She stretched and moved her legs, feeling her wetness spreading around.

The ache was becoming more apparent with each pulse she felt between her legs.

Quietly, she let out a painful moan.

Kyle noticed she was hurting and said, "I will get you something. Be right back." He zipped up his pants and got up slowly.

Adara looked at him as he walked past her, going to the kitchen; his chest was bare and his shirt was loose on his sides.

She heard the water running for a while.

He came back with two crystal glasses and the champagne.

With a loud pop, Kyle opened the bottle and filled the glass with sparkling golden liquid.

He gave one to Adara and toasted. "To us."

They both took a sip. And another.

Adara smiled at him and cringed in pain.

He looked at her with a glimpse of guilt and kissed the inside of her hand again.

Smiling, she warned him, "That better not be regret I see in your eyes. Pain is momentary and unimportant now; it will go away soon enough." Her eyes glimmered in the dim light.

Kyle got up and poured more champagne. The crystal clinked as the glasses made contact.

"To our forever." He toasted again.

Adara sat up and lifted her glass. "And always," she added, slowly drinking it all.

He poured her another, which she drank as well.

"Helps with the pain," she added. The buzz from the champagne eased the pain, and the throbbing turned dull and distant.

"And speaking of forever," he said and reached for his jacket, which was on the sofa. He pulled out a ring from the pocket. "I have been carrying it with me for a while."

He asked, "Will you spend your forever with me?" The three round stones shone brightly in the dim light. "Three stones to represent us as friends, lovers, and soul mates for eternity."

She sat up and hugged him, smiling brightly. After a moment, she eased the embrace and sat up again. After wiping few tears from her eyes, she took the ring.

It gleamed brighter, now that her eyes were still wet from the tears. She could see the sparkles dancing around. Adara lifted the ring and placed it on her left hand. She nodded and said, "I am yours, and you are mine. Always."

❖

The fireplace radiated warmth throughout the room.

Kyle was in the kitchen, busy preparing a light snack, when he heard the shower running. He put the plate on the coffee table by the fireplace and went to the bathroom.

Adara was almost done with the shower.

He undressed and joined her.

The water was warm and calming.

He did not want to touch Adara because he knew he would have a hard time stopping himself after feeling her body on his skin.

They dried themselves off, put on soft thick robes, and went downstairs, both knowing that the night was not yet over.

Grapes and a sandwich, paired with champagne, tasted delicious.

They lay down in front of the fireplace on the pillows they pulled from the bedroom earlier.

Adara turned towards Kyle and pulled out a small glass vile from the pocket of her robe.

Looking at the little bottle and holding it up to the light, she explained, "Charlotte used this on me when I got that nasty scrape on my knee when I was six. The pain was gone instantaneously. Even though she told me I could not take the bandage off for few days, I knew my knee had healed right after she put this on my skin. I don't know what's in it, but I know it works."

Kyle looked confused.

Adara opened her robe and let it slide off her body.

She got up and poured more champagne into their glasses, handed him one and said, "Bottoms up."

They finished and set the glasses down.

She took the bottle and poured a bit in her now empty glass, she then set it aside.

Adara put few extra pillows on the floor and rested on them.

Kyle knelt by her legs as she handed him the vile.

He spread her thighs, opened the vile, and let few drops fall between her legs where he entered her before.

Short sting... and the pain was gone.

She lifted her hand and touched where the pain had been before.

Nothing. No pain. Just a soft, warm and sweet sensation, followed by a dense longing, spreading across her hips.

Seeing her run her hands between her thighs, he felt it too.

Kyle leaned over and kissed her soft lips.

He whispered, "I wanted to have you for such a long time. I fantasized about touching your skin, so soft and warm. The more I thought about you, the more it hurt when I couldn't have you... but no more. You are mine."

He followed her hand with his as she touched herself slowly. He spread her with his fingers... he could feel how ready she was for him. After taking off his robe, he knelt by her feet.

Adara moved her hips impatiently, but he did not proceed. Not yet.

She wanted to pull him towards herself, but he resisted, teasing her.

Kyle took the champagne flute and slowly poured a little bit of the golden liquid between her legs, letting it spill around her opening.

He looked at her. She was breathing heavily... he lowered his head down. His tongue sliding up, spreading her crease, tasting her and the champagne.

Oh, god, what sweet ecstasy.

I cannot wait any longer. I need to feel you.

She spread her legs even more and grabbed his dark hair, as he was moving his tongue between her inner lips. She felt his tongue move up and down and in all directions, rubbing against her bud, his breath cooling her skin with each deep exhale. Adara did not want him to stop, but she also wanted to feel him inside her.

After few moments, he turned her around. With a sense of impatience, he knelt, and made her kneel in front of him, with her buttocks pursed up. He held her hips firmly and pushed himself inside her, in one move... all the way in.

She gasped.

...He came out... and entered back in... again... and again...

Her moans came in the rhythm of his moves. She could not hold herself up, pleasure overpowering her, so with his hand, he grabbed few nearby pillows and placed them under her stomach.

He gently, but firmly, pushed her shoulders down, keeping her buttocks up, as he entered even deeper... her behind puckered upward.

She was so hot and wet... he pushed in again and kept thrusting... faster... and faster...

With each move, her moans became louder, and finally, he heard himself join her. He did not know who screamed first in the sweet release.

Morning came too soon.

Sun was already high up in the sky, when Adara heard a knock at the door.

She stretched under a thick soft blanket. Her muscles were achy, yet relaxed at the same time. It was warm and cozy under the cover; she felt warmth radiating from Kyle's back—she truly did not want to get up.

Another knock.

Oh, just go away, she thought and pulled the blanket over her head.

Kyle was asleep and did not move a muscle.

Another knock.

Whoever it was, was *not* going away.

She lifted her head from under the blanket and looked towards the foyer where she could see a narrow, frosted-glass window by the door.

Yep. Someone is still there.

Reluctantly, Adara moved from under the covers and grabbed the robe, which was nearby. While still halfway under the blanket, she quickly put the robe on to catch as much warmth under it as possible. With an annoyed groan, she got up and headed to the foyer, wishing she could go back under the warm covers.

She turned the lock. The heavy door moved smoothly without a sound.

Standing there, in the bright light of the midday, was Brayden. He looked somewhat uncomfortable.

Adara glanced over his shoulder at the gorgeous lake-side view. In the distance, on the right, she could see the Water's Edge. Then she looked around. Seeing all the driveways filled-up, she realized that all the guest houses were occupied.

It had always been convenient to have guests stay on the property; there were plenty of cottages by the lake in case all the bedrooms got filled at the main house.

She smiled, a bit embarrassed to see Brayden at the door. "Good morning," she murmured with a coarse voice and cleared her throat.

It was apparent that Brayden felt uncomfortable, looking at Adara standing there in her white robe and with messed up hair.

He apologized. "Sorry to disturb you, but your parents are looking for you."

"Is everyone alright?"

"Yes, everyone's fine. It's just that your parents wanted to talk to you at the party, but you were nowhere to be found. I noticed your car in the driveway last night. I decided to catch you in morning to give you the message. You did not answer your phone, so I figured you were asleep."

Adara realized she left her phone in the car and suspected that Kyle did the same.

Brayden looked at Kyle, who approached them and stopped behind Adara, embracing her shoulders.

Kyle smiled and kissed her cheek. While still close to her face, he whispered, "Good morning." Then he turned to Brayden and said, "I see you are already up after such an intense party. Happy Birthday." He adjusted his white shirt, which had few small, dark, blood stains on the bottom, and tucked it into his grey trousers.

Adara guessed that he must have gotten dressed after she left to see who was at the door.

Kyle continued, "I didn't get a chance to wish you my best yesterday. I hope the party was a success."

Before Brayden could answer, Kyle added quickly, "I will have to call Ethan. We left without wishing him a happy birthday—"

Brayden interrupted, "The party went well. But I wouldn't bother calling Ethan. He left immediately after. Something about helping with a case at Marcel's New York location, as continuation of his internship there." He lied.

Brayden was still a bit sore after last night's confrontation with Ethan.

Earlier that night, Brayden had found the place where Adara stayed with Kyle.

Most cottages were still empty, as guests were enjoying the night at the mansion.

Ethan also had driven towards the cottage that night. As he approached the driveway, Brayden swerved in front of Ethan's car. That made Ethan stop across the lawn, nearly hitting the tree, and sending dirt and grass flying across the yard.

Brayden got out of his car, approached Ethan, and swung open driver-side door, nearly damaging the hinges that creaked dangerously.

Fuming with anger, Ethan stormed out of his car and shoved Brayden across his chest, making him stumble back.

To catch his balance, Brayden's hand landed against the tree that was behind him. The tree made a cracking sound; and where Brayden's hand landed, there appeared a scrape in the trunk, as if it were hit with a heavy object.

"Get out of my way! This doesn't concern you. You are not part of this," Ethan yelled.

Brayden grabbed Ethan's shoulder and stared into his eyes. He said slowly, trying to keep Ethan calm, "Yes I know you are hurting, but you at least know that your love is here, and that she is safe. Isn't that what's important? I don't even know where my Emma is. She has not been reborn in any of the houses of our allies. But what I fear now, is that she had been born within one of the Dark Lord's families. We have no access to them; not unless we are willing to reveal ourselves."

Ethan stood there looking at the cabin. He heard everything that was said, but it was apparent that he could not get his mind away from Adara.

Seeing how Ethan was only half-listening, Brayden shook Ethan's arm, and that made Ethan look at him again.

Brayden continued, "Now, after our Awakening, our people will talk. The word will get around. All our allies know who we are. Eventually, it will spread to our enemies too." He raised his voice, "We need to put our mission as a priority. Sure, I could go and look for Emma within the Dark Lord families, but that would surely reveal who we are. So what do I chose? I chose to live in agony of not knowing where she is, and if she is, or will be reborn behind the enemy lines. You at least know where your love is and that she's safe."

Brayden put his hand on Ethan's shoulder and said, "It's not just about what we want. We cannot put ourselves first. We need to remember the mission." Then he added, "You will not get her back by barging in there now."

"But she is my Adara, my... wife," his voice broke as he stared at the cabin, just several yards away.

Brayden said, "You don't have to tell me that, my friend. Your love had been an inspiration for everyone. But that was then, and this is now. She does not belong to you anymore; at least not yet."

Ethan was obviously distraught as he forgot to place a block on his thoughts. Brayden heard how Ethan weighed the potential of his actions. Ethan realized that by walking through the cabin door, he would only push Adara further away. If he stayed away, he could at least be close to her, and to be her friend—like when they were kids. He knew that was logical but he was still infuriated with his impossible decision.

He deplored, "But he's there with her. Do you realize what he's doing... with her."

Brayden stood unmoved.

Ethan knew it was pointless. Brayden was right.

After a moment of silence, Ethan asked, "Why have we done this in the first place? Why have we come here?"

Brayden knew what Ethan meant. He knew Ethan did not mean this road; he meant Earth. Brayden answered him bluntly, "To bring freedom."

Ethan did not say anything to that.

"That means freedom for everyone. But you are denying Adara her freedom. The same freedom we came here to give back to the people. Everyone has a right to be free. Even Adara." Brayden said quietly.

"But she doesn't know what I know. She doesn't know any better."

"That's what our people said to justify oppression and control over us and humans."

Ethan did not respond. He just looked towards the cabin, which stood nearby. He could see a dim light in one of the windows. So close, yet so far away.

Their thoughts could not penetrate the barrier that was around the cabin. Maybe for the better.

"Let her go. For now at least. Let her make her own choices," Brayden urged.

"I can't," Ethan uttered breathlessly, hurt chocking him from within. His vision was getting hazy from few tears of hurt and anger, pooling in his eyes.

"You know she'll hate you if you try forcing her to remember."

Ethan just stared at the cabin.

Brayden observed him.

Hurt, disappointment, and desperation were painted on Ethan's face. He stood quietly, but on the inside, he was scramming.

Brayden could hear Ethan's internal rage, fury, and pain each second he stood near his best friend. The internal screams were overwhelming.

"Give her time," Brayden said. He took Ethan's shoulder and turned him away from the cabin. He then straightened his own shirt that was torn where Ethan shoved him earlier.

"This is not fair," Ethan said, almost inaudibly, and got into his car.

The tires screeched against the road as he sped away.

That was last night.

By now, Ethan was far away. At this point, nobody knew where he went. He just said he needed time. And distance.

Now, Brayden was here by the cabin. The sun was shining brightly and the tension from the events of last night seemed to have lifted with the morning fog.

Brayden looked at Kyle, then at Adara, and added slowly, "But going back to the reason for why I'm here. Adara, your parents need to discuss something with you at home; with both of you."

Adara blushed and said in a quiet voice, but she could not hide the chuckle, "I hope they didn't get too upset over me spending the night outside the house... with Kyle."

"No. It's a different matter altogether. In fact, they'll be glad to find out you two are still together."

Before Adara got a chance, Kyle asked, "What do you mean *still together*?"

Brayden quickly corrected himself. "That's not what I meant to say. What I meant was that she's here, safe, with you. They were a little concerned after they didn't see her at the end of the party." He lied again.

Adara gestured to Brayden to come inside.

Hesitantly, he accepted.

The room was a bit messy, with the pile of pillows and blankets by the fireplace. Champagne bottle, glasses, and few plates were still on top of the coffee table.

"Excuse the mess, but there was no time to clean up." Adara lead them to the kitchen.

She took the cups out of the cupboard.

"I will make some coffee," Kyle offered and kissed her forehead.

"And I will go change into something more company-appropriate." She smiled and pointed to her robe. She placed the cups down and left the kitchen.

Kyle pointed to the round, glass table surrounded by four metal chairs.

Brayden did not sit down, but instead he shook his head. He stood there for a moment, with his back against the counter, looking at the chair, and then spoke without raising his eyes. "Kyle, I need to ask for your assistance."

The gravity in his voice was obvious.

"It must be serious enough. You're not even looking at me," Kyle replied, sensing that something was wrong. Cold fear was slowly creeping up his spine. He tried pushing the thoughts away; to no avail.

Brayden looked up, and the expression in his dark sapphire-blue eyes reflected the seriousness of his voice. "Adara is in danger."

Before Kyle could ask anything, Brayden continued, "We received a warning of a threat from one of Marcel's clients. Marcel, as the attorney who won the case against the... never mind the details. Now the brother of the convicted is seeking revenge on the one who is dearest to Marcel, and who is most vulnerable. And that is Adara."

Brayden did not have a problem lying about the story. He knew that the threat was real; that is what counted.

Kyle looked in the distance through the wide kitchen window. After the initial shock, he replied, "We need to get her out of here." The fear resonated in his voice.

"That's the plan," Brayden confessed and sat down.

Kyle joined him, forgetting all about the coffee.

"We arranged the way for the two of you to get out of here while we take care of the problem," Brayden stated.

"Adara will not run away. You know her; you know that she will not leave simply because of fear. She's pretty stubborn that way. She would rather face whoever was threatening her. She will not agree to run. That woman can protect herself." Kyle chuckled, but the fear for Adara's safety was booming across his mind.

"My point exactly," Brayden concurred, his eyes fixed on Kyle. "That's why we found the way to get her out of here and to ensure she would not stay in one place for too long. In the meantime, we'll do what's necessary to take care of things here. We will inform you when it's safe to come back. It may take a while though."

Kyle looked at him with a question in his eyes, not following what Brayden meant.

Brayden smiled and took out an envelope he had in his jacket pocket.

Kyle looked at the white envelope Brayden placed on the table and was sliding towards him.

He took it and looked inside. After few moments, he looked up and enthusiastically declared, "That just might work."

At the Water's Edge, Adara was looking at the contents of the envelope Michael handed her few moments earlier.

"A trip," she exclaimed, enthusiastically studying the papers inside.

Eva added, "An around-the-world trip."

"But it will take ages to visit all those places," she stammered hesitantly, suspicion rising in her voice. "Are you trying to get rid of me or something?" she asked with a chuckle but also with a hint of uncertainty; she looked at Kyle.

Michael reached into his blazer and pulled out an identical envelope. "This one is for Kyle." He handed him the papers and said to both of them, "We know how much you wanted to travel. Also, we know that being home-schooled had never been your favorite thing, so this is our way of saying *thank you,* and encouraging you to go out there and explore. You will have a chance to catch up on what you have always wanted to do, but never had time for because of family obligations or volunteering we all did."

Adara looked at Kyle.

He was smiling, unable to hide the excitement.

She closed the envelope and said in a comically serious voice, trying not to laugh, "Europe it is then. Around the world with my favorite traveling companion."

Seeing that Adara did not question them further, everyone there felt relief but also uncertainty. She would be away from her home; away from people who were always there to protect her. Now she would have Kyle keeping her safe from those who could potentially hurt her.

Later that night, at the cabin, Adara and Kyle stretched in their comfortable bed, looking at the lake through the second-floor balcony window.

Adara was having second thoughts about leaving.

Kyle said, "We are so fortunate. We can simply get in the car, or the plane, or the boat, and go wherever we want. Not everyone has a chance at such an exciting life."

"You're right; not everyone can do that. Normally, people cannot just drop everything and leave. But what about the firm, your job, or my school?"

"It will all be waiting for us when we get back. It's a family business after all. I will have a place there whenever I come back. And your acceptance letter does not have an expiration date."

After few moments, she smiled brightly and exclaimed, "It's so exciting. Visiting all those wonderful places. But, I also want to go where we can do some good with our time. I want to see how other people live. I want to do something meaningful." She sat up, eyes wide open; she was ready for their adventure.

She looked as if she was about to leave right then and there.

Kyle laughed, "Easy. Let's get some sightseeing done first, and then we can see what else we can do."

The opened envelopes were on the nightstand; Europe, Asia, Australia, Africa...

CHAPTER EIGHT

Struggles

FOUR YEARS LATER...

Kyle's mother was sitting in the sunroom of her estate with Charlotte and Eva. They were drinking tea and looking out the windows that opened towards the rose gardens on the east side.

Jennifer pondered while looking at her almost empty cup, "I do not understand young people these days."

Eva smiled and answered, "They do visit every year, and they will be here for Adara's birthday."

Jennifer sighed and continued, "Yes. I know." After a brief pause she added, "I know I had already said it before, but I am grateful for how your family has taken the situation. I mean, we were all fine with them traveling; but getting married without a warning, just like that... His father and I were terrified that it would ruin the friendship between our two families. I'm glad that it didn't cause any bitterness; after what Kyle did."

Eva smiled and noted, "What both of them had done." Then she continued, "They have been married for almost a year now and are busy doing what they always wanted—traveling and helping others. None of us know what the future holds for them and how things will go; we can only hope that it will turn out for the best. For everyone."

Jennifer wondered out loud, "It was just like Kyle. Getting married in that small village somewhere in Africa, god knows where. I don't even know where to find it on the map. We did not even get any pictures. What a shame. They could have invited us. Africa is only a flight away."

Charlotte laughed. "Jennifer, they are young and in love. They love what they do; and as Adara announced over the phone, they were completely overtaken by the atmosphere there. It felt right."

"Yes, you're right," Jennifer agreed. "Adara will be twenty-two and my Kyle will be twenty-seven. They were inseparable since they were children; it is only fitting. It was about time they got married; I just wish they had done it here," Jennifer looked into the distance.

Eva added slowly but regretted her words the moment she uttered them, "I am sure if I talk to Adara, they will agree to have a formal ceremony here, with their family."

Jennifer lit up like the Sun, "Yes. Oh, please ask her. That would be marvelous."

"Don't start planning just yet. We need to talk to Adara and Kyle first," Charlotte tried to curb Jennifer's plans but knew that it was futile. The thoughts that were inside Jennifer's head were a dead giveaway. She had already started making plans.

Charlotte looked at Eva, and they both thought the same thing. Adara will be celebrating another birthday, and they will again wait to see if she *awakes* this time.

Some started doubting, and the plans had been postponed. They all wondered if Adara would ever regain her memories and join the rebellion.

Charlotte pondered the reason for Ethan wanting to join them for this year's celebration. He said he had a gift for Adara. Something he needed to return to her.

Brayden, after hearing about that, also offered to join them. He sounded nervous when they spoke, not that long ago.

In the meantime, there had been no communication from the Sentinels. Everyone was getting restless. And now, Ethan was finally giving signs of life after such a long separation from the family.

Even though he had not mentioned Adara even once since his Awakening, Charlotte knew he was not over her. *How could he be over her, anyway? They have a history that goes back centuries—all the way to the beginning. No one forgets that.*

Charlotte wondered about the gift Ethan mentioned.

❖

Few weeks later, the house was again bursting with energy in anticipation of Adara and Kyle's arrival.

It was a late evening when they pulled up to the Water's Edge mansion. The lights outside the building created a beautiful sight as each pathway was illuminated. You could see all the way to both gardens, deep within the estate.

Adara exclaimed, "It has been so long since the last time I saw this house."

Tonight she was celebrating her twenty-second birthday.

Now, sitting in the car, she felt so nervous. The cream colored envelope, containing the invitation letter, rested on her lap. It was the formal invitation to her own birthday party that was to be held at her childhood home. She received it last week and did not let it out of her sight ever since.

After so many years away, with sparse visits on her birthdays, she started missing an actual place she called home.

In their travels, they moved from city to city and never stayed anywhere longer than few weeks. The yearly birthday visits were only few days long, as each time they visited, her family had some emergency or a prior engagement that they could not reschedule. Therefore, they ended up staying only few days each time.

The birthdays were celebrated rather simply, with just her parents, grandparents and, occasionally, Kyle's parents. This time, the family wanted to make her birthday more of a formal celebration, as Brayden and Ethan would also be attending.

Three birthdays together. Again.

Adara wondered what warranted such a grand celebration this time.

It felt strange when she realized how much she missed being with her family and friends even though they spoke on the phone quite frequently.

She was looking forward to seeing everyone again.

She missed them all. She was homesick.

Adara opened the passenger side door and got out of the car. Slowly, she fixed her long, olive-green gown. The rose-gold diamond necklace she had around her neck was shining brightly in the light of lamps leading the way to the front door. Her long, red-brown hair was lightly pinned up to the side.

She stood there by the car, looking at the steps leading towards the entrance. The stone steps looked taller than she remembered. So many steps.

Adara knew it was her nerves, but why did she feel so anxious? She tried concentrating on something else. She looked up at the mansion.

It seemed that all the lights were lit inside the house; it was completely illuminated from within. She heard laughter and music coming from the hallways and from all the opened windows.

Kyle took her hand. "Are you ready?"

She kept looking at the main door, wide-open and welcoming, but strangely daunting.

"I don't know. But... we're here, so I better be ready." She looked at him and added, "I want to come back home. I want to have a home of our own. An *actual* home; a place where I go to sleep every night and where my things are unpacked; and can stay unpacked. I am tired of going from place to place." She had no idea why she just said all that. She realized that she missed her home, but something must have shaken her soul as the emotions hit her hard after seeing this place again.

Looking at the house, she continued, "I thought I could travel forever. But something is calling me back home. Something is missing."

Kyle looked a bit distant, as if not knowing what to say. "I'm sure your parents will be thrilled."

After years of traveling, he almost forgot the reason why they had left; though, he was reminded of it every time they came back here. Only few days at a time.

He missed his family too. But he did not have any regrets. Anything to keep his wife safe. He did not know how much longer it would be before it was safe to come home, but it looked like Adara made up her mind. They will have to deal with it somehow. *If anyone resists her, she will start asking questions.*

He said, "We can talk about it later. Now, let's just go in and say *hi* to everyone. They are all here for you." He approached her and kissed her forehead.

Adara smiled. "Well not exactly. You know that this time, Brayden and Ethan will grace us with their presence," she added with a laugh. It seemed odd to her that they were never there when she visited. As a matter of fact, she realized, she had not seen Ethan since their eighteenth birthday. It felt weird, now that she thought about it. All four of them grew up together and saw each other almost on daily basis when they were kids. However, it was strange thinking about that time. Even the memories were so distant.

She took the first steps. *This is what I wanted, so I should already be running up those steps. I don't know why I'm not.*

Adara looked at Kyle and her mind wandered.

Her marriage to Kyle was everything she could ever wish for, and more. The only thing missing was the children. They wanted to start a family almost ever since they began traveling, but it had been four years of trying, and still nothing.

In their travels across the globe, they saw few specialists, who concluded that there was no reason why

Adara and Kyle could not have children. They were two healthy individuals; they were perfect.

Adara recalled her wedding night in Africa, not that long ago. She had woken up before dawn and stepped out of the hut.

The village was asleep, but she felt restless.

She walked along the huts and sat by the fire pit, which was still burning after the celebrations. The flames were dwindling down, so she took few pieces of wood and threw them in to rekindle the fire. She sat down, looking at the dancing flames.

Sitting there, Adara heard a woman's voice behind her, "You want something that is already yours, yet out of your reach."

The woman sat next to her. It was difficult guessing her age. She was short and slender, with dark, ebony skin. Her short hair was adorned with various beads, matching the necklaces that formed a heavy design across her neck.

With proper English but with a heavy accent, the woman continued while she stirred the ashes using a long cane, "You want a child, but you are blocking it. You need to open up. However, you cannot open that which you do not know."

The woman paused, and the cane froze in the flames. She looked into the ashes more closely and continued slowly, "There is a great journey ahead of you. When you discover who you truly are, you will be free to open yourself to everything. To anything." The woman looked at Adara and added after pausing for a moment, "There will be no stopping you." The woman looked confused and kept staring at Adara as she asked, "Who are you child?" But seeing a complete confusion in Adara's eyes, the woman did not pursue that any further. The woman looked away and started moving her cane in the ashes.

After a moment, Adara smiled, as she saw hope in what the woman had said.

But the woman shook her head as she stared at the flames, "The journey... you should not go alone. It will be difficult. In both good and bad times, we can see different sides of each other. Choose your companion carefully. Know that the journey may reveal something... too hard to handle. You will need to be strong for yourself and for people around you."

Few weeks later, when they were already at a different location, Adara told Kyle about what the woman said; after hearing it, all he did was hold her and remind her that he would be right there, next to her, no matter what happened.

Adara looked around the illuminated estate. Going up the steps of her childhood home made her feel as if she was reaching a checkpoint. She felt drained and energized at the same time. It felt like she was about to embark on the new journey.

No better place than here to discover who she was.

Adara stopped for a moment.

Kyle caught up with her and kissed her cheek. "A kiss for good luck. Not that you need it; but any reason is a good reason, as I always say." He looked at her and realized she was deep in her thoughts. "Where was your mind wandering? What were you thinking about?"

Something is definitely ending, she thought.

When he looked at her, he noticed that her eyes were dark, and the usually bright sapphire-blue color seemed to turn black in this light.

Adara gazed at Kyle and said, "I was just thinking about the night when we left to travel. I was always surrounded by people I knew and people I trusted. After that night, everything changed. Don't get me wrong, I know it gave us a chance to start our lives together, but lately, I have been feeling emptiness inside, like something is missing. Like something should be with us."

After she said that, he embraced her, his strong arms wrapping around her.

She placed her face on his chest.

He kissed the top of her head and said, "We both want to have a family; to have children. I'm certain it will happened one day. Maybe now is not the right time." He too wanted to start a family and was baffled by how long they had been trying without success.

Overpowered by sudden and unexpected fear, he said, "If anything ever happened to you, I don't know what I would do. I don't even want to think about the possibility that you would not be by my side. You are my life. My *everything*. You give me the reason to live and to wake up in the morning."

Slowly, she lifted her head, looking at him, and noticed that his eyes were shining in the dim lights. Then she stood up on her toes and put her arms around his neck as he leaned over to kiss her.

After a moment, she whispered, "Please don't ever let go of me."

He looked surprised and noticed that she also was puzzled by her own words.

They looked at each other. They saw love, fear, and devotion—all intertwined.

In the distance, as if beyond time, they heard a familiar voice.

Kyle's mother was making her way down the stairs; her arms extended towards them, as if trying to gather them up and embrace them.

Jennifer exclaimed, smiling towards Adara and Kyle, "They are here. Everyone! They are finally here."

The party was a success, full of laughter and old stories being revisited. As their friends listened attentively, Kyle and Adara were sharing tales of their adventures.

Brayden and Ethan were there as well. Adara knew they were now part of Marcel's business and spent their time traveling extensively. However, when asked about their travels, they responded by saying that it was mostly for business and that they had nothing exciting to add.

It was nice talking to both of them after such a long time of being away. They all grew up together, and being separated felt quite strange. It surprised Adara how easy it was to simply pick up where they had left off. The conversation created itself. It was effortless. The only thing that felt out of place was an odd feeling that Ethan was balancing between being talkative and strangely quiet. It was as if he was catching himself being too open, and then automatically trying to withdraw his involvement in the conversation. However, she did not have time to think about it, as she was being pulled in so many directions that evening.

It was almost time for the birthday ovation.

All three of them were getting ready to blow out the candles, all at once.

Kyle, holding a glass of champagne in his hand, was standing next to Adara.

She smiled at him. "I hope this night will be as magical as the one we had when we celebrated my eighteenth birthday."

Kyle kissed her lips softly and whispered, "Make a wish."

Her face beamed as she announced, "I still wish for the same thing every time, but this time, I will add something else. I also want us to be blessed with a new life. I want us to have a family."

She blew out the candles and kissed him again.

The room got loud from the background music and the ovation in their honor. As Adara opened her eyes and looked at Kyle. For a moment, she did not know where she was; as if her mind wandered off.

She touched her forehead and said, "That is so weird. For a second there, I forgot where I was."

Kyle looked at her and saw she was genuinely surprised and somewhat uneasy.

After what seemed like endless hugs from friends and family, Adara saw that Ethan was approaching them, pushing through the crowd.

As Ethan stopped next to them, Kyle extended his hand, embracing Ethan's, and wished him all the best.

Ethan politely thanked him but seemed to not take his eyes off Adara.

She smiled, embarrassed, and mentioned the unusual timing of their birthdays falling on the same day, almost to the minute.

Kyle noticed that Ethan did not have a glass to toast with, so he offered to get him one.

Ethan looked in the direction where Kyle was walking away and said to Adara, "I realize that we do not do gifts, so I hope you will not get upset, but I brought you something."

He reached into his vest and took out a red silk pouch. "I had it for you, for few years now, but never got a chance to give it to you."

He gently took her extended palm and placed the silk bag on top of it. "I thought I better do it now before I lose it." He continued holding her hand.

As he held her, she felt electricity pulsating throughout her arm, radiating towards the rest of her body.

Slowly, she retracted her hand and, with a quick glance at him, pulled the string apart, opening the pouch.

She stared at the necklace inside.

Ethan explained slowly, "It belonged to someone very special to me. Long time ago. It's an old family heirloom. It was given to me for safe-keeping. I thought it was time for it to be worn again."

Adara was looking at the necklace inside the bag. She touched the diamonds and sapphires, pulled it out, and set the pouch aside, not taking her eyes away from the exquisite piece of jewelry.

It felt heavy on her hand.

The necklace was simple, yet extravagant at the same time, with a pattern of round diamonds and sapphires set in platinum; the stones gradually increased in size as they got to the middle. The center piece was a very unusual stone, double-casted in what looked like a ring. The stone was round and perfectly cut. It seemed to shine with its own light—white, with sparkles of blue, pink, and violet. For a moment, she thought that she saw all colors of the rainbow sparkling within. It was like nothing she had ever seen before; or was it? Thinking about it, she thought she recognized it from somewhere.

Adara lifted the necklace and noticed how the sparkles went in all directions. "It... um, thank you... it is..." She could not find words.

It looked so familiar.

She could not understand what was going through her head.

She saw it before; but where? Her mind got filled with images she did not recognize.

Adara tried collecting her thoughts. "Thank you, it... it is beautiful, and... it... um, it..." She did not know what she wanted to say, or she did, but it did not make sense in her head.

Ethan looked up at her and announced calmly, "It is yours."

"Thank you," Adara added quickly.

"No. I mean it is YOURS," Ethan emphasized, took it slowly from her hand, and walked behind her. He took off the rose-gold, diamond necklace she had on her and placed it in her palm. Then he gently laid the sapphire necklace around her neck. When he secured it, he pointed to the mirror on her left.

Adara turned around slowly and approached the large mirror.

She was staring at her reflection.

The short necklace was sparkling, beams of colorful light going in all directions. It felt cold and heavy, yet strangely comfortable. After a moment, she could feel how it warmed up on her skin and, at that time, it felt like it became weightless.

The reflection in the mirror. It was her... but not her...

"It is mine," she whispered.

Ethan approached her and added, "It has always been yours." He stood behind her and, with his hand, swept back a lock of her hair that fell on her shoulder.

His warm fingers softly touching her skin sent a tingling sensation down her spine.

Adara looked at his reflection in the mirror. Then at her own. Then at him again.

She ran her fingers across the necklace, back and forth. And then she remembered.

"It is mine," she echoed staring at it.

Adara felt Ethan's warm hands on her bare arms as he embraced her.

He softly kissed her right shoulder.

She looked at their reflection. His blue eyes next to her blue eyes. They shone so brightly.

Adara shifted her gaze and, in the distance, saw Kyle standing next to Brayden.

It looked like they were in the middle of the conversation with each other but paused when they saw Adara.

She noticed their faces were turned towards her—Brayden's blank, and Kyle's frozen in painful realization.

Confused, she turned around and took a step towards Kyle.

She wanted to explain what had happened; but what was she going to say? What should she tell him? She herself did not understand what just took place.

With each step she took, the room got quieter and brighter. She did not know what was going on.

Adara stopped and looked around. *Is that fog, or smoke? No, it looks more like a white veil.*

She extended her hand as if she were going to touch it.

She took another step, but everything was almost completely gone.

She looked back at Ethan, but he was disappearing too. Or was it she who was disappearing.

Feeling fear surrounding her, she took few more steps towards Kyle. Everything was gone.

Adara noticed that with each step, everything seemed to slow down as well.

The last images she remembered were of people frozen behind a white veil.

CHAPTER NINE

Reveal

ADARA WAS SURROUNDED by the dense, white fog. Now that she looked closer, she noticed that not everything turned white. A faint outline of the room with people in it was visible when she focused her eyes. But everyone was frozen, and when she took few steps forward, she was not actually moving at all, as everything stayed where it was. No matter how many steps she took, she remained in the same spot.

She got startled when she heard a voice behind her say, "Fascinating. Isn't it?"

Adara turned around and saw a tall man standing behind her, within arm's reach. He was towering over her. She had to look up to see his face.

His clothes were simple and made out of a fabric resembling some sort of thick silk.

Adara asked, "What is going on? Who are you?"

He bowed his head and said, "Dear Adara, your people refer to me, and to others like me, as Sentinels. You can call me by my name, Margram. We are the keepers of this System."

Before she could ask anything else, he continued, "It is an honor and a privilege to welcome you and to show you your true self. The time has stopped. It has stopped to allow me to give you the knowledge about your life, the world, and most importantly, about the reason for you being here."

Adara looked around.

The man continued, "You are not like the others who got *initiated*. Your time has come, and you are ready for the impending battle."

Adara looked confused, "I am sorry, but what are you talking about?"

Margram inquired curiously, "The necklace, did it not give you back some of the memories?" Without waiting for her answer, he smiled and added, "May I?" He extended his hand towards her forehead. "This will open your mind, and you will see the rest... all that has been hidden from you in this life."

"*This* life?"

She wanted to take a step back, but as she gazed in his eyes, she saw there was nothing that indicated danger; there was only peace and happiness.

As he touched her forehead, she saw images flooding her mind—images of times that have passed long before. She saw oceans and lands that were moving and changing shape. She saw animals that were long extinct, and plants that were not here anymore. The stars that shone at night looked out of place.

But the most fascinating part of the vision was the people she saw. They were different. She realized that, although they looked human, they were something else.

She could see them for who they really were; she could see their minds and read their thoughts. They called themselves the Dusana-Tykim, or the Soul Travelers.

She knew where they came from and the reason why they were here. Earth was their new home. This planet was where they settled after they had been forced to leave their planet.

Adara knew she was one of them. She felt so strong and all-knowing.

But she was also aware of the danger and of her enemies.

In her vision, she saw herself talking with a group of people from her Family House. They spoke about the fight they had been preparing for. The conversation happened long before.

They had a plan. She had made that plan, and she volunteered to be the one who would lead them.

It was to be a daring and dangerous mission, but there was a lot on a line if they had not decided to act. The freedom of their people and also the future of the human race was at stake.

In the images, she saw herself drinking something and then falling asleep, images fading away from her mind. There was someone with her. Ethan.

Adara blinked couple of times after the vision stopped.

She looked at Margram. "Was that me? Did that happen to me?"

He looked worried and asked, "Do you remember me? Do you remember your life before this one?"

Adara thought for a moment and answered with a bit of hesitation, her voice sounding empty as she spoke, "I don't remember you. But I do know that I am a Soul Traveler. I am not human, and I know I have a mission that I agreed to lead."

Margram smiled, but sadness filled his eyes. "I see that you truly are different. We did not know what to expect. The prophecy was of you: *...From, and with the blood of a human to lead the fight and even out the scale of justice and power...* We still believe in you and the others to do what needs to be done. You see, after you got *initiated* you were to instantly remembered who you were before this. But in your case, I can see that it is not so. You know who you were before, but that is where it ends."

She acknowledged with a heavy heart, "I know who I am, but I don't remember being there. I remember it like a story that I have seen, not like something I have lived." Adara looked at him and added, "You are not telling me something important. What is it? How do I know that...?" She felt like she could see into his mind.

Margram answered with a sigh, "It will take a while for me to explain this to you."

She looked around. "I guess we have all the time in the world."

He chuckled at her humorous remark and continued, "There are things we do not communicate through the mind. It is the part that only the Lords know, and the chosen ones are given. I already transferred some of that knowledge, but let me give you a bit of perspective."

"When you came to this planet, the humans had already been living here for thousands of years at that point. You came here because your home had been destroyed, and we, the Sentinels, who seeded this planet, granted you asylum, so you and your people could live here if you agreed to help humans in their development. You all concurred. And as a way of getting ready to come here, you sent out a group of your people to prepare this place for your kind and to see how it would be to live here. The group consisted of few hundred individuals who volunteered to start a new life on this planet."

Adara listened attentively as he continued, "It was an alien planet for your kind. The energy fields were unlike anything you had ever experienced before. Therefore, you wanted to test it out first before more souls made the move. It all started as a test.

"During the first Earth years, we had noticed that something has gone terribly wrong. The planet had changed your people who came here; those who were good, stayed good; but for those with a seed of darkness in their soul... it made that evil grow within them. Instead of helping humans, they wanted to dominate them and to rule over them.

"Your bodies did not age, you did not die. Your race became known as Titans, gods, and other *heavenly* beings because of your abilities. You could control people with your minds; you had extraordinary strength and speed, and, in the eyes of humans, you were immortal.

"Those of your people who stayed behind in the Void, a similar place to where we are in now, needed to find a way of putting a stop to the terror of your kind; so they had asked us for help. We told them of a way that could erase evil from your people. We gave them a prophecy... and that is why you are here. You are going to lead the fight and take away the power from the Dark Lords."

Adara stood in silence, trying to process what she was hearing.

He continued, "I know that you have seen the images. All the evil that you saw is the result of what the Dark Lords had done, and are still doing. They need to be stopped. But they will not give up their powers and dominance over Earth; not without the fight.

"The Dark Lords had separated the realms and stopped all communications with us. They had claimed the planet as their own—to do with it as they please."

Margram took a pause, and before he continued, Adara asked him, "You mentioned there was a way to stop the evil in our people. What do you mean by that?"

He smiled, pleased that Adara was interested in his story, "Yes, there is a way to do that. Only the Lords, who came here at the beginning, turned truly evil if they had evil inside them. Their children would be born with either tendencies but could evolve beyond that if exposed to goodness. Sadly, if they were raised by the wicked, they only knew wickedness. For the Dark Lords to become good, they have to be reborn on Earth."

Her voice sounded hollow when she said, "But to be reborn, they first need to die."

"Yes. And they are not willing to give up the power they possess," he stated.

Margram continued his story, "All of you came to Earth in pairs. You all had mates. You were to start a life here together—to form a society similar to the one on your beloved home planet. But an interesting thing happened after coming here though. Everyone was affected by the urges of this wonderful alien planet. Living on Earth had consequences on all the Lords.

"Earth is a pretty interesting place to live on; creatures living here have this irresistible urge to feel, to procreate, to live, and to hang on to life. There is this need to give life and spread life; it is something that even the Lords cannot resist. When you all came here, you made a pact of rules for yourself and your children and their children's children to abide by. Your descendants would be given that knowledge on their eighteenth birthday, called Awakening. To limit the explosion of the new souls coming here, a temporary rule was set, stating that only the Lords would be granted the right to bring more than one child to this world. The children born on Earth would abide by the Rule of One—only one child per couple.

She introjected, "Wait. So there are more of our people waiting to be born?"

Realizing that the *infusion* left more gaps than he expected, he answered, "Yes my dear Adara, there are thousands of souls waiting to be born to this planet. They live beyond time and space. They are waiting to be released and to live outside the Void." He looked around.

Adara followed with her eyes to where he was looking.

Everything remained frozen.

He continued, "But most of them want to be born into a free world, with no Lords controlling their lives. They want to be free, and we want the world to be free of the Darkness.

"Some choose to be born during this time anyway; they say that life, any life, is still worth living.

"Those who decide to be reborn now, are not born with the knowledge, but instead, the knowledge is given to them. However, there is a trick to that too. The pact limits, or filters, the knowledge given by blocking some of it when the person a*wakes* from the *initiation*. So the person *awakes* with the generic knowledge that was originally agreed upon at the time the pact was made. Nothing else remains after the Awakening. So during the *initiation*, we stopped giving the knowledge that would be taken away by the pact made by you and your people. Your people are allowed to be born to Earth with limits and ignorance."

Margram wanted to take another pause, so Adara got her chance to ask a question. "You mentioned that the pact limits the knowledge our people get when they get *initiated*. So what's the point of all this if the pact we all made will erase my mind anyway," Adara questioned, surprised at herself that she was taking it in so easily.

Radiant smile brightened Margram's face, "Oh, but this is where you come into play, my dear. You are not like the others; you are special. Or to be exact, the circumstances during which you were conceived were special. You were conceived during the Alignment—a time when all the barriers are down. Those who are conceived during that time have a free soul and are not bound by any rules."

"So why not let everyone be conceived during the Alignment? Then everyone would be free," she raised her voice, feeling the tension rise within her.

"Yes, but they would not be free of the Dark Lords and what they had done. We needed someone who could discover the source of their power. Killing them would not release their hold over Earth. For that, we needed people with fire in their heart; people who would not waiver during the times of uncertainty."

"What do you mean people?"

Margram added after a moment of silence, "In the vision, you saw that you had not come here alone. There were four of you, but now, there are only three. The incident with the fourth baby was a tragic event. You see, we do not have control over everything, and even though we planned things so well, we could not have prevented that fatality."

Adara looked puzzled, so Margram elaborated, "It happened in one of the other Family Houses. They died in a family conflict shortly after the Alignment. Maureen was carrying a baby as well, but it was too early for anyone else to notice. Maureen and her husband went against their family; that conflict lead to a confrontation. They lost few of their people; among them, Maureen and her husband, along with their unborn daughter, Emma, who was one of the Chosen Four.

"In light of those events, after your birth, your parents, and the rest of your family, became extremely protective of the three of you. That is one of the reasons why you were home-schooled and were not allowed to travel much outside the estate. The only sure safety was on the grounds of Water's Edge and few other protected Family sites."

Seeing he was not done, Adara remained silent.

"You are different than the other two. We also needed that perfect mixture of human and Dusana-Tykim in your blood."

She stared at him, not knowing how to ask for clarification.

"You see, your grandparents, Charlotte and Marcel, made a great sacrifice for all the pieces to fall into place. You are part human. You have human blood flowing through you veins. This is very unusual I have to say because one of the limitations, which are put on your people, is that your kind does not have children with humans. Your people can only successfully mate with your people; Soul Travelers are not able to bond, procreate, nor feel love for humans. During the *initiation*, you get the knowledge of who you are, and at that moment, if there were any romantic emotions felt towards a human, they would all be taken away. You are not able to have children before *initiation*; and after, you can only have children with our kind."

He paused and looked at Adara.

She looked tired and overwhelmed, but he could see there was anger building within her.

He continued slowly, "So you see, your existence is the symbol of a great sacrifice and a precious gift; both, from your grandparents, and the Sentinels. You are part human. That is as unique as it can be for your people. I say *your people* as you are mostly Dusana-Tykim, and only partly human."

Margram stopped when he saw that Adara had a question.

"But how was it possible for them to have a human child?"

"You were a rare gift from us. Nothing like that can happen without our intervention. But you must not forget your grandparents' sacrifice. It was not easy for Marcel to know that the child Charlotte carried was not his. But he loved his wife, and he loved the child inside her, your father. You are one of the pieces to the victory."

"So the fight has already started?"

"Yes. Technically you have started it a long time ago when you decided to be reborn here; to be reborn during the Alignment. You are one of the original Lords, Adara; you are the one who had started the opposition."

Margram noticed she got quiet.

She looked at her left hand and confessed with a grimace, "I know what you're going to say next; I can see it in your mind. The vision you showed me earlier; I came here with my mate who would fight alongside me. I know it is not Kyle." She paused for a moment. "Ethan was my mate," she whispered with resentment in her voice as she looked up at Margram.

He confirmed, his voice sounding clear and resonating around her, "Yes. You are right. This is also where it gets complicated. The original plan had been to get you *initiated* at your eighteenth birthday, the same day as your mate; however, we decided that you needed more… humanity in you, for your soul to become more human."

Adara looked at Margram. Her eyes widened when she understood. "My eighteenth birthday; Ethan." She grinned saying his name.

"Yes, Ethan. He has been waiting for you since then. He also has the full knowledge, but to his disadvantage, he was not born human like you. However, he has other advantages, which we felt would be useful in the fight. There are other beings here beside humans and your people…"

Adara did not want to think about the reality of Ethan being her mate, so she changed the subject. "So what about Brayden; where is his mate? I feel he is also part of our pack. Did he not find his mate after the Awakening?"

Margram explained, looking in the direction where Brayden was standing before everything got shrouded by the white veil, "Brayden is still looking for his Emma.

We do not have access to the Dark Lords; we cannot see past their... blockades. She may have been born there, but if she has, she will not have her memories because she was not conceived during the Alignment."

Adara whispered, as more images from the past flooded her mind, "Life for life."

"Yes. I see you are getting more of your memories back. I think it will all eventually come back. Sooner or later."

Adara knew he was right. Standing there, she could feel other things come back. Dragon's Blood.

That is how she, how they, ended their existence as Lords. A sip of that substance, and they faded, embracing each other tightly.

Before she got a chance to ask another question, Margram raised his hand slightly, letting her know he wanted to continue, "The combination of how you came to be makes the three of you more powerful than other Lords. But you, being part human, are the most powerful person we know." He could barely contain his excitement.

"I don't feel powerful. But I guess, I just don't know what I feel now." The last words came out quiet and muffled.

Margram took a step forward. "Oh, but you are; dangerously powerful. In addition to all the powers Lords have, you, Brayden, and Ethan have a power that none of the Lords possess. You have the ability to give life but also to take life." He took a pause, and then continued slowly, "You see, when the Lords came to Earth, one of the rules they agreed to, as you now know, was that they could not take anyone's life. For them, it was life for life. If they took a life, they had to give their own life in return. If they killed someone, human, or even one of their own, they would die themselves. It was like a protective measure that was put in place to keep the balance. But the Dark Lords had found a way around that. They used coercion and manipulation of humankind to have humans do the killing for them; not directly mind-controlling them but still having them do their bidding."

Adara looked puzzled, so he continued, "Being born during the Alignment gives you the power to bring balance to this planet."

It took her a moment to realize what he meant.

When she finally understood it, she said with disgust, "So basically you want us to kill for you."

Margram admitted frankly, not breaking eye contact with her, "If it comes to that, yes."

Adara's eyes turned dark. "It doesn't sound right. How could I have agreed to that? I made a choice for me to be reborn with the ability to kill?" She was getting pale.

Margram got quiet for a moment and looked into the distance. Then he declared, his voice steady and strong, "Before you left your previous life, the four of you had talked about this mission. Adara, it was you who pressed for a powerful approach and a swift resolution. You said you would not stop at anything to win this war. When asked, you declared that the Dark Lords spilled enough blood, and now, it was their turn to have their blood spilled if they did not submit."

"We chose this to save our people and humans?"

"They are your people too. There is more to being a human than you think. Humans are just like Soul Travelers, with all their flaws like greed, hate, and thirst for power and control. However, unlike some Soul Travelers, they have a strong counterpart to those emotions. Humans, and those who are reborn here, have the ability to love unconditionally and to spread that love so it grows exponentially and is never divided. The Dark Lords, because of the evil in their soul and because they were not born to Earth, as their bodies were given to them, are limited in their ability to *share* love."

Flashback images flooded Adara's mind when Margram continued the story, "Over the millennia, Dark Lord's tyranny created uproar across all realms. The Council decided that the choice had to be made for them.

"That is why you are here. You see, we, Sentinels, can only create life. It is not in our power to take away life. We are unable to do that even if we wanted to. But you, Ethan, and Brayden are the secret. The secret that has been revealed after your eighteenth birthday.

"Adara, dear, I do not know if you understand what we are asking of you. The freedom of your people is at stake here, and I don't mean only your Soul Traveler side, I also mean your Human side. Try to remember what the Dark Lords have been doing to humans for all those thousands of years.

"Behind every major event there have been Lords, manipulating and scheming to keep an upper hand over humans. That is not right. It has to stop. We think that everyone should have the right to be free and to not be enslaved. You were the one who started the rebellion; it was your choice and your plan."

Adara looked somewhere in the distance and asked in a chilly voice, "So how do you presume we *help* the Dark Lords leave Earth?"

Margram took a slow, deep breath and said bluntly, "The same way you left it."

She raised her eyes and stared at him in silence.

"As you now know, your Star Race is not immortal. The answer to that is in the legends and the tales you have probably heard before. There is only one thing that can end the life of a Dusana-Tykim—a plant called Dragon's Blood."

Adara knew that story. It was one of the tales she had heard as a child. Back then, she did not realize it was a story about her people.

The legend talked about dragons that were feared by everyone; and of one mighty family that did not want to have competition when it came to fear. *They* wanted to be feared and respected.

The family had ordered all dragons to be hunted down to extinction. But they had not realized that the first dragon they slayed was a Sacred creature. It was said that the curse had been placed on the descendants of the people who killed it; and for every drop of blood that the dragon lost that day, a thorny bush grew where the blood fell; it would be poisonous to the descendants of that family. The sweet-smelling flowers would lure and tempt; and when inhaled, could put one to sleep; when ingested, would kill. The plant was almost impossible to be removed, as the roots spread deep and wide; and whenever it was dug up, it would almost always regrow again.

Margram interrupted her thoughts. "But I got away from what I wanted to tell you. I don't know if you saw it in the vision, but each Lord had been given a Gem."

Adara touched her necklace and the shimmering stone in the middle of it.

"Yes. That is one of the Gems. This one is yours," he noted; then he added, "And to make any kind of change to the pact, all the Gems have to be rejoined, and a new pact needs to be made. The Dark Lords will not give up their stones without a fight. They had power over their Houses for far too long. But as I said earlier, killing them is not the main initiative. You need to find the way to undo, and release, the hold they have over Earth. The evil that has been spreading has its roots somewhere. You need to find the way to stop it."

Adara just stood there, frozen and tired.

Margram continued, "I could stay here and remind you of all other stories, but they will come back to you on their own, eventually. For now, there is a matter that needs you attention." He made a gesture with his hand, and the veil started to lift gradually.

Everything was still. People were standing, stopped mid-conversation, motionless, frozen in time.

Margram pointed to Kyle and then to Ethan.

He stated in a clear voice, "Ethan is you mate. For life."

"And we live forever," Adara added bluntly, anger rising within her again.

"You had come to Earth as mates and lived your life as husband and wife, up until you left together with the intent to be reunited after being reborn. Your love inspired people throughout centuries. Your devotion to humanity had no bounds; and together, you had proven it by sacrificing your existence in order to lead the rebellion—"

"I do remember Ethan, but I don't feel love for him." She turned to face Kyle. "He is my *only* love. I do not care what you say; I will not leave my husband."

Margram waited a moments and said, "Kyle will be in danger if he stays with you. He is a mere mortal amongst Titans. He will eventually break your heart by leaving you. His existence is just a blink of an eye in the eternity of time—"

"If you say I am this... all-powerful being, then I chose to stay with Kyle. I will be able to protect him."

Margram added slowly, "But you cannot stop death. Kyle will meet his end eventually."

Adara's eyes turned black, and she snapped in a quick reply, her voice determined and cold, "So we better hurry up with this fight for equality because the clock is ticking. He dies, I die." At that, she looked at Ethan, who stood frozen, just like everyone else. She took off the necklace, placing it in her pocket.

She declared, "If you want my help, you will find a way for Kyle and me to stay together. I will promise you my allegiance, but only if you promise me that I will be allowed to stay with Kyle and that he will be allowed to live with me for as long as I live."

After a moment of silence, Margram conceded. "Agreed. On one condition. You and Kyle need to prove it to each other and to Ethan."

"Prove what?"

"That you truly love one another... unconditionally."

Adara was confused by what he said. It took her a moment to realize what he was telling her.

Then she asked, "But how the hell do I prove it. How do I prove something that is a feeling, deep inside my soul? How do I show proof of *that*?"

She was angry and confused.

He declared, "It is up to you. But both you and Kyle will have until the next moon change to show Ethan your proof. But do know, until then, Ethan will not stop. Since you have already released yourself and Ethan from the bond, now Ethan needs to release you and himself; only then will you be free of the commitment.

"You made him promise you, before both of you left this world together, that he would never let you go; you made a promise that the two of you would find each other and reunite. Know that he will keep that promise, no matter what. Now that you have *awaken*, he will do everything in his power to remind you of your love for each other. And if you give in, it will be the proof that you are not committed to Kyle. But in the meantime, Kyle will have his own choices to make. When both you and Kyle decide to separate, you will be bound to Ethan again."

Adara felt a sudden fear grip her heart. She remembered that feeling she had for Ethan. It was coming back along with other memories. Sudden longing, hurt, and pain returned for a split second. The aching, thirsty love she felt for Ethan. She was starting to remember. *No. I will not.*

Her eyes turning completely black, staring in disbelief at the person in front of her, she exclaimed, "That is ridiculous. I can already tell you that I do not want Ethan—"

"Don't you get it? You and Ethan had been together for centuries. You made a pact to come here; your love is endless and stretches across centuries. Your love knows no bounds... it will always prevail—"

"Enough. My love for Kyle is endless. That is what I know. He has always been there for me, ever since we were children. I will never leave him. Ever."

Margram replied quietly, "Your choice to prove it. You will be allowed to keep Kyle in your life if you prove that you are worthy of each other's love." He looked around and opened his arms slowly as he said, "Let it begin."

Adara saw that people around her started moving again, and the noises filled the air.

She looked and noticed that Charlotte and Marcel were looking at her with a question in their eyes.

"I am back," she stated, calm and determined. She knew they heard her thoughts. *And I am staying with Kyle.*

CHAPTER TEN

The Proof

ADARA LOOKED AT where Kyle was last standing, but she only caught the sight of him leaving through the opened doorway. She wanted to follow him but was stopped by someone speaking her name behind her.

She remembered that voice. She missed it so much. Adara froze for a moment, and then she turned around apprehensively.

"I have been waiting for you, what seems like forever," Ethan said and put his arms around her in a loving embrace.

Adara felt a strange, but familiar ache, her knees getting weak. While he was holding her, she remained motionless and stiff, but then her arms gave in a little.

He released her slowly and looked at her mixed reaction with sadness in his eyes.

She smiled, confused and embarrassed of her own reaction to his embrace.

He seemed to notice her expression right away and said quietly, "You feel it too, don't you. They told me about that, but now, I actually get what they meant. It feels like two pieces of a puzzle getting back together."

Adara said, her voice shaky, "No it doesn't. And besides, how do you know what I felt?"

"We all can do that, but I'm even more sensitive to those thoughts. I can feel what people love or want. Even if they don't admit it to themselves. I can sense the hidden desires."

Adara thought about what he just said. Then she felt it.

Effortlessly, she thought about what he was thinking. Then she *heard* it.

His thoughts. His feelings for her.

He was not lying.

The love, the longing, the commitment, and the pain he felt at this time, and for the years going back. It was real.

It was too much for Adara. She pushed the vision away. Then she declared, "Well, I definitely can say I did not want it. We are childhood friends, nothing more."

Sadness and pain spread across his face.

He said, "Our kind can sense and hear the thoughts of others if we are near. You can also choose to block them... if you wish; that way no one can get in. It gets loud in our heads from all the thoughts crossing the space. *Blocking*, helps keep things quiet." After a short pause he added, "And speaking of thoughts, what I felt there for a moment, coming from you, was a clear and unadulterated longing."

Adara looked away and said, "It was not. I do not love you, nor want you. I did see our past, but it is, as I said, the past..."

Ethan declared in a quiet voice, "Our love is endless. I will find the way to help you see yourself as you had been before. You are my Adara, and I am your Ethan. I made you a promise before we left. You made me swear that I would find you and never let you go. I intend to keep that promise. I know you are in there," he ended and gently extended his hand to touch her cheek, but she moved her head slightly so his hand stopped midair.

"I need to talk to Kyle," Adara said and left to where she saw her husband walk few moments ago.

She needed to leave. But she had not done it soon enough, as the strong sensation of longing had already filled her; the longer she spoke with Ethan, the more overpowering it became. She needed to get away from him.

But knowing that Ethan could sense what she felt did not make her feel any better.

It took her a while to find Kyle. He was in a completely different part of the house and was finishing what looked like a heated argument with Ethan.

Adara was surprised that Ethan found him first.

Brayden, Charlotte, and Marcel were also there, standing in a distance.

When Kyle turned around to face Adara as she approached them, she felt there was something different about him. He was avoiding looking her in the eyes.

A sudden fear surrounded her. "What happened? What's wrong Kyle?" She had a lump in her throat. The fear was choking her and making her voice shake.

He said, "I just had an interesting conversation with your... with Ethan. He told me about your family... your special kind of family; and about who you are, compared to... us." He paused for a moment to clear his voice. The he said, looking straight at her, "I think it would be a good idea for you to spend some time here with... your family." He was choosing his words carefully, and it was apparent that he felt uncomfortable looking directly at her.

"What do you mean, *spend time here*? What about you? *You* are my family."

Kyle looked at Charlotte and Marcel, and then at Brayden. He was completely avoiding looking at Ethan.

Then he said to Adara, "We both know I do not belong here. I kept you safe. Now you do not need protection. You are the one they have been waiting for; you can protect yourself now."

Adara had tears in her eyes. "What the hell are you talking about? What are you saying?"

Kyle cleared his throat, took a deep breath, and spoke, his voice shaky, but slowly turning cold and empty, "You will be at home here with your people. I am not cut out for this—to be a part of this whole... thing. This is just too crazy and too messed up for me. And this whole business with Ethan. I don't think I can do that."

She wanted to say something, but Kyle blurted out quickly, "Take care of yourself Adara. You are loved by so many here." Then, with both hands, he embraced her face and kissed her forehead. He turned around and quickly walked towards the hallway.

She stood there, frozen, not able to make a sound.

After a moment, Ethan followed Kyle as Adara kept standing there, unmoving, not understanding what just happened.

Few tears ran down her face, and a big lump was forming in her throat. She did not know if she wanted to burst out crying, or scream with frustration, so she just stood there.

Those standing around were looking at her, not knowing what to say.

Marcel and Charlotte were not sure what had happened between Kyle and Ethan, but they knew the separation was inevitable.

After a moment, Adara quietly asked in disbelief, "What the hell just happened? Why would he leave like that?"

Charlotte put her hand on Adara's shoulder, "Not everyone is resilient enough to face the truth and stay strong. It must have been too much for him." She did not know what Ethan said to Kyle, but after that conversation, and shortly before Adara got there, she saw that Kyle was furious.

Adara looked towards the door where Kyle and Ethan left. "What the hell did he say to Kyle?" she yelled, angry and disappointed. "What did Ethan say to him?" she demanded.

No one knew.

They got there few moments before she did, and at that point, Kyle and Ethan were already done arguing.

Not getting any answers from them, she ran out of the room looking for Kyle, leaving the rest of them behind.

❖

As Kyle approached his parked car, Ethan caught up to him and said, "That was a right decision you made. She will be happy here."

Kyle turned around and took a swing at Ethan.

The punch landed on Ethan's cheek. As the blow hit his face, Ethan took few steps to regain his balance. Still holding his jaw, he was stunned wondering why Kyle's punch hurt him so. *How did he make me lose my balance? He is merely a human!*

Puzzled, Ethan agreed slowly, "I guess I deserved that." He wiped the blood off his lip. Staring at the sight of his own blood, on the back of his hand, he looked confused.

Kyle opened the car door and announced, "For your sake, I hope Adara shows you mercy if one day she finds out the truth."

Ethan's bright-blue eyes turned dark. "She and I belong together; you are simply a short chapter in her life," he snapped, his voice cold and sharp, cutting through air like a knife.

Kyle looked at Ethan and declared, pain and sorrow spilling with each word he uttered, "She is my whole life, and she will never truly choose you. You do not know her as well as you think you do. If you push her too hard, she will make your whole world crumble. But I guess that is what you deserve."

"I only do it because I love her!" Ethan's now dark eyes turned black. His heart was breaking, as he knew that he put Adara through so much pain.

Sitting down in the car and slamming the door shut, Kyle whispered inaudibly, "And I do *this* because I love her enough to let her go." He meant it for himself, but Ethan still heard it through the window.

The tires skid on the gravel as Kyle sped away.

Ethan stood there, the cut on his lip slowly vanishing. He wiped off the blood that remained.

The car was quickly disappearing behind the curve leading towards the front of the building.

Ethan could still hear Kyle's last words resonating in his head. With each heartbeat, they were echoing in his ears. They were getting louder and louder.

Adara found Ethan walking into the mansion through the back entrance. He was facing the heavy door, slowly closing it behind himself.

He stood there, still facing the door, with his palms on the wooden surface, unaware that Adara was behind him.

"What did you tell him!?" Adara spoke slowly through her teeth. It felt so strange. The fury she felt when she saw him was suddenly being replaced with something different. She could not stop the strong sensation of wanting to get closer to Ethan. She pushed her thoughts aside and yelled, "And stop that mind control, I told you I do not want this!"

Ethan turned around; his tired face now showed pure surprise. "I swear; I'm not doing anything. It's not me. It's just us. It's who we were; who we are still. It's you coming back to me." He wanted to embrace her but feared that she would push him away again.

He missed her so much. She was so close, yet never this far away.

"No. What did you tell Kyle to make him leave?" she demanded.

"Whatever he found out, it doesn't matter now. You are free. He made his choice for both of you. Now you are free to be whom you were meant to be. I know that you will remember us and our love."

Adara saw Marcel approaching them.

She took few steps towards him and asked what happened with Kyle.

He answered, "Follow me Lady Adara."

She remembered he called her that many times in the past, but now, it had a different sound to it. Now she knew what he meant.

Ethan looked on as Adara and Marcel walked away.

Charlotte, who was right behind Marcel, stopped next to Ethan and said, "My old friend. It is so hard seeing the two of you going through this. We are all fighting for the same cause, but here we are, manipulating Kyle into submission."

After a moment, Ethan said in an empty voice, "He did not submit. I tried to control him, but it did not work. She must be protecting him somehow. So when control did not work, I lied to him to make him leave. I don't know how, but he made the choice himself. I explained to him that the only way to keep her safe, and to save her life, was for him to let her go. So he did. He let her go... to save her."

Standing still, Charlotte said, "A selfless act of love. Does Adara know about that?"

Ethan blurted out, tired, unsure, and battling his emotions, "Of course not. He was told to make it believable. And he did." He added almost inaudibly, "If she had found out about his sacrifice, our promise to each other would have been voided. I would have lost her."

Charlotte looked at him. "So now it's her turn to choose."

He looked back at her, pain in his eyes mixing with determination. He walked away without saying a word.

Adara was standing in the study, looking at some books on top of the desk, when she heard Marcel say, "I assume Kyle was told the truth about who you are. And he did not take it too well, I presume. The part I heard Ethan say to him, when they stood in the hallway, was that you would never have children with humans." Marcel was going through the piles of books and boxes on the desk, looking for something.

"How many times do I need to repeat myself? I do not want Ethan," she replied, tired but still angry.

"It does not matter how many times you say it. You are slowly, but surely, falling into each other. You will eventually become one. It is unavoidable. Not even you are powerful enough to separate two neutron stars gravitating towards one another."

It looked like he found what he was looking for on the desk. He said quietly, "I still have some things you gave us for safekeeping before both of you left. This is one of the items here." Marcel pointed to the object he was holding in his hand.

Adara looked at it, not knowing what to say.

He continued, "I see that Ethan has already returned you necklace." He gestured to the pocket of her gown and chuckled, "We, Lords, have the power to sense the presence of the Gem if it is near us." He extended his arm and handed her an old jewelry box.

Adara opened it and took out the pendant that had an inscription on the back.

The words were written in some strange-looking runes. Surprised, Adara realized she knew how to read those signs. She saw her tears slowly dripping onto the inscription. It read, *Our Love Story.*

She took a deep breath. "Can I ..."

"I'll leave you alone. We have missed you so much. I'm so sorry for what you're going through. None of us foresaw this." He left and closed the door.

The knob made a clonking sound as the doors closed shut.

Adara held the pendant in her palm, took a breath in, and closed her eyes. Slowly, the images flooded her mind...

She was there with Ethan. They were standing on the balcony, looking at the calm sea. White curtains were billowing in the wind.

The air felt fresh and a bit salty as it blew across the shore while he stood behind her, kissing her neck. She remembered what she said to him, like it was yesterday, *I want our children to be born to the free world; I will not have them be limited by the Darkness.*

She started the quest for freedom, not only for humans, but also for her people; to make sure they would not be bound by the rules set in the past.

Adara remembered seeing Ethan's face as he smiled and kissed her before they left the world to wait in the Void; to make it to the Void, as opposed to other realms, they had to leave at a specific time set by the Sentinel. So much time had passed in that endless place. She saw him when he kissed her for the last time before they were reborn into this life, little over twenty some year ago. She felt the love they had. She felt it burn in her heart and spread across her body.

Sitting in the study, holding the pendant, Adara opened her eyes. Warm, salty tears ran down her cheeks. She wiped her face with both hands and whispered, "No. I will not. That was a long time ago."

She looked around the room and remembered the time when she was a little girl running through this house, playing hide and seek.

She put the pendant down on the desk and walked towards one of the bookcases. Gradually, more memories that had been lost started coming back. She smiled at the old memory that came back to her and realized that she was made to forget it.

As a child, she used to play hide and seek in this house, and one day, looking for a hiding spot, she ran into this room. While running in the dark, she tripped on the carpet, lost her balance and, to prevent falling, she pushed herself against the cabinet and the books on the middle shelf. She heard a click in the cabinet as the books slid inside. Slowly, she stood up and looked at where the set of books used to stand.

In their place was a brass lever. She straightened her skirt, took few steps towards the bookcase, and, after a moment of hesitation, pulled on the brass handle.

Another click.

A floor-length mirror on the other wall slowly opened, revealing a lit room filled with more books and various bottles. She went inside and looked around. There were scrolls and books, neatly organized on multiple shelves. Some were laminated, and some neatly rolled and stacked inside a wooden grid.

On one side, there were few shelves with a variety of colorful bottles decorated with ornate-looking carvings.

The bottles were quite small, between an inch and three inches high, and arranged by color and pictures.

She was admiring all different designs and images that adorned them. They looked like pretty jewels, sparkling in the dim light.

She wanted to look at one of the vials with a red apple on it, and as she stood up on her toes and reached out to get it, she heard a voice behind her.

"Adara, you always find a way. How did you manage to find this?" Charlotte smiled and playfully messed up her hair.

Adara asked, "What is this?" and pointed to the pink bottle with the shape of an apple carved into it.

"This, my curious Lady, is a very powerful extract; nothing to be toyed with."

"Why do you keep those bad things here?" Adara had questioned, looking worried but intrigued.

"Oh honey, this is not a bad thing at all. This one here," she pointed to a yellow vial on the other shelf, "has the power to send bad thoughts away, so a person can see the good things in life. It can help brush away those clouds that keep people from seeing the beauty and happiness in their lives."

"So these are all good things that help people?"

"Sure," Charlotte answered shortly. Then quietly added, "Most of them." Looking at Adara, she opened a small bottle with some intensely smelling herbs inside and said, "This one here... helps people forget."

Adara sniffed to see what was inside the bottle. "Forget what?"

"Nothing."

Standing next to Charlotte, Adara looked around and said, "Something smells so nice and so sweet... and blissful. How can something smell so heavenly and sweet?" Adara wondered.

Ignorance can be blissful. Charlotte chuckled and said, "It is probably the ice cream and the apple pie that is waiting for you in the kitchen. I came here to find you because the other kids decided to stop the game and are currently rummaging through the pantry for some goodies instead. If you don't hurry up, there won't be much left."

Adara jumped up and exclaimed, "I hope they don't get to my secret stash of cookies I keep behind the rice box." She ran out of the study and headed down the hallway.

Being here now, it was so odd realizing what had happened next in that room. How can she recall what she had not even experienced? Adara *remembered* Charlotte putting away the bottle on the shelf. She saw Charlotte glancing at the room as the door was closing and saying, "It will be safer for you if you do not remember what you found here. Ignorance can be *sweet* and *blissful*. It can be *heavenly*."

Adara looked at the pendant on the table, and then at the bookcase. She pushed the books, just like before.

She remembered.

The lever was revealed, just like the last time she was here. She pulled it and proceeded to the room that was opening before her.

Adara thought, *Kyle made his choice and left. One sniff from that bottle, and I can forget and move on without pain in my heart. Or I can forget Ethan. Or even better, forget both of them... I don't know what I want... I just want to not think about anything.*

She looked at the shelf and took the tiny glass bottle. Hesitating for a moment, she opened it and smelled the liquid inside.

As she inhaled the scent, she kept concentrating on Kyle and Ethan. The contents of the bottle did not smell as sweet as before. In fact, she did not smell anything at all. She felt another wave of tears coming over her. "Why aren't they working? Maybe this stuff is too old," she sobbed helplessly.

A voice by the door startled her.

Charlotte's voice slowly filled the room as she spoke quietly, "It is not too old. It never loses its potency. But this potion doesn't work like you think. You cannot make someone simply forget love, just like that. Love is magical. And reciprocal love, like in case of you, Ethan, and Kyle, is binding."

Adara felt numb and completely exhausted. She put the bottle down, closed the secret door, walked out of the hidden room, and joined Charlotte.

Together they walked to the hallway in silence.

Charlotte said, "Ethan is looking for you. Will you speak with him?"

Adara felt paralyzed and empty inside. She looked at Charlotte and answered, "Yes. I will talk to Ethan."

As she said it, she realized she forgot the pendant from the study. She stopped and said, "I forgot something. You go ahead; I'm gonna catch up with you soon."

Charlotte smiled and gave her a hug.

Adara turned around and walked back to the study, knowing exactly what she needed to do next.

The pendant was on the table where she left it. She picked it up and placed it on her hand. Looking down, she saw the sparkle of her wedding band as the light from a table lamp reflected in the golden surface. She placed the pendant back on the table and touched her ring, spinning in around her finger.

Adara closed her eyes and recalled their wedding day when Kyle took off the promise ring that he had given her years back and, on their wedding day, replaced it with the wedding band.

She looked at her pinky finger and the ring—her promise ring.

She went to the window and looked outside. The sky was dark. People were still sitting in the garden by the bonfire that was built there for the celebration.

Adara completely forgot that it was her birthday. She wished this day to be over.

She looked towards where the tree line was usually visible during the day.

It was there, on the trail through the woods, where Kyle promised her his devotion. She was just a little girl when it happened, but she remembered it vividly.

She was about nine years old, and Kyle was fourteen. They were walking through the woods on their way back from the river and a full day of swimming and playing with other children. The others were ahead of them when Kyle said he wanted to talk to her. They were on the edge of the forest; the meadow was visible nearby.

Kyle sat down on the fallen tree trunk and pointed to the spot next to him.

"Adara," he started and looked at her, "do you know why I follow you everywhere you go?"

"Because I am fun to be around?" She giggled.

"No silly you. I mean, yes, you are fun to be around, but that is not what I mean." He looked like he was sad and happy at the same time. "A while ago, I had a dream. I was told to protect you and to never leave your side," he added quietly.

"Well that is rude. So you only play with me because you were told to do so?" She looked hurt.

"No you silly goose. Don't you get it? I want to be near you because I care about you. I was asked if I agree, or if they should look for someone else. I got angry with them and told them that no one was good enough to be worthy of you. I said that I... well... that I cared about you and that you were my best friend." He ended quickly.

"You did the right thing. I do not want anyone else but you; you are my best friend, for life," she said with childlike conviction. Then she added, "What a scary dream." She gasped after she thought about it for a moment. She sat up on his lap and hugged him, her long, still damp, hair, covering his shoulder, falling on his back as she hugged him.

Kyle embraced her arms tightly, his face in her tangled hair. Hesitantly, he let her go and stood up himself. He saw her eyes beaming brightly; he took her hand, and they continued walking together.

As they walked, hand in hand, Adara's bright-blue eyes turned dark. She exclaimed, "It must have been very scary for you to have such a frightening dream. I'm glad it was only a dream."

"Yeah. Just a dream," he concluded slowly. Then he added, "The thought of not having you as a friend scared me more than anything else."

They almost caught up with the rest of the kids, when Kyle added, "I have something for you; so you can remember that I am never going to leave you and that I will always do whatever it takes to protect you."

She stopped and laughed. "You are silly." Then she added with gravity in her voice, "How can I ever forget you?"

He smiled and waited.

Adara laughed, and urged impatiently, "Alright, alright, what is it? What did you get me?"

"I found it in our house, in the attic, and asked if I could keep it. It turned out that it didn't belong to anyone, so I was allowed to take it. I want you to have it." Kyle reached into his back pocket and pulled out a shiny golden necklace made out of various size, flat, golden circles connected together, forming a long chain.

He took Adara's hand.

The sparks that reflected in the polished surface dispersed in all directions when the bright sunrays fell on it.

She gasped and exclaimed in excitement when he placed it in her palm. "It's beautiful. I love it!"

It was way too long for her to wear around her neck, so she looped it around her wrist. Extending her hand to the sun, she marveled at how it sparkled in the light. She said, "I will never take it off." She stood up on her tippy toes and gave him a quick smooch on his cheek, and then she joyfully skipped to join the other children, still sneaking a peak at her circle bracelet.

She looked behind her and saw that Kyle was standing there, holding the side of his face.

That was the first time she stole a kiss from him. Later, when she was fifteen, she stole her first *real* kiss. Then, on her eighteenth birthday, she stole their first night together. All of that because he stole her heart. She had been living on stolen days. Looking at her wrist and the golden bracelet, she thought, emptiness filling her heart, *And now I am done. No more stealing. Everything worth taking had already been stolen. There is nothing left to give or to take.*

She approached the bookcase, opened the secret room, went inside, and looked for the bottle that caught her eye before. She reached for it and held it in her hand before putting it in her gown pocket. She pulled on the lever and heard the mirror move back in its place.

She stepped towards the window and looked outside.

Some people were already driving away from the party.

Adara was ready for this night to be over. She felt terrible. She was empty.

She was broken.

Her love for Kyle was burning a hole in her heart. But the flooding sensation of longing for Ethan was overwhelming her senses. She hated the fact that, with each minute, she felt the connection between her and Ethan getting stronger. She missed him and wanted him near her.

She hated that.

The anger drained all her strength. She felt she was losing control.

The bottle she has been grasping in her pocket warmed up under her touch.

Margram, Marcel, and Ethan were right; she and Ethan were gravitating towards each other. She could feel his presence near.

Adara was standing there for a while when she heard someone open the door.

Ethan walked in and said, "I was looking for you; then I saw you through the widow." He walked towards her. "Not the birthday you expected."

"Birthdays are the beginnings, but they can also be considered endings. For something to begin, something else has to end. Life finds balance even if we don't realize it," she muttered, looking at him.

After a moment of silence, Ethan said, "Would you dance with me?"

"There is no music," she stated but still took few steps towards him.

Her body was longing for his embrace. She felt the pain tearing her apart from inside.

"Your heartbeat is my music." He smiled. He saw the pendant laying on the table. He picked it up, went behind her, and placed it on her neck.

His hands remained behind her neck and slid down slowly, gently touching her back.

Adara made a soft sigh when he got closer and held her tight.

She thought, *It feels so familiar, so right, but so wrong at the same time. I have missed him so much.*

Still behind her, Ethan whispered quietly, "I have missed you even more. All this time knowing you were here, so close, yet unreachable."

He went around to face her. He gently held her neck and face in his hands and studied her eyes.

Adara felt the warmth spreading from her stomach, going in all directions, the air around her getting dense.

Still looking in her eyes, Ethan slowly, as to not scare her, leaned over and kissed her.

She kissed him back.

His strong hands went to the back of her dress and undid the top buttons.

Adara was shocked by her own reaction, as she suddenly wanted him to rip the dress off her body. At that moment, she felt him starting to pull the back of the dress apart.

Unable to control herself she sighed, but then, she firmly pushed away from him and said, "I cannot do this. I do not want to. This is not right. Please let me go," she pleaded.

"But I am not holding you." His voice was full of hunger and pain.

Surprised, she realized that she was the one who was holding him close.

He whispered, "You are here because you want to be here. Don't you realized it is you who wants to be here... with me?"

Confused with her own feelings, she looked at him and saw his eyes getting watery from the tears he had been holding back. She saw both pain and happiness as he was looking at her.

Her voice broke, "I do not want it. I do not choose it. I would rather die than leave him." She did not realize, but her hand slid into her gown pocket and tightly grasped the little glass vial.

Holding back the tears, Ethan pleaded, uttering the words slowly, "But he left you. He chose to be away from you!"

Anger started rising within him. Anger at Kyle for loving her enough to let her go; and anger at himself for not being able to stop fighting for her. Who was better? Who was worthy of Adara?

It did not matter anymore. Adara made her choice.

She felt the rage exploding inside her. "I don't care! I know that Kyle did not choose me, but I am choosing him. If I can't have him, then I do not want anyone else." Her voice was breaking with each word she spoke. Taking a step back, she instinctively looked down at her pocket and made a tighter grip around the bottle inside.

Ethan followed that move with his eyes. Then, terrified, looked up at her face.

He froze.

His now black eyes, full of anger and tears, filled with fear as he spoke slowly, "What do you have in your pocket?

Adara answered quietly, without looking at him, "You know damn well what I have there. We both know we are not immortal."

Ethan's face got pale.

Adara's mind flooded with another wave of memories. "Those tales from when we were children; the little princess who asked the dragon to set her heart free. The same dragon that is on this bottle, with the liquid that can bring freedom to the soul."

Slowly, she was taking her hand out of her pocket. "The same kind of bottle we used to help us go to the Void."

She pulled it out.

Looking at the bottle, he spoke, his lips trembling, "You would not drink that..." But he knew that she would; he saw it in her eyes. "Please don't. Not that. I could not live, knowing that you were not here," he pleaded breathlessly.

Helpless sorrow swept across her face and heavy tears streaked down her flushed cheeks. "It's too much. I will not live my life knowing that you will pursue me while I still love my husband... and knowing that he left me. I want him back... but I don't know why I want you more and more each minute that passes. This is too much. I can't live like that. There is not enough room for that here." She pointed to her heart and took few steps back.

Without hesitation, she reached for the little cap and pulled it, opening the bottle and letting the sweet sent fill the air around her.

Terror gripping his heart, Ethan exclaimed, "He did not leave you. He still loves you. Please don't drink that!!" He took a breath and continued slower, "He thought that the only way to save you was to let you go." He paused again, then added, "Now I know what he meant when he said how much he loved you."

Ethan saw her hand lowering. He saw her standing there with her arms limp on her sides. His heart breaking, he repeated, "He told me that he loved you enough to let you go. Now I know what he meant." Ethan realized that he has lost her; that she has chosen another.

Adara looked like someone woke her from a nightmare; she was relieved, yet still not realizing it was over.

She said, "But knowing that you will never stop trying to rekindle our love... that is unbearable." She looked at the bottle. The smell was so pleasant and intoxicating; she wanted to have a little taste, just a little. It would all go away.

Ethan got very still and avowed, dense fear chocking him, "I swear on everything that is holy to me, I will never try convincing you to come back to me. I release us from the promise. You are completely free to live your life how you please and to make your own choices. The only thing I cannot do is stop loving you. You cannot ask me for something I'm unable to do. That is beyond me."

For a moment, they stood there in silence. Adara looking at the bottle, and Ethan looking at Adara.

"He did not leave me. He..." Adara repeated almost inaudibly.

"He has been promised your safety if he left. He did it because he..." The last words were hard to say, "...loves you."

She looked at her hand that held the cap.

Ethan asked, "The bottle." He pointed to the opened vial.

She handed it to him.

"He is at the guest house, in the—"

"I know which one." She interrupted and headed towards the door.

With her hand on the doorknob, she stopped and turned around. Slowly, but without hesitation, she took off the pendant and walked to Ethan, handing it to him. She said, "Thank you. Thank you for... letting me go."

Adara left the door opened and ran through the hallway.

CHAPTER ELEVEN

Gift

WALKING TOWARDS THE car, Adara realized that it was the pendant, in combination with Ethan's presence, that was bringing back her memories and feelings for Ethan. Now that she was away from both, she felt the feeling fading into a distant memory—like a flame on the match, slowly flickering away.

The mansion was almost empty. Most of the guests had already retired for the night, but she still did not want to bump into anyone, so she took a long way around to the back garage, where the family cars were kept.

She drove around the house and found her way towards a winding road leading to the guest houses by the lake. After driving for few minutes, she saw the cottage with their car parked in the driveway. She slowly pulled up next to where Kyle had parked.

Adara turned off the engine and just sat there. All her energy was gone; she had no power to get out of the car. She felt as if all her adrenaline had burned out. Placing her face in her palms, she noticed she was crying.

Soft knock on the window startled her.

Adara wiped her face, opened the door but remained in her seat, letting the few remaining tears dry out in the gentle breeze that blew in through the door.

Kyle smiled at her. "So, after you kick my ass for *leaving* you, do I have your permission to kick his ass for making me *leave*?"

She got out of the car and rested her back on the side of it. Then, with profound relief and pure joy on her face, she spoke slowly, "There will be no ass kicking. But how did you know I was coming here?"

"I got a call... from him. He explained everything; briefly," Kyle said and embraced her as they walked towards the cabin. "I have your favorite wine opened. I think we both need something to help us relax."

The cabin was exactly how she remembered it— welcoming and cozy. The warmth of the fireplace had already spread through the house; the bottle of wine was on the table, almost completely empty.

Adara said, looking at the table, "I see that you had already started without me."

She approached a wine rack by the fireplace, pulled out a bottle, and placed it down on the table.

Kyle held his wife close and said, "The reality of being away from you was more than I could handle. I do not ever want to live through that again; it ripped my heart into a million shards. I didn't know how to pick up the pieces when I was here, sitting and hoping that this nightmare would end. I kept thinking that I would wake up and see you next to me."

He squeezed her tighter, her head on his chest. He said quietly, "I promised you that I would never leave you, and that I would do everything in my power to protect you. I never actually left, and I never will. I will never let anyone come between us. Ever again."

Adara could hear the anger and determination in his voice.

She closed her eyes as he kissed her slowly. The taste of his lips, and his breath on hers, weakened her knees. She took a breath and kissed him hard and put her arms under his, embracing his back.

He kissed her long and hard. Then he slowed down a bit; he looked in her bright-blue eyes, and whispered, "I love you to your Star and back."

They both laughed at his intentionally cheesy statement.

They stood there for a moment when Adara said, feeling the weight of the evening crashing over her once again, "I need to get out of this dress."

She took it off as she made her way to the shower.

"So much to wash off," she stated, thinking about the long day they had. She saw that Kyle was walking behind her, loosening his collar and unbuttoning his shirt.

The water was warm, and the lather felt soft on her skin, calming her, helping wash away the tension.

"I love being with you," she whispered between her breaths as the water slowly washed over her face and shoulders.

"I love making you happy." He kissed her stomach. Water was dripping down her breasts and falling on his head. He slowly kissed his way lower and lower.

He always had a way of putting her in a good mood and getting her mind off whatever worried her.

She giggled. "That does make me happy indeed; but I was thinking about something that we both wanted for a long time. I feel that this time is different."

He looked up and, with both hands, wiped away the water that was pouring over his face. He smiled playfully, giving her a mysterious look. "Well, for that, I need to go up." He slowly kissed his way up her stomach, her breasts, to her neck and lips. He lifted her up and pressed her back against the wet stone shower wall. He smiled and asked in a comically serious voice, "A boy or a girl," holding her thighs on his hips.

"How about both." She pulled herself closer to him, embracing his hips with her thighs, crossing her ankles behind his back.

"Are you sure you're up for that? That may take all night," he warned and looked at her jokingly.

"We have all night; and more."

He carried her out of the shower and laid her on the bed.

Their bodies were sticking to the silk covers. He knelt down by the bed and kissed her thighs, spreading them apart. His lips quickly found a way between her, and he felt how soft she was down there. As he moved his tongue, he could hear her moan softly, and he felt her fingers running though his hair. She was so wet.

After few minutes, her increased breathing and her stiffening back indicated she was close. He knew what she liked, and he knew exactly how to give it to her.

Just as she was coming, he used his fingers, along with his tongue, and made her come quicker and harder.

She grasped the covers in the intense wave that flooded her senses.

Now it was his turn, but he knew she wanted more. She always wanted more. One was never enough.

He loved making her come.

She was moving impatiently on the bed waiting for him to give it to her again. He turned her around to her knees and stood behind her on the floor; he spread her legs apart to match his height. He thrusted himself into her.

She gasped for air as he pushed in.

He pushed again and again, just the way she liked it, slow, deep, and steady in the beginning. He could feel her giving in.

Not long after, he heard her asking him to go faster. He held her hips and thrusted hard and fast. He felt her buttocks stiffen as he entered deeper with each move. Now he could feel her back arch and tens up, as he thrusted his entire length deep into her. Then gradually, he felt her muscles relaxing as she angled her bottom towards him and seemed to open herself even more. He looked down and gasped at the view, his penis entering her, sliding in effortlessly into her opening.

He thrusted his penis in and out of her, each move, and the sight of it, sent pulses down his spine. She was in front of him, taking all he gave her and asking for more. Seeing that, he could not hold back any more. His movements were forceful and rhythmic. He felt her clinging to him and pressing onto him as he was pressing onto her. The release swept over him suddenly; he filled her, holding her hips tight, as she fought to keep her buttocks pursed upwards; his body was overtaken by intense pleasure.

❖

It was almost noon. Adara stretched between the blankets. At some point that night, they had made their way to the living room and settled in front of the fireplace.

The fire was still burning slightly, and the smell of fresh firewood filled the room.

Adara felt the bitter sweet pain in her lower stomach. She stretched again and enjoyed the feeling of the strangely sweet tenderness around her thighs. *A night to remember,* she thought.

She noticed that Kyle was not in the room.

Refreshing aroma was coming from the kitchen. "Is that coffee I smell? Is that coffee? If it is, than why am I not drinking it?" she yelled jokingly towards the kitchen.

She stretched beneath the covers and pulled a blanket over her arms.

Being comfortable and warm, she remembered what Kyle whispered in her ear before they fell asleep:

..."I listened to them, and I pushed you away when I thought it was the only way to save you. It was like pushing the last bit of air out of my lungs—painful, unbearable and scary, illogical, unnatural sensation. The thought of not being with you was like not existing.

"Now, having you in my arms, I want nothing else. I just want to be with you, to kiss your body, to be in you, for you, to hold you close to me. I never want to let you go. This is what it feels like to be complete. The thought of being banned from being near you is unbearable to me."

She whispered to him, almost inaudibly, "And I love you more than ever. I know I will never leave your side for as long as the stars are burning in the sky. I will love you till the end of times." The last words were muffled as she drifted away...

That was last night.

Now, the sun was making its way through the curtains.

Kyle brought a cup of steamy, black coffee and sat down on the blankets, next to his wife. "A cup of coffee and breakfast is the least I could do to thank you for a nice wake-up you gave me this morning. That was a good comeback. I don't know what came over you, but you won't hear me complain." He chuckled and handed her a cup.

She took a sip and admitted, "I woke up before dawn and though it would be a perfect way to start the day. I figured that you were tired after last night and knew that you love me on top. I know that you like the view. But truthfully I wasn't sure if you would be up for it after what we did at night." She chuckled, thinking that Kyle took the baby-making so seriously and spend the night fulfilling that request. She then laughed and mentioned that to him, highlighting the fact that they were both sore after last night.

They both laughed and thought about the busy night they had.

Kyle smiled and kissed her forehead.

She thought about what they did that morning.

Adara had woken him up when the sun was almost out. She had started slow and gentle. She sat up on him and gently moved herself up and down. Then she let him move and push up on her for a while, and she used her fingers to touch herself. As she got closer, she put her hands on his thighs, arched her back a bit, and started moving harder and faster.

As he held her hips firmly, she moved herself back and forth until she came. She did not stop moving though; she wanted to make him come as well. While holding his face, Adara leaned over slightly and rocked harder, and made him look at her as he came.

When they drifted off to sleep, the sun was shining its first morning rays. Adara slowly touched her belly and smiled. She was almost asleep, but then she heard voices... distant voices. For a moment, she thought she saw faces that were smiling at her through the fog.

She fell asleep trying to remember where she had seen them before.

Now, she and her husband were sitting by the fireplace, drinking coffee, memories of the night still fresh in her mind.

Adara smiled. "Almost like our first night together."

He smiled back and took a sip of coffee. "It only gets better with time," he said inhaling the aroma that arose from the cup.

Sitting next to Kyle, she thought about the night she had just spent with her husband. Those voices she had heard. Somehow, she knew they were important.

She touched her belly. *Could it be?* She remembered the words that an old woman had spoken to her in Africa.

Adara wanted to have her own family. They both wanted children. *I guess time will tell.*

Kyle noticed how she touched her stomach; he moved closer to her, gently embracing her hips. He gave her belly a soft kiss. "I want it too." He then kissed her forehead and embraced her, wrapping his strong arms around her shoulders.

They sat there talking about this new situation they were in, discussing the new responsibility they were facing, now that Adara's past had been revealed to both of them.

After a while, still sitting huddled together, Adara noticed something through a narrow window by the door.

From where she was sitting, she saw a movement.

She expected to hear ringing of the doorbell or the knocking; but nothing happened.

There was silence.

She voiced her thoughts to Kyle.

"Maybe you just though you saw something," Kyle said, looking towards the door. "We are sleep-deprived after all," he said, making a joke.

Adara was puzzled. "No. I definitely saw someone, or something."

She stood up and, wrapping a robe around herself, walked to the door.

Kyle remained where he was and looked at her as she opened the door. Then he heard her say, "What the...?"

He got up to see what she was talking about. As he walked, his smooth, bare torso catching early sunrays, he fixed the pajama pants and stepped outside.

Shielding his eyes from the bright sun, he saw Adara looking at something in front of the entrance.

She bent over and picked up something sparkly.

"What is that?" he asked.

"It's a necklace," Adara answered and looked closer at it. The gems were just like the main stone in her diamond and sapphire necklace, shimmering brilliantly in the sunlight. "And a letter," she added, reluctantly looking away from the sparkling necklace.

She handed him the necklace and opened the letter.

Kyle looked at her when she was reading it inaudibly.

She froze mid-sentence.

"What is it?" he asked.

"We are being congratulated on the addition to our family; we are also invited to the welcoming ceremony for our children. The necklace is for me; apparently I am the guest of honor." She stared at the letter.

"Did you say, our children? But—"

"They... the Sentinels, already know I am pregnant... after last night. And they want to welcome our children during the Blessing Ceremony," Adara was stunned, still looking at the letter she was holding tightly in her hand. "Our children. We will have... I am pregnant!"

He took the letter from her and studied it carefully.

"Adara," he said looking down at the paper, "it does say *children*. Not a child, but children."

He embraced her and twirled her around.

Adara exclaimed, as she realized the news, "You are not fazed by all this!?"

Kyle chuckled. "No. I'm just going with the flow. After last night, and what I found out about your family, nothing surprises me anymore. I don't care what happens, as long as I'm with you. We might as well be living on Mars for what I care."

Adara smiled at him and whispered, "We are going to have a family. Our own family."

Kyle smiled back at her, picked her up, and spun her around again. Her robe whooshing in the air as he turned her round and round, her long hair softly moving in the air with each turn.

He stopped, embraced her face in his strong hands, and said, "I love you so much; I can't wait for us to share our love."

They did not know it yet, but the news of their blessing had already been sent to other family members.

CHAPTER TWELVE

Crystallized

CHARLOTTE OPENED THE kitchen door that led to the stone terrace, when she noticed something sparkle in the distance. She stepped through the door and walked across the path. The light was coming from the low, round, altar-like, stone table behind the garden. It had heavy cast iron chairs surrounding it after yesterday's celebration. The metal fire pit insert had already been removed by the staff and, in its place, there was a white marble plate that matched the gravel landscape surrounding the table in a massive circle.

In the center of the massive table was a crystal apple with a beige envelope under it.

The crystal was a dead giveaway.

Charlotte briskly walked towards it, already suspecting who left the correspondence. The white gravel stones were in contrast with the blinding green color of the lawn. The entire image was surreal—white path, leading towards the circle-shaped, white stone landscape, all surrounding a massive, round table with the crystal apple in the middle of the white marble insert.

The light coming from the crystal, and the sunlight that was piercing through the clouds above, was blinding.

Charlotte covered her eyes with one hand as she walked. She heard the stones crunching under her feet as she approached the table. After reaching for the crystal apple, she picked up the letter.

The seal had an impression of a large letter *W* pressed into the bright red wax.

Charlotte took a deep breath.

She knew who sent it.

It had been a long time since she last saw one of these correspondences. She broke the seal and read the message.

A faint smile appeared on her face. She thought, *New life. They are precious gifts; they must be so important since the entire planet is welcoming them. This was not foreseen.*

This was not planned. Or was it someone else's plan all along? Time will tell. Time reveals all.

When she walked home, with the letter and the crystal apple in her hand, she saw Brayden in one of the doorways that opened up to the terrace.

He looked at her, as if he knew exactly what was in that letter. Charlotte looked down at it and slowly nodded. Brayden turned around. That was when she saw that Ethan was in the room.

She stopped for a moment, looked at the letter again, but then continued towards them.

Charlotte kept her mind in check. They needed to read it for themselves.

She handed the letter to Brayden who, after reading it, handed it to Ethan.

As Ethan was reading through the letter, they could see how his hand started trembling slightly.

After he read it, he looked up at them. His face was pale, with expression they were unable to name. He turned around and slowly proceeded to the hallway, placing the letter on the nearby table.

Charlotte called out towards him, "We all need to be there."

Feeling the rising tension, Brayden exhaled slowly and rubbed his forehead.

He said to Charlotte, "He knows. He will be there. He simply needs time to cope." Brayden looked out the terrace doorway and gazed into the distance, towards the forest that was surrounding the property. "The

Blessing Ceremony is still some time away. He will come around until then; I will talk to him."

They heard a faint sound of an engine roaring in the distance and later a screech, as if the tires lost the grip with the asphalt.

Brayden continued, "The babies are important and will be protected by all those who let us call this planet, home. A meeting like that has never taken place. It makes me wonder if that was the plan all along. What if we are not the ones who were to win the fight, but the ones who will bring the true warriors to the frontlines. I know I don't feel complete without my Emma. We are all broken."

Then he laughed and continued sarcastically, "The Sentinels probably realized the mess we were in and decided to send reinforcements. Or maybe they never had full trust in our success. I guess, rightfully so. They knew we would need help."

Brayden was tired.

The negotiations had not been going well, and the Dark Lords were almost ready to bring the battle into the open by publically confronting the human race. Brayden knew that humanity was not ready to face the reality. People needed to be slowly introduced to the fact that they were not alone. The surprise attack would only create chaos and would start waves of violence, crime, and mass panic. It would shake the world, and, as a result, countless lives would be lost. He knew they needed to introduce the new knowledge gradually—to create awareness in small steps. That is what his family had been doing for a while now—talking to major players in all sectors, slowly raising the awareness. But that took time. Humans are creatures of habit, and most are not used to such revelations; they find it threatening.

The Dark Lords would thrive on chaos and mass hysteria. Brayden knew that the Dark Lords were planning on doing a reveal, but that also required forming alliances and gathering enough Gems to make that happen. Sentinels were ready to use the only protection against such a reveal, but no one wanted to be frozen, stuck between the heartbeats. Everyone knew that Sentinels were ready to stop time for those who were about to break the rules. That was the only thing preventing the Dark Lords from attempting the reveal without having all the Gems. Once the Gems were collected, whoever had them, had a complete control over what happened next.

Each side wanted to get the Gems first.

Charlotte whispered, "How did it all get so complicated. It was not supposed to happen this way." She sat down on the sofa and continued, "The Dark Lords are openly attacking our way of life. Their manipulation, corruption that leads to killings, crime, and atrocities are spiraling out of control. They are letting humanity destroy itself. What is happening to the world?" She placed her face in her hands and rested her elbows on her knees as she took a deep breath.

Feeling exhausted, Brayden said, "All we can do now is uphold our negotiations and keep the peace until we are ready to strike. If we attack now, it all may be lost. We need to wait until we have enough force to win. We just need to hold on a little bit longer."

Ethan jumped into his car and started the motor. Flooring the gas pedal, he sprayed surrounding bushes with gravel. The acceleration forces of the supercharged engine pushed his body into the seat.

As he looked back through the mirror, he saw two deep grooves left by the tires. *Just like Adara and I now*, he thought. *Separate*. This thought enraged him.

The powerful engine propelled the car forward like a bullet. His internal screams clouded his mind. He fumbled with a seatbelt, with no success. "Oh, who gives a fuck!"

The entrance to the estate was disappearing in the distance. Few miles later, Ethan was speeding through the winding road. He could not breathe.

His heart was pounding ever since he saw that letter. The words were burned in his memory

... pleasure of requesting your presence... honor of welcoming the heirs of the Light... children of Adara and her mate, Kyle... keys to freedom and balance...

He could not stand it anymore; whenever he closed his eyes, he could see the words.

It hurt so much.

He and Adara had always wanted to have children, but they decided to wait until the freedom and balance were restored. *Why would she choose to go ahead now? And with him!? He's a mere second in the eternity. And she chose him!*

"Why!?" Ethan yelled and hit the wheel.

He glanced at the speedometer. Seventy.

I am going too fast.

Ethan did not even touch the brakes on the wet, slippery asphalt. He turned the steering wheel as the road bowed. Too sudden, too much.

The big, heavy car left tire marks as it skid sideways. As the tires began to loosen the grip on the slippery asphalt, the car started spinning around. The road took a turn to the left, but the car launched straight as it span.

Ethan did not care... as if in that instance, everything became clear to him.

He looked around.

He saw it all in slow motion. Car skidding sideways, patches of grass flying from underneath. He was beyond time. He knew he was not human, but instead, he was who he had always been.

As the car spun, and right before it hit the tree, crushing the entire passenger side, Ethan *shifted out* of the car and through the physical elements.

Loud explosion of the air bags boomed across when the car smashed into the tree, passenger side completely wrapping around the thick trunk.

Moments later, he stood next to the car that was bent around the tree.

Sudden silence.

He looked at the wreckage.

The smoke was rising in the air.

Ethan was remembering his thought from a moment ago; *Kyle is a mere a second in the eternity.*

He voiced his thought slowly, "Kyle is simply a second, and he will fade just like everything else here. We are going to be the ones who remain. Adara will forget him in the perspective of time." He added quietly, "It will all pass."

Ethan found comfort in knowing that the curse of Eternity was also his salvation. Everything passes, but they remain. They will always have each other.

He smiled, his eyes getting lighter and turning bright-blue again.

Being without her had left a gaping hole in his heart. He was not himself. But now, his heart ached a little less, knowing she will eventually be his again.

He declared, "I am a Soul Traveler. It's about time I started acting like one." On that last word, he smiled, looked at the wreckage again, and *shifted out*, disappearing and leaving everything behind.

❖

He *shifted back* and appeared at the doorway of the mansion. Walking steadily, he bumped into Charlotte who was walking towards the study.

Surprised, she stared at him.

She said, "I know how hard it must be for you, seeing them together. I wanted to remind you that there is a way to break the ties between you two. There is—"

"No need. All is good. I never want to forget my love for her. That is what gives me strength. The reason to live. Please do not mention that again." He smiled. "Really, all is good."

He continued down the hallway to the study.

Charlotte just stood there, trying to understand what he meant. But he was long gone.

Ethan opened the door to the study and saw that Brayden was reading one of the books.

Brayden looked stunned when he saw Ethan walking towards him. "I thought you left. Is everything OK?"

"Never better, old friend. I needed a moment to think and get my thoughts together. All is good now. I will need to get a new car though." He chuckled.

Brayden glanced through the window in the direction Ethan was looking. The smoke was rising in the distance above the trees.

"What the hell? Are you OK?"

Ethan grinned and explained, "Never better. I just needed to vent. I am all done venting now. And besides..." he raised his hand and slowly waved it through the heavy credenza under the window.

The hand passed through it, as if the cabinet were not there. "Who are we kidding? We're only pretending, so we can fit in and not freak anyone out."

He looked at Brayden, nodded at him, and then at the cabinet.

Brayden exhaled with resignation, lifted his hand up, and did the same thing as Ethan. His hand passed through the cabinet, as if it were moving through air.

Brayden said, "We need to fit in to not invoke fear. But you're right; we should take a stand. Let's get this mess over with."

As they walked, Brayden announced, with hope in his voice, "I think I am closer to finding Emma..."

Ethan looked at his friend and gave him a pat on the shoulder as they got into the hallway. He was truly happy about his best friend having a chance at finding his lost love.

In the meantime, Adara was taking a relaxing bath while Kyle took a jog around the lake. She felt so completely relaxed when she dipped her head under the clear, warm water.

She opened her eyes. The waves in the tub made the images blurry and distorted. The thoughts of her plans flooded her. How was she going to approach what was ahead of her, now that she was pregnant? She was thinking about the future, when she realized she had been under the water for a while now. She wanted to emerge to take a breath but then realized she did not need to.

She looked around and saw bubbles escaping from her mouth. Adara did not need to take a breath. Slowly, she looked at her wrist watch, but the image was too blurry, so she placed the watch under the water. Looking at it, she saw how seconds turned into minutes. The hands on the watch kept ticking and moving round, and around.

The water got cool.

Feeling emotionally numb, she surfaced slowly, put on the robe, and went to the balcony, where she sat down in the chair.

The wind was blowing around her, and it started to drizzle... but she was not bothered by the cold. She felt the fear filling her from within... she did not want to say it; she did not want to think it.

"I was looking for you. Come inside, it's getting chilly out here." She heard Kyle's voice as he stepped onto the balcony. He leaned over and kissed her cheek.

Adara turned in the chair, stood up, and faced him.

He saw she was crying.

"The cold does not bother me," she replied.

Kyle embraced her shoulders and felt how warm she was.

He tried to lead her inside, but she resisted and said, "I do not need to breathe. I do not need it to live."

Saddened, he looked at her as he realized what that meant.

She knew it before, but it did not sink in—until now.

Adara raised her voice in fear, "Do you know what it means? I can't die. I do not need air… but you do." Her last words turned into a silent sob.

He embraced her and held her tightly as she clanged to him. He looked in the distance and kissed the top of her head.

After he swallowed a lump that was forming in his throat, he cleared his voice and said, "It will be alright. No need to think about it now. Let's just enjoy what we have."

She felt so drained. "I will not let you leave me," she said, her cheek still on his chest.

He laughed. "I am not going anywhere. I am not even thirty years old; I am healthy as a fucking horse. You will not get rid of me that easily." He kissed her and led her inside.

They walked into the bedroom and went downstairs to the kitchen.

He poured her a cup of tea and set it on the table.

She stirred it with the silver spoon and looked at the tea leafs swirling in the cup.

Her mind was calming down; she knew what she wanted, and now, she knew how to get it.

CHAPTER THIRTEEN

The Bond

MONTHS FLEW BY quickly.

Adara and Kyle situated themselves at the Water's Edge while their new home was being built nearby on the far north side of the property.

The Blessing Ceremony was to take place that night, so the staff was given few days off. Charlotte and Marcel did not want anyone asking questions or being exposed to something that would reveal their true identity.

Outside, some distance from the terrace, the white stone path that led to the garden table was lit with waist-high torches, making a wide circle around the massive stone table.

In the house, feeling tense, Adara was pacing back and forth. "I didn't expect to be so nervous for this ceremony. I thought it would be more... simple." She looked at the empty terrace. Peering in the distance, she did not see anyone by the massive stone table in the garden, but she knew they were not alone. She was told *they* would join her when she crossed the torch-lit circle.

Eva handed her a glass of water and said, "It's all a formality; they will be there to welcome you and your children. Normally, the Blessing Ceremony takes place after the child is born, but the Sentinels insisted it be done now. They are recognizing you as the key person."

Adara drank the water and set the empty glass on the granite countertop. To cool herself down, she placed her warm hand on the chilled surface. It felt like her body was getting hotter from inside, and the cold countertop was not enough to cool her.

Eva continued, "It's not just a Blessing for the children. It's the Blessing for you and for the road ahead of you." Eva placed her palm on top of Adara's hand.

The sun almost completely disappeared over the horizon.

Adara gazed in the distance at the round table surrounded by smoking torches. She thought anxiously, *So why am I so nervous. It doesn't feel so simple.*

Upstairs, Kyle was walking through the hallway, holding Adara's wedding band, which she left in their bathroom that afternoon. He stopped by the sitting room that had a view of the terrace. In the far distance, he could see the outline of the cherry trees; closer to the house, he saw the round stone table surrounded by smoking torches that made a vast circle around it. Torches were spreading smoke low to the ground. The sun had just set and the ceremony was about to start soon.

He looked at the wedding band in his hand and twirled it in his palm. He was nervous. As if something bad was about to happen.

Kyle heard someone behind him.

Ethan stopped few feet away from him and looked through the window. He took few steps towards Kyle. "Looks beautiful," Ethan uttered in amazement, touching the glass. "They are all here for her. They chose her to be the leader." Then he looked at Kyle.

Kyle kept staring through the window and, for a moment, thought he saw a movement in the garden; but when he looked again, he did not see anything. "They are here for our children. It is a Blessing Ceremony." He shifted his eyes to look at Ethan.

Then, he turned back towards the window again and saw Adara walking down the white path. "Damn it. I took too long. She's already there."

Adara had already walked past the terrace and was now on her way to the stone table.

Kyle's first instinct was to run downstairs, but then he noticed that the view was excellent from where he was standing. His hand still on the window pane, he stayed and glared at Ethan, who stood next to him.

Ethan's face was frozen and emotionless.

Kyle watched how Adara made her way through the long, winding, gravel walkway towards the table. He saw her get close to the circle entrance and stop.

She looked so fragile.

Her white, flowy tunic billowed softly in the gentle breeze.

Then, he noticed that the circle was not empty. He could see movement inside.

Everything was somewhat masked by the smoke coming from the torches. Suddenly, he noticed that somebody appeared inside the haze-outlined circle.

Adara stepped inside.

After few moments, he could not see anything because of the wall of smoke that rose up unexpectedly.

What is going on in there?

The smoke was dense. He could not see inside, and even though the breeze moved the smoke outside the circle, somehow, the view was still obscured.

From where he was standing, the middle of the circle seemed to be clear, but the smoke was moving high up in the vortex, going around and spreading to the sides, few yards above the ground.

He froze.

Breathless, Kyle turned around wanting to run downstairs, but Ethan grabbed him by his arm and commanded, "Do not interrupt. She is safe there. She is the guest of honor."

Kyle yanked his arm from Ethan's grip and rushed downstairs.

In his mind, Kyle could hear her calling his name. She needed him.

In the garden, Adara was making her way to the stone table.

She was nervous.

Kyle did not come back, and she was told she had to cross the circle before the last sunrays disappeared. So she headed out without seeing him.

Adara knew Kyle would be watching her, but still, she needed some encouragement before going into the unknown. She did not know much about what was about to happen. From what she remembered, the people who would meet her there had their own way of showing appreciation and respect.

But that was not much information though.

She was given a delicate, white, tunic-looking dress to wear for the ceremony. Now it was being lifted up by the gentle breeze. Looking down, she saw her pregnant belly.

She was about five months along and her bump was fairly prominent. She gently patted the dress down and placed her hand under the base of her stomach.

Inhaling the smoke-infused air, she smelled different herbs, and firewood. The scent was intoxicating. She felt a strange sensation in her lower stomach.

"That is odd," she said to herself, surprised. She felt aroused all of a sudden. The wetness between her thighs felt so good. Her knees were getting weak. She remembered that the white tunic and the white panties were the only thing she had on. *Why did I just think about that now? What does it matter?* Her thoughts confused her.

Crossing the torch circle, she saw the figures standing around the table. They were definitely not human.

A blond man pointed to the stone table.

Adara saw that it was covered with thick, fur pads; she had not noticed them before. She went around the table and faced the people who stood there.

Each of the human-like figures approached her and placed various objects by her feet. She heard different languages that were spoken but did not understand what they were saying. Or did she? Somehow she was starting to realize what they meant.

They were bowing their heads while approaching her.

When they spoke, it was as if they were not talking to her but rather through her; like she was there just as a bystander.

The blond man gestured to her stomach.

After a moment of hesitation, Adara opened her tunic and exposed her pregnant belly. The murmuring voices turned into a rhythmic chant.

One after the other, they came to her and touched her stomach with different, herb-like smelling substances. She felt weak in her knees from being aroused by the sounds and by the dense air that surrounded her. She looked around and noticed that the smoke swirled all over the perimeter of the lit torches, and she could not see anything on the outside. She felt relieved, knowing she was concealed. That relaxed her a bit more.

But why?

The excitement sent a contraction across her belly; the intense pleasure was pulsating between her thighs. She leaned back on the table.

The voices and the rhythmic beat filled the air. She knew that it was not only about her but also about the life growing inside her. Adara remembered that all ceremonies like that were about fertility and life.

Is that why I'm so aroused?

The voices boomed stronger and flew faster.

Adara felt intoxicated.

She was woozy from all the smells of various herbs, but she did not want to leave. The air was thick with lust and primal urges. Slowly, she lay down, her breathing becoming heavier.

She looked down her stomach, bending and spreading her knees. Feeling confused, she realized that she did not know what was happening to her.

Still in a daze, she could see one of the creatures approaching her between her legs. She wanted him to stop.

He stopped.

The yearning in her stomach begged for release. She saw him approach her again. Right before he did, she made a soft groan. She sounded scared and impatient at the same time.

Then, she understood that they were following her thoughts and unspoken demands. It was she who was making it all happen.

The man stopped and looked in the direction of the house. She looked in that direction too, but the smoke cover was thick, and she could not see past it.

"Kyle" she whispered. She kept repeating his name over and over. "I claim Kyle." She was breathing heavily. "He is the price I demand." The voices stopped, but the rhythmic drums continued.

She realized that the drums were beating in accord with the rhythm of her heart.

Kyle stepped out of the terrace to follow the stony path. Strangely enough, no one was stopping him. Not that he expected opposition, but he was aware that he was about to intrude on the ceremony.

The white path ended by the table. He could not see past the torches, as the smoke surrounded that entire area. Kyle was getting glimpses of the silhouettes, and for a moment, he thought he saw her.

The torches were burning yellow and orange, and the glow was spreading over the smoke that twirled around and rose above, before dissipating in the air.

Then he heard her. This time not in his mind but her actual voice.

She called him. Adara called his name.

He stepped through the smoke and saw Adara on the stone table, lying on the thick fur covers, her knees bent and legs spread apart. He saw how her lips moved, saying his name, "I claim Kyle."

He looked around and noticed different creatures standing around the perimeter of the smoke wall. Some of them were the most beautiful beings he had ever seen, whereas others were dark and scary. It was bizarre, but he knew they all were friendly. And from the overwhelming feeling he sensed in his body, they were probably too friendly.

Now he felt it too. The raw urge. That sensation sending his body into a frenzy.

Adara was moving impatiently on the thick fur covers. Her fingers were grasping the soft, long fibers as she arched her back. Looking in her eyes, and seeing how she was shifting her body, he understood what she wanted.

Kyle did not know what was going on; his mind was getting hazy; all he felt was the urge to take her, to feel her skin against his.

Next thing he knew, he was on top of her, pulling her white dress above her hips and ripping off her underwear. He felt how ready she was when she pulled herself closer to him.

It was all a blur. After he first entered her and dove into the intense pleasure, everything blended together. He was on top, but then he realized she was now on top, thrusting her hips hard on him. He heard her scream in ecstasy. Then he was taking her from behind, her legs spread wide as he pushed himself into her, holding her hips tight to his body. Looking down, he saw how his penis smoothly slid inside her each time he thrusted; and each time he did, it was coming out wetter and more slippery. He did not know when one orgasm ended and the other one began. He had heard of orgies, but this was surreal.

This was an out-of-this-world experience. He was satisfied with each time he came, but he still wanted more. The more he got, the more he wanted.

The time did not exist for them. He could not count the number of times she climaxed, nor the number of times he did.

He was not tired. He did not feel out of breath, he did not need to rest. The only time he was not in her was when they were switching positions, and even then, Adara impatiently rammed herself onto his penis, or if he was quicker, he ripped into her slippery, wet opening, filling her countless times that night.

Everything was spinning.

The fog was all round them and stretching across the grounds.

Kyle was in a dream state, not dreaming any more but still not awake. The voice come from a distance but seemed as if it were by his ear.

Am I dreaming? Kyle thought.

What are dreams anyway? But if that is easier for you, then sure.

Where am I?

Good question. You are where you fell asleep. I cannot shift you away because you are still human. So we are meeting in this dream, as you call it.

What do you mean still human? What else would I be?

You have been welcomed to our realm, but you have not yet left the human realm. You cannot be in both. At least not yet. You need to choose.

I had already made my choice.

Yes. You will still have to make it known to your kind. So you can be released from your bounds and from your realm.

What do you mean, my realm. We don't have things like you do. We just live and die.

Really? Just few months ago, you did not know we existed. What makes you think it's all there is. We were not the first ones here. The same goes for you.

Kyle was silent.

The voice continued, *Be ready to make your choice known when the time comes, but know that there are consequences.*

What do you mean?

A topic for another time. But for now, welcome. We are pleased with her choice.

The voice faded. And the fog slowly started receding towards the lake in the south.

Kyle woke up when the sun was slowly peeking above the horizon. The torches were still emitting thin ribbons of smoke but not enough to shroud the table, like the night before.

It was surprising, but he did not feel cold on that foggy morning. There was an aura of warmth around him and around the stone table. Slowly, he pulled his arm from under the soft, fur covers and placed it outside the table.

The temperature was much lower there.

He looked at Adara; she still had her white dress on her, but it was rolled up all the way to her waist.

Slowly she stretched, and then curled up on her side.

Kyle's clothes were on the ground. Reaching for them, he saw that Adara's wedding ring was between one of the white stones on the ground.

It must have fallen out of my pocket last night.

Slowly, he got up and picked it up. His body was aching as if he ran a marathon; each move sent a painful reminder of the previous night.

He bent down again, picked up the clothes, and put them on, after which he sat up on the table and slowly curled up next to his wife.

Kyle put the ring on her finger and pulled the fur covers over himself and Adara. He embraced her from behind and closed his eyes.

He needed rest.

Sleep came quickly.

Far away, Ethan was sitting across from Brayden, watching the sunrise from the private jet as it was taking off on the runway.

"Thanks for coming with me on such a short notice," Brayden said, looking at his best friend sitting in front of him.

Ethan nodded in agreement, raising a glass, filled halfway with clear, square ice cubes and their family-brand of liquor.

Brayden realized that almost every time he saw him, Ethan had a drink in his hand. Not just a regular alcoholic drink that had no effect on them and was drank to enjoy the flavor—but rather the alcohol infused with substances that enabled them to get the same kind of buzz as alcohol gave humans.

Brayden decided not to bring it up now because, unlike humans, their people did not risk becoming physically addicted, where their body would crave it even if their mind did not want it. But still, their dependence came from having a relief and numbness after drinking enough of it.

Brayden knew that Ethan was self-medicating himself and numbing the pain and hurt. *I'll talk to him, just not now.* Brayden understood that Ethan needed numbness after what happened last night.

Brayden's thoughts were interrupted.

"No problem," Ethan answered. Then he asked slowly, "But why a pilot if it's such a sensitive trip? We could have flown by ourselves, or we could have just *shifted in* over there."

Brayden leaned back in his seat and explained, "I thought it would be a good idea to leave flying to someone else, plus we do not want to raise any suspicions. That is the rival Family we're talking about. The less they know about our abilities, the better. But mostly, I wanted to talk to you about what happened earlier last night. I am sorry. I should have been more sensitive. I thought that what I did... would eventually help you realize the reality of how things are now... to help you move on, that is," he added while looking at Ethan.

With a tired voice, Ethan replied, "No worries. I guess I needed the wake-up call." He took another sip. Then, in one gulp, he finished the drink, leaving the crystal-clear ice cubes on the bottom, clacking against the glass as he moved his hand.

Brayden started talking about Emma and about the news of where she has been reborn. As Brayden spoke, Ethan heard bits and pieces about Emma's eighteenth birthday that was coming up in couple months.

It was difficult for Ethan to concentrate.

Brayden said that Emma was getting close to her Awakening, and that the Sentinels recognized her presence and wanted to share that with the Family. The pact with all the realms, which was just sealed, made it possible for Emma to be located before she got her full powers.

While Brayden was talking, Ethan still could not get the image of Adara and Kyle out of his head. He rubbed his eyes and looked out the window.

After a while, Brayden stepped out to talk to the pilot.

Ethan looked down at his hands. They were trembling. They felt so empty. He closed his eyes again and saw images from last night.

They flooded him.

He pulled his head back, trying to fight the tears. But few escaped.

The memories flooded his mind again...

It started few moments after Kyle ran out of the house to go to Adara. Ethan saw him cross the circle and approach her. Everything happened so quickly.

The smoke cover lowered and, for a brief moment, was not high enough to obscure the view from where Ethan was standing—so he could see inside the circle.

He did not want to watch.

As he turned around wanting to leave, he saw Brayden approaching.

Ethan stopped; his back was to the window.

Brayden commanded in a stern voice, "Turn around and look at them."

Ethan did not want to look but still did so, turning instinctively. He saw Kyle on top of Adara as she pulled herself close to his body. He saw them kiss passionately and caress each other. Just those few moments, and he wanted to turn around, but Brayden snapped coldly, "Watch them and realize what is happening."

Ethan wanted to turn away from the widow and leave, but Brayden grabbed his arms back and held him, forcing him to look out the window.

Ethan prayed for the smoke to rise again, but he was not granted mercy; the cover remained lowered and the table was visible from where they were standing.

Brayden continued, "They are together; they are married. They have bonded in this ceremony and are recognized as one union, by all the Realms. He is her husband, now in the eyes of *all*, and she will never leave him."

Ethan wanted to break free, but Brayden was holding him in place.

Brayden continued, but it was apparent that his voice was on the verge of breaking, "Look at her belly. Look at it!" He raised his voice when Ethan, once again, tried to break away. "It is filled with the life they have created together."

Ethan looked at Adara's uncovered stomach as she moved rhythmically on top of Kyle who was holding her hips and thighs. The delicate, white tunic she was wearing had untied almost entirely from the bottom up, exposing her belly. Ethan gazed at the tight skin of her prominent round shape that started right under her rib cage. He saw how Kyle glided his hands from her hips to her stomach. Emotionally crushed, Ethan felt a sting of pain deep inside is soul. *I am the one who should be there; these were supposed to be our babies. Our life together.*

Ethan stood there, frozen, as all the strength left his body. He realized that he was powerless when his struggles to get her back fell fruitless. Now, he simply stared at them helplessly. Paralyzed. His eyes dry. His heart ripping apart.

Brayden repeated relentlessly, "Did you hear what I said; they have created that life. Those babies inside her are their love manifested. No Soul Travelers conceive a child unless they have mated, for life. Those babies are a miracle. They are *our* miracle. Our salvation. Even you cannot deny that." Brayden took a shallow breath and, now with a plea in his voice, said, "You need to realize that your personal quest is a lost cause. If you make her leave him, she will hate you forever. We cannot afford any more setbacks. We need to unite for the battle ahead."

Ethan gave up trying to break away; he was exhausted.

Brayden loosened the grip on his arms.

Ethan stared out the window and felt how tears filled his eyes until he was not able to see clearly, which came as a relief. But the image of the two bodies intertwined, naked, moving in unison was burned into his mind. He heard himself weep helplessly as he collapsed to his knees.

The realization of defeat struck him harder than he imagined possible. He turned around and rested his back on the wall by the window, unable to get up, with no energy left. He wanted to leave but had no more strength to stand himself up—so he just sat there, staring aimlessly at the room in front of him.

He did not even notice when Brayden had left the room. He desperately wanted to forget what he saw, but the images persistently kept creeping in and replaying in his head.

Sometime after that, he was still sitting on the floor by the window, when they got the news about Emma. Somehow, he found the strength to collect himself. Without looking back, he left the room.

The release of information from the other realms was also a reminder that, thanks to Adara and Kyle, the pact had been sealed, and the communication between the realms was now open.

So here he was—sitting with Brayden on the jet, flying to Spain to see if it was indeed Emma who had been spotted.

Anything to get away from his life and his pain.

CHAPTER FOURTEEN

Release

ADARA LOOKED AT the gorgeous mansion with a Spanish sunset sky illuminating it in the backdrop.

It had been several weeks since Brayden and Ethan made their trip to Spain to visit the family where Emma was said to have been reborn.

It was Emma indeed. Her hair was not as dark and her face was paler, but it was Emma.

Ethan could see how Brayden struggled to hold himself back when he saw her few weeks ago. Brayden wanted to run to her, take her in his arms, and never let her go. But he just stood there, still, looking at this red-haired beauty walking past him. He almost reached for her hand to pull her close to him and tell her everything, but he knew she would not understand; she did not even know him.

Brayden took solace in knowing that Emma was to be given all her memories on her eighteenth birthday—an unexpected gift from the Sentinels.

She would not have the powers as the other three, but she would be allowed to remember her life from before.

That is why it was so important for the other three to be present during her Awakening. They had the power to ensure her safe passage, in case things took a wrong turn.

Emma's eighteenth birthday was tonight and they were here on the premise of negotiations.

The Awakening time brought a lot of tension and some uncertainty to the Dark Lord families, as it was not uncommon for young adults to leave their family after *initiation* when they learned about the oppression. Conversely, sometimes, there were few members who wanted to join the Dark Lords because they felt superior to humans.

It was a time for the newly *awakened* to choose a side.

So here they were, walking up the footsteps of this exquisite mansion. They knew they were going into the lion's den.

Adara remembered this mansion from her other life. This rivaling family was the most powerful one in that area.

All three of them were invited because the Lords were curious about them, since no other Lords have ever been reborn after they passed to the Void. This family here did not realized that Adara, Brayden, and Ethan kept their memories and had become more powerful. So tonight's mission was about to change all that. Once Emma *initiated*, nothing would be the same. She would have to be granted a safe passage, and for that, they needed to act quickly.

Lord Steffan's family extended the invitation on the condition that Adara would attend as well. He was curious.

Openly curious.

As they slowly walked up the steps, Ethan was getting restless.

He had a feeling that things may not go as planned. He worried for Adara because her current state prevented a quick getaway. *Shifting* was out of the question for Adara at this time because of her pregnancy, as that would send the babies' souls back to the Void. They were told that being pregnant was one of the limitations to *shifting out*; also, any traces of Dragon's Blood and Life Water could not be transported that way. The other dimensions did not allow such *pollution* to pass through. Those were the prime substances of this realm, and they had no place in the Void even if only just passing though.

Ethan was seriously worried about Adara, whereas Brayden, on top of fearing for Emma's safety, was nervous about the mission in general.

The only one who had been calm thus far was Adara herself. She felt the inner peace and excitement of something new about to take place; she was motivated to get Emma back.

Adara knew they would not fail. The only thing that worried her was the thought that Kyle was upset about having to stay home.

Before they left, Kyle had eventually acknowledged that if he came with them, they would not be able to fully concentrate on the mission because he would be yet another vulnerable person in the group. They could not afford that. With a heavy heart, he gave in and stayed behind.

Right before Adara left the car, which was parked by the stairs leading to the mansion, she spoke to Kyle on the phone, reassuring him they would see each other in a day or two.

Now, she was stepping through the enormous, stone doorway leading into the expansive, open foyer decorated with beautiful ornate lights.

Her short, black dress was attractively fitted to her body, showing off her prominent, pregnant belly. She still had several weeks left, but the babies made her belly look round and full.

Ethan instinctively held her hand as she walked up the stairs. She did not need help because, for them, pregnancy was not the same as for humans. It gave their women resilience and connected them to the source of energy and strength.

Nonetheless, Adara took Ethan's hand, knowing that her state awoke the image of fragility in the eyes of those around her.

Now that she passed through the doorway, she realized something that started to worry her. She knew that, just like the pregnancy, the birth was not the same either. She heard that it was rather quick and was extremely personal. It took place with the partner's presence for the reasons of intense physical responses that did not involve pain. There was no pain, but instead, women would go through phases of ecstasy. That process was said to be as intimate as making love.

Thinking about that, all of a sudden, she felt not so comfortable anymore, being away from Kyle. Adara knew she was weeks away, but the thought of not being with Kyle during the birth scared her.

She looked at the glass doors in the distance and said with conviction, "Let's get this over with."

Ethan and Brayden looked at each other, feeling the tension rising. They followed close behind her.

All was going well. They were welcomed with reserved and cautious smiles, and as the party progressed, they were involved in intense conversations with various family members.

Brayden stayed close to Emma to be ready to help her *leave* after she *awoke*, and it was Adara and Ethan's job to distract Lord Steffan when Emma would go through the Awakening.

It did not look like there would be a problem with keeping Emma's father, Lord Steffan, occupied because he was completely engrossed in the conversation with Adara, trying to inconspicuously gage her awareness of who she was in her previous life.

Adara knew he recognized her, and she sensed that he was not sure of how to act around her.

He suspected that they had been reborn, but he also believed they would not possess any memories of the life before. He had never met anyone who had been reborn. All souls that came here as descendants were new.

But the three of them did not look new at all. They looked like their old selves.

Lord Steffan recognized them the instant he saw them. It arose many questions across their Families. Plus those intense-blue eyes on all three of them; the eye color of the Lords.

Adara could hear that, in the main room, the champagne was being circulated. Lord Steffan arose and wanted to head back to the main hall for the ceremony. That was the sign for Adara and Ethan to ensure that

Steffan would not be present in that room when Emma *awoke.*

Adara stood up, slowly approached the table, and pulled out a velvet pouch from her pocket.

She declared leisurely, "As you know, we are asking all the Lords to submit their Gem to revisit the Waters of Life. The purpose of our visit here was to see you and ask you for your support in joining the freedom movement to unite our kind and humanity."

Steffan looked at her and laughed. "Dear Adara, we are not going to submit to those demands; we are happy with how the world is. We also have great plans for the future. Just wait and see. It will be beautiful. Magnificent. When we are done." He stepped away from the door and approached the table.

Seeing that, Ethan moved closer to Adara.

Steffan looked at him and said with a false smile, "Ethan, no need to be nervous; we are all family here. Our kind should stick together." He looked at Adara's belly. "And what a joyous time for both of you. New life that you bring to this world. Our world." He studied Ethan's face carefully and saw a flash of painful grimace shoot across Ethan's face.

Steffan was watching both of them to see how they would react to those words. Now he knew.

He saw Ethan's reaction. He saw how the hurt spread across Ethan's face even though Ethan was trying to hide it by looking away.

Steffan smiled slowly in surprise. "Oh. Well. I mean to say that you two were... Never mind. Don't mind me. Such a blessing either way. Maybe when he or she grows up, it will choose correctly and join *our* Family."

With curiosity in his eyes, Steffan looked at Adara and asked, "What name does it go by?"

Adara was caught off guard, "We don't know yet."

Steffan tilted his head slightly to see if she was telling the truth. He stared in disbelief, seeing pure surprise and truth in her words.

Before Adara could move back, Steffan extended his arm and placed the tips of his fingers on the top side of her belly.

"Now that is interesting..." he said, but then quickly jerked his arm back, as he was struck with excruciating pain. The intensity of the pulse made him fall to his knees and collapse to the ground.

Startled, Ethan looked at him, but then he noticed that Adara's face showed that the pain swept through her body as well. She grasped the bottom of her belly with one hand and reached for Ethan's arm with the other.

Grabbing her hand, Ethan froze for a moment when he saw fear in her eyes as she looked at him. He could sense the surprise and panic that she felt at that moment.

Adara took a deep breath and declared to Steffan, "I think that the choice is obvious to us all."

Still kneeling down, and with one hand pushing himself off the ground, Steffan looked up at her. "It is not just *one*. There are *three* babies. But that is impossible," he murmured still stunned by the pain.

Ethan looked at Steffan and took Adara's hand. He could hear Steffan's thoughts; he could hear what plans went through Steffan' head.

They needed to get out. It was not safe here anymore.

With a stern, yet calm, voice, trying not to show panic that was building inside him, Ethan declared, "As we have informed you earlier, we want you and your family to come over to our side. But now, I guess, it would be best if we left as you contemplate your allegiances. But I warn you, do not underestimate our abilities."

Steffan stood there, rubbing his shoulder, still feeling the burning pain in his body. He glared at them as they were leaving the room. Thoughts were rushing through his mind.

Outside the door, Ethan said to Adara, "Brayden has Emma. They are safely home. He *shifted out* with her just few moments ago."

He held Adara's hand, and they ran down the hallway towards the back door where the cars were parked.

Adara stopped suddenly and gasped in pain. She looked at him, not knowing what was going on. The fear in her eyes was bewildering.

Ethan stopped. "What are you feeling? Where does it hurt"?

She pointed to her belly and her back as she was breathing through the pain. Gasping for air, she exclaimed, "It feels like they are trying to rip their way out of me!"

Ethan looked around, fear in his eyes almost blinding him, and he said, "You are going into labor, but you should not be in pain; something is not right."

After a moment, Adara stood up straight and started moving again.

They ran to the last corridor when Adara gasped again, cringing in pain. Another contraction swept through her body, and she held his hand, trying not to collapse.

Ethan muttered to himself, "But she's not due for few more weeks."

He picked her up and carried her the rest of the way to the back of the building, towards the private garage.

Ethan needed a fast getaway car. He approached the Koenigsegg and did not pay attention to the fact that it was one of the most expensive vehicles there.

Fast is fast, he thought.

After helping her into the passenger's side seat, he swung shut the futuristic looking doors, a gun-like muffled snap resonating around the garage.

Ethan pressed the start button.

The supercharged engine begun to growl ominously. He shifted into first gear and lifted his foot of the clutch pedal. Vehicle launched forward, and slid out of the garage through the doors that opened just in time.

Tires begun to squeal when he went around the corner of the mansion, still accelerating.

The driveway ended abruptly.

Ethan sped off, turning onto the main road leading to the city, all while Adara was breathing through another contraction.

He pressed the pedal. More gas. Shift to second gear. Still more acceleration. Clutch, throttle off, and gear lever went to third as he took the curve at 92 miles per hour.

Ethan pushed the car to the limit.

Another bend on the road. Carbon ceramic brakes did their job and the car slowed down just enough to stay on the road.

On the apex, Ethan floored the accelerator. Seconds later, he shifted to fourth gear.

120 miles per hour.

Adara was breathing heavily. More contractions followed, one after the other.

Then she yelled, "Pull over, they are coming!"

Ethan saw the side road by the hill leading to the vineyard close by.

He hit the brakes. Speedometer needle dipped down.

He turned the steering wheel left towards the dirt road. The vehicle started to drift on the soft, dry soil. Small stones hit the carbon fiber body, as tires coped with the grip.

He drove for few more minutes, trying to get as far away from the main road as possible. Then he hit the brakes again.

The car stopped abruptly.

There were no lights by the dirt road. It was pitch black. All he saw were the car's bright headlights illuminating the rows of grapevines stretching up the hill. He went around to Adara's side and helped her out. As he held her hand, pulling her out the car, Adara's water broke and trickled down her legs and on the grass.

She wanted to lie down but Ethan led her to the front of the car. "I can't see anything here; lie down by the headlights."

She did just that and continued breathing through another contraction.

But that one did not seem to go away.

Adara cried out in pain unable to hold it any longer.

Ethan went around and helped her sit up. He knelt behind her back and gently rubbed her shoulders.

His head was close to her cheek as he whispered to her, over and over, "Adara, there is no pain. Remember? We do not feel pain."

She listened but still cried in agony as blood was gushing from between her legs.

After few moments, she relaxed her body as he gently rocked her back and forth and continued whispering in her ear, "Breathe. Feel how relaxed you are getting. There is no pain. Remember? There is only pleasure," he repeated, his cheek now on hers. Supporting her body from behind, he lifted his hands and gently placed them on her belly. He moved them slowly up and down on her sides.

Adara felt the pain melt away, the contraction turning into soft pleasure, which soon turned into deep and long sensation, underlined with ecstasy that reminded her of her orgasms.

Ethan fought the urge to kiss her neck. He took a breath in and slowly stood up.

She propped herself up when Ethan went to the front.

He pulled her knees apart and pushed them close to her sides.

She did not know how to react.

As her body was relaxing, she felt that the baby was coming out. And with another strong pleasure-filled contraction, the baby ripped its way out of her body. It seemed like the blood was flowing everywhere.

The contrast of the green grass, the paleness of Adara's thighs, and the bright-red blood that covered everything was chilling.

Ethan lifted a crying baby girl, who was completely covered in blood, and placed her on top of his shirt that he previously spread on the ground. The dark-haired baby girl seemed to calm herself down, and they could see her bright-green eyes opening and closing.

Adara smiled. "This is Nerissa," she said after hearing the baby's name in her mind.

There was no time to rest as Adara looked between her legs and tensed up with another contraction.

Ethan firmly pushed her legs apart again. As he held her knees separated, he noticed that Adara's body tensed up and with the next contraction came another baby. A boy.

Looking into her son's bright-green eyes, Adara was surprised when the name was revealed to her. "Rainer," she announced between her breaths.

Then shortly after Rainer, a third, last baby was born; a baby girl, named Kayla; with strawberry blond hair, now covered with blood, but with the same emerald-green eyes like her siblings.

Ethan looked at the three babies lying on his blood-drenched, white shirt. After a moment, he realized something strange about them, and about their birth. Without voicing his thoughts, he wondered if she noticed it too. *None of them have... No time for that now.*

Looking at the babies, he felt numb and empty. He wanted to embrace Adara; he wanted to hold her and tell her he loved her so.

But he did not do that.

Ethan smiled at her and said, "Let's go home. Now we can *shift out* safely." He handed her Rainer and Kayla, and he himself picked up Nerissa.

"You go first," he said to her. "I'll go right after."

Moments later, he saw her *shift out* with Rainer and Kayla in her arms.

Holding Nerissa, he stood up and looked around. The car was still running and the lights illuminated the ground where Adara gave birth just moments ago. Red streaks covered the short, green and yellow grass.

He muttered to himself, "I will be back for the car later." He looked at the baby in his arms and noticed he was covered in Adara's blood. The fabric of the undershirt, which the baby was wrapped in, clanged to his body; his arms and torso were sticky and wet from Adara's blood.

He slowly inhaled and *shifted out* to where Adara went.

All that was left was a running car and a pool of blood illuminated by the bright headlights.

Not long after, that same night, everyone gathered around Adara and the babies.

Questions seemed to have no end.

Ethan stood there, looking at everyone from a distance, when he noticed Kyle approaching him.

"Thank you for what you did there. Thank you for bringing them home safely. I am forever grateful," Kyle said.

Ethan glanced at him quickly and answered, "I wanted to keep her safe. But I bet she would have been fine without me. We are a strong race. She simply needed a little reminder of who she is."

Kyle thought about Ethan's words for a moment and said, "Nonetheless, thank you for being there for her when I couldn't." Then he looked at his wife sitting on the sofa, surrounded by the family.

"Anytime. And congratulations." Ethan replied. Then he added quickly, "I better go and take care of the car we left by the vineyard." Ethan gave Kyle a short pat on the shoulder as he turned around and left.

After few steps, he *shifted out*.

Kyle remained there, looking at where Ethan stood just a moment ago. He looked down and took a deep breath, feeling strange tension after talking to Ethan. He then turned around and walked to join Adara in the living room.

That same night, the house finally quiet after all the commotion, Ethan was walking the hallways of the mansion and looking at different artwork that hung on the walls. He remembered all the pieces from before. They were all from such a long time ago.

He stopped by the door to one of the sitting rooms on the lower floor. The door was cracked open, and he could see that someone was there.

Gently, he pushed the door slightly and looked inside.

Brayden and Emma were standing by the fireplace, closely leaning on each other. They held hands and looked at the flames. They seemed to be fused to one another.

Ethan took a step back and moved the door to where it had been before. He exhaled heavily and leaned his back on the wall.

He was tired.

Seeing Brayden and Emma, he realized how lonely he had been all these years.

He needed warmth.

The gap in his soul burned painfully. He needed to feel closeness.

Any closeness would do at this point.

He knew where he needed to go, but before that, he needed to take care of one more thing.

The wall sconces lit the hallways with a dim light. Ethan went up the main staircase and turned right. Few doors down, he stopped and knocked softly.

He knocked again.

After a moment, Charlotte opened the door and stepped out to the hallway.

Ethan apologized for disturbing her and then said, "I am planning to go away for a while, but before I go, I wanted to let you know about something that I forgot to mention earlier."

Charlotte pointed to the leather bench down the hallway. They walked towards it and sat down on the brown, leather cushions.

Before Charlotte got a chance to ask a question, Ethan said, "You have to keep the babies safe. I saw what was in Steffan's mind. He was not even trying to hide it. He completely forgot to guard his thoughts."

Charlotte's face showed emotional exhaustion as she rested her back on the wall, exhaling slowly.

Ethan continued, "By now, everyone knows that Adara was expecting triplets. But at least they don't know she has already given birth. I removed all traces from the road. Adara and the babies are safe. For a while."

Charlotte reassured him that Adara and the children would be just fine. They were safe here. No one can enter the grounds without being allowed in. It's not possible to physically, nor mentally pass the barriers set by Sentinels.

Ethan knew that, but he simply wanted to make sure they knew the danger was approaching.

He stood up to go, but Charlotte grabbed his hand and pleaded, "Please be careful. Do not do anything you could later regret."

Ethan stopped and announced slowly, each word echoing in the hallway, "I need to get out of here. Away from Adara. This is too much."

"I know you are hurting but take it easy. Don't just jump into a relationship—"

"I'll be back to visit in a while. It will be like an overdue vacation." He smiled as he turned around and left the hallway.

Charlotte waited few minutes before going back to the room. She knew what his plans were. But it was his life; there was nothing she could do to stop him. She hoped he would realize that escaping into the arms of another woman would not heal the wounds of his heart.

CHAPTER FIFTEEN

The Roulette

MONTHS PASSED. To Ethan, it felt like an eternity, but it had only been about two years since he left. He stayed out of the way as he promised. It was hard, but he kept busy by traveling constantly and visiting the opposing families, negotiating treaties.

The few Gems he had been promised got them closer to a formal reset they strived for; but there were still more Gems to be collected.

Different week different city, country; different woman. But the gaping hole in his heart remained.

Since he left, he had been communicating with his family, and especially, with Brayden, informing everyone of the progress he was making. He had also been getting updates about the work from the other fronts across the world.

From conversations with Brayden, it was curious to hear that Adara's children were quite peculiar.

He had visited the house a few months back when Adara and Kyle were away on a trip. When he saw the children, he could not believe his eyes.

They were almost two years old then and were developing very differently. The youngest one, Kayla, was a happy baby girl, cheerful and giggly. However, Rainer and Nerissa were growing unnaturally fast. They were growing at an accelerated rate.

Nerissa looked and behaved like a seven year old, and Rainer was not far behind.

Right after the children were born, no one noticed anything unusual, but after few months passed they had noticed that Nerissa was growing exponentially and Rainer was trying to catch up to whatever happened to his older sister. The only thing that reminded the family of the three being triplets were the intense-green eyes. Besides being completely puzzled by the unusual growth, everyone was baffled by the eyes, as the green color had never appeared in their people before.

As for the appearance, Nerissa had wavy, dark brown hair with streaks of red woven in between the locks. Her dark hair complimented her delicate, olive complexion.

Rainer's skin was light caramel color that matched his straight, jet black hair. A complete opposite was Kayla, who was a fair-skinned redhead, with her hair almost as red as Emma's, but completely straight.

No one expected any resemblance to the parents, as parental genes did not play a role in how children looked. The complete mutation made the children look totally original.

That is why the green eye color was an interesting phenomenon. It reminded them of the surprise everyone had after seeing blue eyes Adara, Ethan, and Brayden had.

Those two years had flown by quickly, filled with heavy negotiations on both sides. Ethan had been traveling alone and towards the east, whereas Adara and Kyle, along with Brayden and Emma, accompanied by other family members, had been traveling west to negotiate the coalition. During that time, the children were staying with the family at the Water's Edge and had the biggest connection with Charlotte and Marcel, just like Adara, Brayden, and Ethan had before them.

As the time passed, Ethan realized that he could not distance himself emotionally from Adara. His love was still burning a hole in his soul. Every mention, or even a mere thought of her name, ripped the stitches out of his heart.

He had been rebelling against this crippling feeling by seeking solace in the company of other women.

Because of his looks and generally charming demeanor, he was surrounded by women at all times. He did not need to use mind control for them to spend time with him; wherever he turned, he found what he wanted; but, apparently, not what he needed.

None of the women had been able to fill the abyss that seemed to grow within him.

It had been a long time since he visited the family, and what seemed like forever since he last saw Adara.

So now, Kayla was somewhere around two years of age; but he wondered how Nerissa and Rainer looked, considering their accelerated growth spurts.

For some reason, he could not fall asleep this night. He was tossing and turning, unable to disconnect himself from the thoughts that were rushing through his head. He felt emotionally drained.

Sleep was the only escape from his torments, but this night, for some reason, the sleep eluded him.

He seldom had dreams, so oftentimes, all he wanted to do was escape from reality and simply sleep. But that was tricky because he rarely felt physically tired, so *sleep* was something he did to disconnect from reality.

But not tonight.

He looked to the left on his bed. The silk sheets were covering the naked body of a woman he took to bed last night. He thought quickly, trying to remember her name; but he could not recall it.

Exhausted and restless, he sat up slowly, as to not awake her. He put his feet on the granite floor. The tiles felt nice and cold on his bare skin. The air was warm and the breeze blew through the opened balcony.

Ethan placed his face in his hands.

After a moment, he stood up to get some air. The silky sheets slid off his naked body.

He felt agitated.

Something was not right... somewhere. He just could not *see* where.

As he made his way to the balcony, he grabbed his pants and put them on, sliding them over his smooth, warm skin.

The breeze was gentle but slightly cooler on the balcony. He rested his naked back on the stone wall of the building as he leaned on it with his head arched back.

The beautiful night scenery of the dark hills, illuminated streets, and picturesque villas stretched in front of him.

What am I doing here? He looked back inside the room where he saw the bed with mangled sheets and a woman whose name he could not remember.

The intense emotion of worry crept up again, and he realized that he was worrying about Adara.

But she's perfectly safe with the rest of them, he thought again.

Suddenly the wave hit him hard. He felt his heart racing, filling with fear. He rested his palms on the wide, stone balustrade as he inhaled deeply, trying to calm down.

It was Adara; she was in trouble. *But how?*

Ethan went inside the room, put on his shirt and shoes, and was ready to leave. He hesitated and stopped by the nightstand on the side where the woman slept peacefully. He felt empty, looking at her lying there like many other women did over the past several months.

It was not her fault; it was all him.

He was looking for love and belonging where he subconsciously knew he would not find it. Not because of the women he slept with, but because of his unwillingness to move on and accept change.

Feeling miserable and guilty, he wrote a quick note and placed it on the nightstand. Then he slowly traced his hand over her forehead. He wanted to make sure she would not miss him; he did not want to leave her wanting something that was not meant to be.

He stood up and walked through the balcony door as he *shifted out* with the breeze that swirled the rising curtain.

Ethan *shifted back* near the terrace by the kitchen.

There was silence.

All seemed calm in the early afternoon. He needed a moment to adjust to the change of time zones as he *shifted back* to the Water's Edge.

He walked to the kitchen and saw few *family* members sitting in the dinette, talking, and drinking coffee.

When they saw him, they all turned and started to greet him, but then they all froze after hearing Kyle call Adara's name as he walked briskly through the hallway.

They all turned towards his voice.

Kyle repeated, "Where is she!? Where is Adara? Have you seen her this morning?"

He was holding a letter in his hand. Ethan took few steps towards him to look at the envelope.

Everyone got closer.

Ethan could sense the danger...

"I found this in the hallway," Kyle said as Ethan took the letter.

Ethan read it out loud.

After a moment of silence, he declared, "She must already be down there." He studied the letter again.

Eva added, "I saw a carrier earlier this morning. I thought it was a delivery, but I guess I was wrong. It must have arrived then. Their house is few hours away."

Ethan looked at Marcel and asked, "Where is Brayden?"

"He and Emma are traveling and are at the Waters of Life mountain range. They are unreachable. Even by thought."

Ethan cursed out loud, turning around and heading to the hallway. "I will get to her quicker if I take the bike." Ethan headed to the back of the building, going to the main garage.

Kyle took few steps to follow him, but Ethan stopped him and said, "You will only slow me down. It's a rescue mission. I have no time to babysit anyone."

"What the hell are you talking about? My wife is in danger; I need to go to her."

Ethan snapped, "It's like going into the lion's den. You will, most likely, not come out alive. Whom do you think will be blamed for that? Adara will never forgive me if anything happens to you."

Kyle wanted to argue, but Ethan repeated again, this time calmly, "You will only slow me down, and we cannot afford that. For Adara's sake."

"Fine. But why use the bike anyway? Just *shift out* of here and *shift back* where she's at."

Ethan looked at Charlotte, who then quickly searched for something in the kitchen cabinet, then he looked down and uttered slowly, "I can't."

"Who the hell cares if they see you and realize the powers you have. It's Adara we are talking about!" Kyle yelled, steaming with frustration.

Ethan raised his voice but slowly lowered it again, "I can't. I need to take the Life Water. Just in case."

Kyle was confused.

Ethan looked at Charlotte who handed him a small glass vile, "We are not able to *shift out* with this on, or in our bodies. Same with the Dragon's Blood. These substances prevent travel through the Void."

Kyle turned pale, his face freezing in fear when he realized what Ethan meant. Adara's life was in danger.

Ethan assured him by saying, "When I get to her and it's safe to *shift*, I will bring her back right away." He turned around and headed towards the back door.

However, before he took the first step, Kyle grabbed his hand.

Ethan turned around and looked at Kyle's face. It showed fear, anger, and helplessness.

"Bring her back safe. Whatever it takes," Kyle implored, his voice shaky, full of fear.

"I'll bring her back." Then he added quietly and turned around, "Or die trying."

"I know," Kyle muttered. "That's was worries me."

Adara was sitting in the family room, admiring the antique furniture, when the maid brought some snacks and informed her that Lord Adrian would be with her shortly.

The maid added, "Is there anything else I can get you?"

"Thank you. I have everything I need," Adara replied, looking at a tray of pastries.

She sat there, looking around the room, thinking if she made a good decision of coming here by herself.

The letter implied that Adrian would only discuss the treaty with her. She knew that others were done negotiating with him, but she believed that she could convince him to join their side without using force or brutality.

"Even more beautiful than I remembered. But then again, you are Adara; your beauty has been known throughout the written history." Adrian's voice carried across the spacious room.

He continued, "I hear that your memory is not completely back yet. Still little hazy about the past?"

"No. Not anymore. And I definitely remember you," she said with confidence in her voice.

He came closer and embraced her like a very good friend, but there was no warmth in his gesture. He pulled back and looked at her, noticing how rigid she remained.

"Oh. Adara, you hurt my feelings. Such a cold welcome. And we were like brother and sister."

He turned around, approached the table, and took few grapes from the plate. With a smooth motion, he gestured for her to sit back down on the couch.

He came over to the wine rack and asked which one she preferred.

"Not a big wine drinker lately," she said, refusing his offer.

"We must celebrate the new beginning." Adrian insisted, pointing to the two bottles.

"I'll have a glass of red then."

He poured two glasses and placed them on the table. Pointed to them and waited for her.

Adara picked up a glass and raised it.

He picked up the other and toasted. "To the new beginnings."

They both took a sip.

Adrian looked at his glass and asked her, "I've heard that the memory issue has been giving you trouble in your Family for quite a while now. A big mix-up I heard. How is Ethan dealing with all that? His mate with another. Sad." He swirled the wine around and took another sip, watching Adara drink hers.

"You need not concern yourself. But since you know so much about what is going on with us, you should know that Kyle and I could not be happier together."

"Yes. The triplets. I've heard. I have not gotten the news of whom their protectors are though. You, on the other hand, are alone. No one is protecting you; not anymore." He sputtered coldly, finished his glass of wine, and placed it on the coffee table.

She felt a shiver going down her spine.

Adara tried to sense his thoughts, but his barrier was up; she remembered noticing it shortly after he had walked into the room.

"Why did you invite me here?" Adara saw him looking at his empty glass. Then it dawned on her, "You never wanted to talk about the way we could come to the understanding," she stated coldly, feeling fear and anger rising within her.

"No. I wanted to get a chance to see which one of us would be lucky enough to survive the roulette." He pointed to his empty glass he just placed on the table, and then to the one she was holding in her hand.

Hers was half empty.

She lifted it up and smelled the dark burgundy liquid. The scent of wine was strong, but now that she thought about it, she could smell something else in the half-empty glass—something familiar.

Then she realized what it was.

Still sitting, Adara felt weak in her knees when she recalled where she had smelled it last.

It was the small, dark-glass bottle with the dragon engraved on the side.

She tried standing up and putting the wine glass down, but her knees got weak, and as she placed her wine on the table, the glass tipped over and fell to the side, making a sharp sound as the glass surfaces made contact. The red wine dripped onto the cream carpet, pooling around before being absorbed by the thick fibers.

Adara got up quickly but had to sit right down again. She looked at the wine stain on the cream carpet. The red drops were spattering as they fell. Everything was in slow motion. The drops traveled slowly through the air before making a splash in the red puddle.

Adara looked up and felt like the whole room was spinning.

After she closed her eyes, she sensed that Adrian approached her. Feeling that she was losing her balance, she lay down on the sofa.

She was opening and closing her eyes slowly.

Adrian sat next to her and just stared at her face.

After a moment, she said to him, "But if you did this to me, then you will have to pay with your own life."

He rested his back on the sofa, getting more comfortable next to her, smoothed her hair, and explained slowly, "Not exactly. I had prepared two bottles; one with poison, one without. You chose the one with the poison. I set down two glasses; one had the antidote, while the other had more poison. I didn't know which one was which. You chose your glass; I took the other. It was either you or me. You chose your faith; I did not choose the glass for you."

He got up and, as he walked away, he added, "When you go to the Void, please let the others know that our House stands strong. We are not giving up the power. We never will."

Adrian sat down on the armchair across the coffee table and watched her slip away.

Adara's eyes were closing and opening slowly; her breaths became slower and shallower.

Everything was fading.

Adrian stood up and poured himself a drink. Then, he heard commotion in the hallway. He put away the glass and saw Ethan storming into the room.

He taunted Ethan in a loud, but surprisingly, shaky voice when he saw him approach Adara's motionless body, "You are too late. She is fading away... if she hasn't already crossed over."

Ethan did not pay any attention to him and rushed to Adara's side. He knelt next to her and wiped few strands of her hair away from her face; he checked her pulse. *Still there.*

He pulled out the small bottle and opened it.

He took a small sip and swallowed it, then steadily tilted her head and gave her his breath; her lungs filled with his antidote-infused breath. He did another one, making sure his breath and the microscopic particles of Life Water reached deep into her lungs. His throat and lungs burned in pain as the Life Water dispersed across his body; the sensation disappeared as quickly as it began.

After tilting her head upwards again, he poured the remaining liquid in her mouth.

He did not feel her swallow it though.

Holding her tight, he whispered in her ear, "Do not let go. You are not allowed to let go. If you don't have enough strength to hold on for me, please do it for him. Whatever you do, please do not let go." He kept his cheek close to hers and rubbed her arms, trying to spread the antidote around her body.

He whispered, his face next to hers, "I want to make this world better for you. It doesn't matter to me who you are with. I want you to live, to be happy and healthy. Hold on. Please, just hold on."

He saw her chest rise slowly, and her breaths become deeper.

She opened her eyes slightly but closed them quickly in discomfort.

Adara whispered almost inaudibly, "Just let me sleep. I am so tired."

"No. Do not let go," Ethan pleaded and rubbed her arms.

She whispered, "It was so nice and peaceful out there. Tell him I love him."

"You can tell him yourself when I get you home," he implored.

Her lips moved slowly. He barely was able to make out her words.

He heard her say, "I love you... I always had."

His eyes were shining with tears that pooled around as his soul was filling with despair.

Looking at her face, he declared, "You will be alright. The antidote is working; you will be home soon, then you can tell him yourself. We just need time for the poison to burn out."

"I love you," she whispered and was again drifting away in his arms.

"Wake up. You cannot fall asleep." He shook her.

Adara opened her eyes slightly.

Ethan stood up, picked up her weak body, and held her in his arms. Then he declared to Adrian, his voice

ice cold and as harp as broken glass, "I am not done with you. It's personal. Not only for me, but also for the entire Family. You just started the war."

Without looking back at Adrian, he left the room with Adara in his arms.

Adrian stared out the window, holding his empty glass. He looked down at his hand and at the golden band on his finger. "Eleonore, I hope it was worth it— starting the war at your command." He poured himself a drink and said, "So it begins."

He looked in the distance and finished his drink in one gulp.

CHAPTER SIXTEEN

The Broken

ETHAN RUSHED THROUGH the hallway of Adrian's house and headed to the back door. He yelled at the servant standing by the door, "Open it... Now!"

Ethan pushed it with his shoulder to open it wider. Then he shouted again for the servant to open one of the cars that were parked along the side.

The servant said, "But what about you motorcycle—"

Ethan stared at him and said, "The car. Now!"

The servant opened the door quickly without adding a word.

Ethan placed Adara on the front passenger side, reclined the seat, and buckled her in. He quickly went around it, got in, and started the engine.

Holding her hand in his, he sped through the long, curving driveway leading to the main street. He was terrified and frozen at the same time. The images from the last time he sped like that made his heart race. *Everything will be fine. Just like last time.*

But this time Adara's life was hanging by a thread.

Speeding along the tree-lined road heading home, he talked to her to keep her from sleeping. He simply needed to keep her awake; otherwise, she would slip away.

He knew that the antidote would soon take its full effect and make the poison burn out. But at that time, she needed to be placed in cold water to cancel the reaction and prevent the skin from reabsorbing the poisonous substance.

It had only been minutes, but the drive seemed to go on forever. As he drove along the beautiful hills and valleys, he kept looking for a nearby inn that he knew was in this area.

"It's not far. You'll be better in no time," he promised. "The poison will dissipate soon; we just need to get you on ice."

He dialed the number to the inn. Slowly, making a pause after each command, he said, "This is Ethan Monsanto. Let the manager know that I will need my room ready; tub full of ice. I will be there shortly."

Few minutes later he pulled up to the back door of the hotel. The manager was already waiting. Ethan picked Adara up and rushed through the door.

On his way to the room, he gave directions to the manager. "No disruptions. Bring high protein food."

The manager had a blank expression on his face and said nothing when opening the door to the suite and, later, to the bathroom.

"Should I get some help, sir?" The manager looked concerned.

"No need. It's not as bad as it looks. It's just the matter of time. She'll be fine."

Manager's face did not even twitch as he nodded and left the suite. Ethan knew exactly what he was thinking though, now that he eased the control over the manager's mind.

Ethan did not care.

The tub was filled half-way with ice, so he poured cold water to fill the rest.

He quickly undressed Adara, who by now was strong enough to sit up on her own. He helped her up and placed her in the icy water. As she lay there, he took her hand and sat on the floor next to her.

"Now we just need to wait." He picked up her hand and kissed it gently.

After few moments, he noticed how hot her skin was getting and knew that the poison had started burning away through her skin. He put her hand in the water and told her to submerge herself entirely.

She slid under the surface.

Her whole body underwater, she kept her eyes open and looked at him from beneath the surface.

Time passed.

Ethan was resting his head on his crossed arms, leaning on the edge of the tub.

They lay there looking at each other.

Ethan whispered quietly so that she would not hear him under the water, "My only sunshine."

After a while, all the ice had melted and the water was steaming. A sweet smell of flowers and herbs filled the air.

Adara was safe.

Ethan sat up, his head arched back against the wall. He heard a sound of her slowly sitting up in the tub. She was smiling at him as she swept her wet hair away from her face.

Adara pulled the plug to let the water out.

She rested against the wall in the tub and said, "I knew you would never leave me. I knew that you would find me." She leaned forward, reached, and touched his face.

Ethan looked at her, confused and not sure how to react to that gesture.

She smiled radiantly.

Ethan opened his mouth to say something, but the words did not come out.

He did not know what to say. *That smile*, he thought; he had been waiting for that smile for such a long time. *No. This is not real. My Adara is gone.*

She stretched and stated, "I am starving."

"It's the reaction after the antidote. I'll get you something to eat when you get out. But first you need to rest. Your body has been through a lot." He shifted his head to face the other wall, trying to avoid looking at her naked body.

She slowly raised herself up.

Ethan instinctively looked at her when she stood up in front of him. He quickly looked away but not before seeing her hips in front of his face.

"I'll start the water so you can take a shower to wash yourself off. Most of the poison has left your body, but it will take few hours for you to get back to normal." He was trying not to think about her naked body next to him.

"Silly you. I am back to normal. I'm perfectly fine." She smiled and stared at him.

"You are not yourself," he said harshly and turned on the water in the shower.

Adara said quietly, "I *am* my old self; can't you see." She touched his face.

There was a knock on the door leading to the suite.

Ethan held his breath and left the bathroom.

As he was leaving, he saw her standing there, looking sad and confused.

Ethan went to open the door to the suite.

Just as instructed, the manager brought a tray full of food. After closing the door, Ethan went towards the bathroom but then, right before coming in, stopped and knocked on the door.

"Come in."

Feeling numb, as he saw her tired face, he said, "You were crying."

She stood in the shower and said, "You will never forgive me for forgetting you."

He walked towards her with a towel. "It's not your fault. And there is nothing to forgive... I never stopped..."

"I love you too," she declared quietly, her voice steady and clear.

"It's just your body reacting to the antidote; you will be yourself s—"

"But I am myself!" she exclaimed and covered her face with her hands. She said quietly, "I know what is coming and I am afraid. All I know now is that I love, and I miss you so much." She looked emotionally exhausted.

Ethan was silent, so she looked up and saw that he was standing in front of her, his shoulders down as all the fight had left him. His eyes were filled with pain.

He looked defeated.

Adara looked away and asked quietly, "Please hold me... I have missed you so much. It feels like I woke up from a long nightmare. But why do I feel so alone?"

He took a step towards her and helped her out of the tub.

She stood there on the cold tiles, dripping wet.

Like in a trance, he gently touched her cheek with his opened palm then slid it to her shoulder.

One more step towards her.

He kissed her softly. Her lips felt so supple and warm. Slowly, he moved his lips down to kiss her neck and shoulder. Her skin tasted sweet and fresh.

Adara whispered in his ear, "Our love story."

He slowly pulled her closer and kissed her with intensity that had been burning in his soul ever since his Awakening.

He was starving for her taste; he remembered it so well.

He hungered for her; and now, tasting her brought back all the memories he had been trying to push deep inside his subconscious.

He could feel her body clinging to his and felt her melting in his arms. There was no space between them.

Her kisses were as sweet as he remembered them. Her skin on his tongue was intoxicating. He felt her arms around him and her breath on his neck.

He knew it was wrong. He knew damn well that he had no right. But he could not stop.

The sun was still high when he was falling asleep next to her. The reality was slowly creeping in, but he kept refusing his thoughts. He did not want to think about what they had done. Not while she was in his arms.

For now, she was his.

Please let her stay herself forever.

But all he heard was silence.

He hoped.

For now, it was only two of them. Their love story. Endless love that had survived millennia. All they knew now was that they had each other.

Nothing else mattered.

As he drifted away, looking at her sleeping next to him, his last thought was: *What have I done.*

It was still daylight when Adara sat up at the side of the bed, her body aching all over.

She hesitantly touched her arms, and slowly felt her hips, and stomach. When her fingers touched the inside of her thighs, she felt a dull ache in her lower abdomen and between her thighs. Then she remembered where she was.

She closed her eyes and recalled how Ethan touched her. Exactly like she remembered from before. Just like she wanted.

His hands finding their way to each place that gave her pleasure. He knew her body and she knew his. They were in unison; moving in harmony, just like they had done in the past; knowing exactly what each other liked and what brought them most satisfaction. She remembered that the intensity of sensations that flooded her body was only matched by the completeness she felt when he filled her with each move he made.

She opened her eyes.

"What have I done," she sighed quietly, looking down at her hands.

She looked at the right hand. The golden ring bracelet on her wrist was dull and dark, almost completely black. Seeing it, she felt empty, like there was nothing left of her.

Each breath brought her pain—each one was a reminder of the reality.

Adara held her breath, trying to stop the flood of guilt and sorrow.

However, it did not prevent the reality from creeping in. Finally, she just let go and each gasp of air mixed in with a silent, helpless sob.

She remembered.

She remembered Ethan.

She remembered Kyle.

She remembered it all. The love, the longing.

Everything.

For both.

Adara got up and reached for her clothes that were hanging over the chair. After quickly slipping on the clothes, she took the darkened bracelet off and placed it next to the car keys.

"Please do not leave." She heard Ethan's voice behind her. He was standing in the doorway to the bathroom.

"I do not belong anywhere. I failed," she said, sounding empty and disappointed.

He tried to say something, but before he did, she said, "I failed our cause and everyone that ever loved me. I was a fool to think I could bring peace by being good. Dark Lords do not deserve good."

She looked at him and continued, "But you and Kyle deserve more than this." Her voice was getting louder, anger resonating throughout the room. "You and Kyle should not be forced to share me, and I should not be forced to choose. I have you both in here," she pointed to her heart and sobbed. "There is not enough room though; my heart feels like it is bursting with pain. That damn poison *awoke* everything but erased nothing."

Ethan got up to comfort her, but she took few steps back and said, "How the hell am I to save the World if I can't even handle my own life. I can't live like that. This is sick," she yelled the last words.

Then she added, her voice breaking, "I want to go home."

"But you are going home. Everyone is waiting for you," Ethan pleaded, pain spilling with each word he uttered.

"No. I want to go *Home*. To our home, to how things used to be. I can't deal with all this. I need to leave."

Ethan took another step towards her and took her hand.

She said, "Please tell everyone that I love them and that I never wanted to hurt them. I will be alright... I just need to get away. I need to think."

Ethan embraced her gently and closed his eyes. When he opened them again, his arms were empty.

She was gone.

CHAPTER SEVENTEEN

Truth

WATER'S EDGE.

Ethan *shifted back* in the hallway and walked through it to the kitchen. He got himself a bottle of wine, opened it, and poured a glass. He drank it and poured another one.

He turned around when he heard a child's voice coming from the family room.

The voice was getting closer. "You can't get drunk with that. This wine does not work on us. You need to go to the back room if..." The jabber continued.

Ethan stood there with his glass empty; he smiled when he saw Nerissa approach him with her cat-like moves.

She gracefully leaped onto the counter, and sat with her feet down and her ankles crossed.

She continued, "Please don't tell Charlotte I'm on the counter; she hates that. 'Ladies do not jump like that; ladies do not get mud on their dresses; ladies this, ladies that...' I keep telling her I am not a lady; and I like sitting on the counter because I can finally look people in the eye. I hate being treated like a kid. I am not a child. When will they get it? Stupid body." She pouted and grabbed an apple from a dish, looked at it for a moment, rotated it in her hand, and took a bite.

For a moment, Ethan forgot all about his troubles. He looked at Nerissa and listened to her monolog.

She was a feisty girl who looked like a preteen.

It was amazing seeing her as the time passed. She was the oldest looking of the triplets.

They were about two years old, but Nerissa and her brother aged differently than Kayla.

When he had visited here last time, few months back, he overheard Nerissa arguing with her brother Rainer...

During that visit, Rainer, speaking to Nerissa, exploded with anger, "Why won't you slow down. What's the hurry!?"

"I am not forcing you to do anything! You can do whatever you want; it's your choice. But I am on the mission," Nerissa replied, annoyed and angry.

"We are all on a mission. But why the rush. Mom is going to handle things. She says that diplomacy is the key."

"Diplomacy my ass. The war is coming, and I will not be caught in this puny little body." She turned on her heal, grabbed a bunch of peaches, took a bite of one, and skipped through the hallway to where Ethan, caught off guard, was standing and looking at the whole encounter.

Nearly bumping into him, she stopped just in time, said *hi*, and skipped along. Then she stopped abruptly, turned, looked at Ethan, and stated, "Rainer is in the kitchen being such a child. I think that he would benefit from your advice on how to be a man and grow up already." She turned again and skipped along.

Ethan stood there, not knowing if he should start laughing or be concerned and mention this to someone.

They all knew that the children were growing at different rates, and at this point, everyone was at peace with it after the initial shock.

All that aside, he was still astonished seeing this little girl speak like that.

After Nerissa was out of sight, Ethan went to the kitchen and saw Rainer at the refrigerator taking out some snacks.

"Is there anything good inside?" Ethan asked him.

"Why are girls so stubborn? She drives me crazy!"

A faint smile emerged on Ethan's face as he thought about Nerissa.

He looked back at Rainer. It seemed hilarious to hear those words come out of such a young boy. But he knew they were not like other children.

Being serious about what he was saying, Ethan had answered, "She has her priories. It looks like her mind is set on something."

"She wants to grow up now, now, now. Why can't she be a good girl and simply stay a kid? It's not like she will need her powers tomorrow," he yelled and smashed the door shut.

Ethan asked, "Why do you follow her? I mean, why do you age as she's aging?"

"I go where she goes; that was our deal. I am the protector until she can handle things on her own. I can't be a protector if I am in my diapers, drinking milk from the bottle." Rainer sat down on the stool. His eyes looked tired and showed his true age, reminding Ethan that Rainer was agelessness.

"Go, have some fun now before she gets older and really starts causing trouble." Ethan rubbed Rainer's head and chuckled.

That conversation was not that long ago.

Now, Nerissa sat in front of him, being at least a foot taller compared to the last time he saw her, few months back.

She was munching on a red apple.

Her growth had accelerated lately. *Why is she rushing?*

"How do you know about the wine and the back room?" Ethan asked, pouring himself another glass and taking few sips.

Surprised, she looked up at him, "There are no secrets as far as I'm concerned. When I left the Void, I wanted to live. I am done observing everyone. I want to experience things for myself." Her eyes sparkled bright-green. Same color as her siblings'.

"I am ready to shake this place up… whether the World is ready for me or not; I'm ready to be here," she declared and pulled her knees to her chin, embracing them with her arms. She looked at him and whispered, "Thank you for saving mama again."

"Again?"

She looked away and said candidly, "Dragon's Blood vial… before I was born. Thank you."

He did not know how to respond to that.

Nerissa kept glaring at him and continued, "Life is a gift, and bodies are sacred. It's a privilege to be alive. We should never waste that gift nor destroy our bodies." She looked in the distance through the glass door.

Exhaling softly, she took another bite and continued after a moment, "Before I came here, I could see everything and be everywhere, but I could not experience nor feel. I saw the Sun but could not feel it's warmth on my skin. I could see this apple but could not smell it, nor taste it." She took another bite; savoring every moment, she chewed and swallowed it, and then she said, "It was all emotion with no physical connection at all."

Looking at the apple in her hand she repeated, "Life is a privilege and a gift; we should never forget that; and should never waste it."

Ethan stood there with an empty glass in his hand. He just stared at her. He could not find words.

She asked him, "Do you remember the time before you were born here again, and after you left your first life?"

He looked puzzled and was trying to think about what she just asked him.

"Do you remember the Void?" she clarified.

He hesitated. "Yes... No. Kind of. I remember it like a place where there is no time. I know I was there for a long while, but it seemed like merely moments," he said thinking out loud.

Nerissa grinned with a bitter smile. "I remember it all; every minute of it," she replied with resentment.

After a moment of silence, Nerissa said, "Speaking of the Void, I know the real story behind the origins of Dragon's Blood, the story that only the Sentinels and the Dark Lords know about." She stared at the remaining half of the blood-red apple she was holding in her hand. She looked up at him as if waiting for him to ask her about the story.

Ethan was caught off guard with Nerissa's quick change of topics. He chuckled. "I'm not sure what you mean."

He really did not want to leave yet. He did not want to face the reality. And he, definitely, was not ready to go and confess what he had done earlier that day.

Talking to Nerissa was a form of escape he needed; a perfect way to postpone what he had to do. Ethan simply wanted to stay here and listen to her cheerful voice.

He said, "The story of Dragon's Blood is known to everyone in our family. It's one of the *fairytales* we tell the children as a bedtime story."

He saw how Nerissa smiled, giving him a mysterious look. *Does she really know something we don't?*

Ethan asked hesitantly, "What do you mean by the *real story?*" He was getting quite intrigued, looking into her bright-green eyes, now beaming with excitement. He could sense she was proud to know something he was interested in knowing himself. He chuckled when he realized that, even though she had an ageless soul, she was still a child, looking for someone to be proud of her and to acknowledge what she did or knew.

Nerissa sat up comfortably at the edge, her legs together on the side of the island and her ankles crossed. She leaned closer to Ethan as her hands gently grasped the round granite ledge.

She leaned closer and spoke slowly while looking into Ethan's eyes, "We all know that the only way to end a life of Dusana-Tykim is to use the Dragon's Blood poison; that is true. We have always been told that when the Dark Lords killed the Sacred Dragon, wherever the blood fell, there arose a thorny bush that was poisonous to all Dusana-Tykim."

She stopped for a moment, making room for a dramatic pause. "What we were not told is the entire story of what happened. Have you ever wondered what happened to all other dragons? The stories only mentions the first dragon—the Sacred Dragon. If you think about it, you will start questioning how, out of all the thousands of dragons that lived here, the Dark Lords managed to somehow kill the Sacred One—the most important one that lived on Earth."

She took another pause. Ethan completely forgot about the earlier events of the day and became entirely engrossed in her story.

As she continued the tale, Nerissa slowly lifted her arm and, with her index finger extended, swept across his forehead.

He realized that her story started coming into his mind, presenting itself as images, as if he was there for the events when they unfolded. There was no doubt; her powers were increasing day by day.

She continued the story and the pictures filled his mind. "The Dark Lords wanted to seize control of the Sacred Mountain where the Waters of Life originated—the place where the Lords had been welcomed by the Sentinels and where the binding pact had been made.

"The mountain was protected by the Sacred Dragon that would breathe fire on whoever had devious intentions when coming there. And you probably don't know, but we are not impervious to their fire. It is not a surprise to know that the Dark Lords did not step into the frontlines themselves, but instead, they used humans to do their bidding. The Dark Lords stood and watched from a safe distance as the Dragon scorched hundreds of humans who were sent to slay him while being corrupted by the Dark Lords. As a payment for slaying the Dragon, the volunteers had been promised riches beyond their wildest dreams.

"The Dragon's blood fell on the ground, and where it landed on the soil, a thorny bush would arise. Dark Lords learned that no matter how many wounds the Dragon sustained, it was impossible to destroy it, as each piercing would close almost instantaneously after the first drops of blood spilled out.

"Then, what they had done, I consider worse than death." Nerissa's eyes turned black. All the green shimmer vanished and was replaced by a looming flicker of a black diamond.

She straightened her back and lifted her chin a little as she continued in an empty voice, "They chained him up. Dragged him to the cave below the Waters of Life fountain. The chains were made from the metal quenched in the Water of Life itself and were, therefore, unbreakable, even for the Sacred Dragon."

She saw that Ethan had a question so, without him uttering a single word, she answered it, "Yes. Dragons can go back and forth between different realms or dimensions, but they are unable to travel for as long as they are bleeding. The blood of the Sacred Dragon would contaminate the Void. As long as their flesh is opened and the blood is seeping, the dragon cannot *shift out*." She looked at him and continued with a gravel voice, "The Dark Lords had heard the Dragon's thoughts of escape from that battlefield under the Sacred Mountain; that is why they did what they did next."

Ethan was moved by what he saw after that. Nerissa's eyes got watery but did not shed a single tear. He could see she was trying really hard to keep her composure.

She continued in a shaky voice, "To prevent him from *shifting out*, they kept piercing his beautiful, green and black scales as they dragged him to that cave."

Ethan could see it all, as if it was all happening in front of his eyes.

Nerissa cleared her voice, took a deep breath, and continued, "They dragged him to the stone alter that had been used for the welcoming ceremony when you all came to Earth. To prevent him from *shifting out*, the Dark Lords chained him to the altar so he could not move. Then, they shoved a jagged metal spike through his heart, knowing that it would not kill him, but just prevent him from escaping. Each beat of his heart sent a trickle of bright-red blood down the altar and onto the stone floor. They left him there after performing magical rituals that were intended to give them power over Earth. And they left him there. Alone and bleeding.

"As the time passed, the trickling blood collected around the altar and formed a shimmering, red pond as dragon blood doesn't dry. Over the ages, it seeped through the stone crevices and contaminated Earth. Dragons are not evil, but the dagger that pierced his heart was intended with malevolent purpose; therefore, evil, treachery, and hopelessness spread as the Dragon's blood made its way throughout Earth."

After a moment of silence, she added, "The Sentinels were appalled by what the Dark Lords had done. And as a result, they had taken away all the magic and the power of rituals from Earth in order to prevent things like that from happening again. Ever since then, the realms have been closed to Dusana-Tykim and Earth in general. As a result, none of the Lords have been able to *shift*. Now you are the only ones who are able to do that. But that's a secret because your enemies still do not know," she whispered, as if someone else was listening.

She continued and the images kept on coming into Ethan's mind, "To help Earth heal, the Sentinels have opened up the Waters of Life, so the power of the Dragon's blood could be negated by the healing power of Life. Light is more powerful than Darkness, as it illuminates that which is hidden. But when you add humans or any other beings into that equation then the dance and the battle begins."

Ethan looked at her, not following what she was saying, so she explained again, "Light always wins over Darkness and the Darkness only appears when there is a third element introduced. The shadows are casted and Darkness surfaces as soon as we come into play. If the light moves, the shadow we cast moves too. So there is always a battle for balance between Light and Darkness."

Ethan stood there, looking at Nerissa's dark eyes. She turned her head and looked outside through the glass terrace door.

She continued without looking back at him, "The dark rituals they had performed closed the door to Earth. Dark Lords thought of themselves as the masters of all that surrounded them. They did not want competition. They knew that they were not the first ones who settled on Earth, but they wanted to be the last. They did not allow anyone else to enter Earth and make it their home. No other kinds were allowed since then. "

Ethan's eyes widened. He had never thought about that before. Nerissa was right. Why did he think that they were *it*? That Dusana-Tykim would be the last ones here.

She smiled, seeing his realization, and then continued, "The Sacred Dragon is still chained up at the Sacred Mountain's Cave of Tears." She smirked, and added, "That's how I named it. I call it the Cave of Tears because when I tried going there in my dreams, I could never get past the sweet-smelling shrubs that line the entrance to the cave. I sit there and cry; I don't know why, but the tears keep on coming when I'm there."

She heard the question that was forming in his mind, so she added, "No one can enter the cave to save him. Not until we have all the Gems. The cave has been sealed by the magic the Dark Lords performed that day. Only after all the Gems are gathered, the seal can be broken."

Ethan realized something about the images he saw during her story. He did not put the two and two together. Until now.

As one of the Lords, his body had been given to him by the Sentinels; therefore, he had not experienced a childhood. However now, having a chance to be reborn, he had gone through all the stages, and everything that came with them.

Like other children, he had been told bedtime stories, one of which was the tale of the dragons. He remembered having nightmares about the cave, of which he never heard of, until now. He remembered the cave Nerissa mentioned, and it was exactly like the one from his childhood dreams. Now that he thought about it, the nightmare was the one mentioned by many children of his people. Ethan had never realized that the cave from his nightmares was the same cave they were welcomed in after being granted haven on Earth.

Nerissa looked at him and, *seeing* his thoughts, she said, "All other dragons, as well as other sacred creatures, left Earth when the magic was taken away."

Ethan's thoughts circled around something Nerissa mentioned earlier. Then he said, "If magic had been taken away, why have the rituals, our family performed, actually worked?"

Nerissa picked up another apple and bit into it.

She answered him, still chewing the juicy fruit, "That is one of the things we needed to keep as a secret. We could not reveal that we had been favored by the Sentinels. That would have created a full-blown war with the Dark Lords; something that we were not ready for, and in a way, are still not ready to face."

"How do you know all this?" Ethan asked, curious and intrigued.

Nerissa answered, all excited, "I was told that during one of my travels. At night." She continued, "They said I will learn more things during the training we're going on."

Ethan looked confused, so she explained further, "Rainer and I are leaving tomorrow. We are going to travel, with Marcel and few others, and visit different places and some interesting people. They will help us get ready for the fight that is near. The war has already started; now it's up to each side to decide where to strike and who will make the next major move."

Ethan had no idea what she was talking about when she mentioned them leaving.

Nerissa realized he was unaware of their travel plans, so she added, "We are leaving tomorrow and will come back whenever we're ready to begin the mission."

Listening to her explanation, he realized what it meant. Nerissa and Rainer were leaving, and their mother was not here. She will not see them off; unless he finds her soon.

Nerissa smiled brightly and assured him, "Mama is alright. You do not have to worry."

She changed topics so quickly.

Ethan knew that Nerissa, even though so grown up and with an old soul, still referred to Adara as her mother. He did not know if she did that for herself, or for Adara.

"She's so lonely though, but I don't want to interrupt her. You should go to her. It was a beautiful home." She looked out the window.

Ethan was trying to keep up with what Nerissa was saying.

"What home?" he asked. He still could not shake the strange feeling of being next to this extraordinary girl.

"You are funny. Of course I mean, Atlantis. How can you forget such a beautiful place? Oh, how I wish I had lived there. Now, it's all gone. Water took everything." She stared out the window.

Before he said anything, she turned to him and smiled with reassurance. "They are waiting for you in the study. I 'm sure they would like to see you before you go to her."

Ethan looked towards the hallway leading to the study. He hesitated.

Nerissa casually stated as she hopped off the counter, "They don't care about that. They will forgive you. They still love her, and they love you too. All of them. I promise." She grabbed few apples, approached the glass door, walked out of the kitchen, and stepped onto the stone terrace without looking back.

Ethan stood there, frozen, unable to move. He watched her leave the kitchen and walk towards the rose garden.

CHAPTER EIGHTEEN

Reset

ETHAN WALKED TO the study and saw them sitting at the table in the corner. Only Kyle was standing by the window, looking into the distance.

Everyone turned towards Ethan as he walked in.

Kyle approached him and said, "I didn't see you pull up. Where is Adara?"

When Ethan did not answer, Kyle tilted his head slightly. He asked, his voice trembling faintly, "Where is my wife?"

Ethan looked at Brayden, and then at Kyle. After clearing his voice, he answered, "Your… Adara is safe.

She... needs time away from... all of us. She said she'll be fine."

Ethan did not look directly at Kyle. It was hard for Ethan to keep eye contact with him. The guilt of what happened earlier burned inside Ethan even more now that he found himself in the same room with Kyle.

"You promised you would bring her back. Where is she? What happened?" Kyle's voice rose in anger.

Brayden approached them. "Ethan. What happened at Adrian's?" He sounded suspicious, observing Ethan, who looked miserable, standing there, surrounded by everyone.

Ethan raised his arm and made a gesture for Brayden to touch the top of his hand.

Knowing what he meant, Brayden grabbed it and stood there, looking into Ethan's eyes.

The images flooded Brayden's mind.

"So it is war," Brayden declared and let go of Ethan's hand.

"There is more," Ethan confessed.

Brayden hesitantly picked up his hand again.

After a moment, Brayden's eyes got still and stern. He looked at Ethan and said, "I know that it will sound cruel, but I expected more from you, my old friend."

Kyle asked, "What the hell are you talking about?"

Ethan extended his hand for Kyle to touch.

Brayden's voice was quiet and gloomy, "See for yourself."

Kyle looked at Ethan's opened palm. It was trembling slightly as Ethan held it up in the air.

Being unsure what to expect from this, Kyle hesitated for a second but then placed his hand on top of Ethan's palm.

And then he saw. Everything.

All that happened since this morning.

Everything.

"How dare you... touch my wife... you unimaginable bastard," Kyle growled in a low voice and, with his open hands, shoved Ethan, ramming him on the chest. "She wasn't herself. She had that damn poison in her body, you asshole!" he yelled, pain and disappointment choking him.

Kyle added in a cold, gravel voice, "But you knew that all along. And you still did it." His words boomed across the room.

Everyone stood in silence, suspecting what must have happened.

Ethan stared back at Kyle and exclaimed, "She is my Adara."

Kyle enunciated slowly, "She is my wife. We grew up together. We are best friends. We belong together and nothing, I repeat, nothing will ever change that. Not even you and what you had done." Kyle slowed down a bit and continued, "You heard me. We. There is no room for *you* in what we have. We were happy together, but then you had to dig up all that ancient crap. It should've stayed buried."

Ethan stated shortly, "Adara and I sacrificed so much already. Our people are doing it all for you. For all of you. Our plan was to free everyone."

"Well, if this is the price of freedom, than I don't want any part of it. And it looks like Adara doesn't want it either," Kyle yelled and turned to the window, trying to control his rage.

But then he turned back around and smirked, "Freedom you say. All this talk about freedom, but you still keep Adara as a prisoner. Why won't you set her free; for a change."

Ethan exclaimed, hurt spilling with each word he uttered, "I had let her go. I did. But then she came back. At least that's what I thought; what I hoped. But I was wrong. Before she left, I had felt it. She chose you. She wants you. I don't understand why, but she does."

Everyone was looking at Ethan.

His eyes were shining as he stared at Kyle. Hurt was gripping his throat.

Few moments of silence passed and the tension was slowly fading.

Then Ethan continued, "But she left, thinking she has failed. She said that none of us should go through this. She said that no one deserves this never-ending heartbreak."

With a hollow voice, Kyle said, "My heart bleeds every moment she's not near me. What happened between the two of you is irrelevant to how I feel about her. It means nothing in the perspective of time. I want her back."

Ethan froze at those words. It was exactly what he had thought about his own and Adara's relationship. He thought that Kyle was just a moment in the eternity of time. But now he understood.

Time was relative. To Kyle, the past that Ethan and Adara had shared was a moment in time, whereas Kyle and Adara had a lifetime ahead of them.

Ethan pondered the difference between a lifetime and the eternity. Both different, but just as powerful if spent with the right person.

Ethan looked at Charlotte and nodded. He knew he needed to release Adara and himself from the bond.

Kyle broke the silence and spoke to Brayden, "Tell her to come back, please. Nothing matters if she's not with me."

Everyone stood still for a while. Then Charlotte came by Kyle and put her hand on his shoulder. "It will be alright. We will have Brayden find her."

Ethan declared quickly, "I know where she is. I'll get her for—"

"It will be better if I get her," Brayden interrupted and looked in the distance. Then he added, "Now I know where she is."

Kyle and Brayden left the room.

As Kyle was walking away, Ethan caught a glimpse of his face. It showed hurt and disappointment; but above all, it showed worry.

Ethan turned to Charlotte and said, "I know I said that I don't want to forget my love for Adara, but this is destroying us. I was wondering if—"

"I will get everything ready. I never thought that things would get this complicated. But at this point, it looks like our House is being uprooted. We cannot afford to be weakened this way, especially now."

Ethan left the room and went to the terrace, trying to clear his head. He saw two of the triplets playing catch in the grass. Kayla sat in a wooden sandbox with Emma at her side.

Nerissa saw him and quickly ran towards where he was standing.

Wow. She can run, he thought.

She was next to him in just few seconds and was clapping her hands, apparently very excited about something.

"Please, please. Show me how you *shift out*. Please show me. Please, please, pleeease," Nerissa begged. "You're going to her, aren't you? Please show me the jump," she squealed with delight.

Her brother walked towards them and said calmly, "She has been bragging that she can *shift out*, but obviously she cannot or she would've showed me that already."

"Well, I almost can," Nerissa boasted quietly. Then added, getting more excited, "But I will do it soon."

"How do you know?" Ethan and Rainer asked in unison.

She looked at them, her green eyes sparkling. "Well... it feels like electricity in the air, and as if you are in two places at the same time. Like you are here, and where you wanna be, all at once."

She looked at Ethan for validation.

He smiled. "You got it. That is how it feels. More or less."

Nerissa gave them a beaming smile. After a moment, she looked past them. "Mama feels very sad. She feels so lost."

She stared at Ethan and said, "You will bring her back, right?" She waited with anticipation.

"Things are a bit more complicated. Brayden is going to get her," Ethan assured Nerissa, staring at her green eyes.

"Well. Maybe you could still show us how you *shift out*. Do you have anywhere else you need go, maybe?" She looked at him, trying to be serious and to sound all logical.

"Ready?" Ethan asked and chuckled. He found it amusing how well-formulated her arguments were.

"Yes. Yes!" she let out a gleeful squeal.

And so he was gone. He could only imagine the excitement on their faces as he *shifted out* from in front of them.

Ethan *shifted back* at the stony shore. The sun was high above him. He could see the tops of pillars peeking through the waves.

Atlantis.

His old home. Now covered by water.

It was odd, but the pillars seemed to be higher above the waves than he remembered. The waters that took everything were now slowly giving it all back, inch by inch.

Even if it comes back, in a few centuries with all the tectonic changes that are taking place, it will never be the same. It will be just another ancient site that is revealed to the world. Things don't stay hidden forever; they surface eventually.

He felt a sting in his heart, remembering the life they had here.

The last day of Atlantis.

Ethan recalled the floods. People leaving. All the memories of things left behind.

His wife, Adara, had stayed the longest. She stood right here, when water rushed through the streets and made its way up the roads and walls.

It was all happening during a sunset—a fiery-red sunset.

The next morning all was covered by the water.

Thinking about that time, he knew that, while she waited for the waters to rise and cover the city, she was safe. But it worried him seeing her suffer through another separation from home. It was difficult watching her stand there, hurting, not wanting to let go of this place. However, there was nothing he could have done to take the pain away.

It was a long time ago.

Now he was here again.

He looked along the shoreline.

Brayden was standing in the distance, looking at the water.

Ethan approached him and asked, "What is it?"

"She's not letting me in." Brayden answered and tried stepping into the water, but the surface did not give in. It stiffened whenever Brayden tried placing his foot in it.

Ethan took a step. Water did not stop him. He looked up at Brayden and walked in.

He slowly made his way through the water and swam to the pillars.

A dive down revealed a beautiful scenery. Old buildings of white stone, so beautiful at one point, now covered by coral and plants.

It was so serene, seeing her sit under the surface at the edge of the building, looking down towards the city covered by the crystal clear water. The image was surreal.

Her body was resting firmly on the stone edge. The only indication that she was underwater was her hair flowing softly around her head as the current flowed towards the shore, brushing the hair away from her face.

Seeing Adara sit at the edge of town made him think of a water globe enclosing a beautiful stone city, and a lonely figure inside, watching the forgotten beauty of the place.

He sat down next to her and took her hand.

She squeezed it tight, without looking at him. *It will never be the same, will it?* Her thoughts loud in his head.

Nope. We cannot change the past. We can only change the future.

They looked at each other. It was not clear if they meant the city, or what happened earlier that day. However, they knew that both things were true.

He stood up and gently pulled her up with him. They slowly swam to the surface, admiring the beautiful city that stretched below them.

Adara emerged and lifted herself over the surface. She sat up gracefully on top of the water and as she was lifting herself up, all the water that covered her and her clothes was falling through her, leaving her completely dry.

With her hand gently sweeping the surface, she made it stiff like a sheet of glass.

Ethan sat next to her and looked at the beauty that revealed in front of him. They looked at the wide streets and tall buildings, now with fish swimming everywhere and coral covering everything in sight.

"It's beautiful." He marveled.

"There is beauty even in death," she stated, her face empty, without any expression.

Ethan took her hand and reminded her, "We are survivors. We have been through so much, and we are stronger because of that."

"When will it stop? Planets, continents, cities, different lives. Can we just stop?" knowing that it was merely her wishful thinking, she pleaded, longing and resignation apparent in her voice.

Ethan could feel the pain that ripped her hear apart. His heart was bleeding too. Sitting next to her, he sensed the choice she had made. He heard it loud and clear. Just like before she left the hotel room.

Ethan knew she wanted to be with Kyle; she just did not know how to separate herself from loving two men.

At this moment, all Ethan felt was pain; everything else was silenced. All he wanted was for that paralyzing pain to stop.

"Charlotte told me that she can help us. Let's give it a try," he suggested and looked at Adara.

"I'm assuming Kyle knows everything by now."

He heard her voice breaking a bit. She could not hide the pain.

"Yes," Ethan answered after a short hesitant pause. "He loves you. He is mad at me, not at you." After looking at her sad, motionless face, he added, "Please come back."

Few moments passed. Adara broke the silence.

"We have been running ever since I can remember. It seems that all I know is how to run. But no more. I am done running."

❖

It was already dark when they *shifted back* near the terrace steps leading to Water's Edge.

Nerissa, with joyful smile brightening her face, ran towards Adara and chirped happily as she ran, "I helped Charlotte prepare. Charlotte said I looked like a little witch stirring that pot. That's what she told me. She was joking, you know. I am not a witch, but I would love to meet one... one day." She pulled on Adara's hand. "It's ready. Come, come." Pride and excitement spilled with each word she said.

Adara smiled.

She loved seeing her daughter so excited. Nerissa was always so curious and full of life. *She's just like me when I was a kid.*

By now, they knew there was no way of stopping Nerissa; at anything.

Seeing her daughter's bright-green eyes, full of excitement and vivacity, reminded Adara how glad they all were that Nerissa was good and that she was on their side.

The thought of having her as an enemy brought shivers down Adara's spine.

Nerissa skipped along the lit terrace.

Ethan and Adara followed her inside.

In a softly lit kitchen, Charlotte was standing by the island, sipping on red wine.

Ethan stayed in the terrace entrance and leaned on the door frame.

The room was spacious and simply decorated with the large island in the middle. Nerissa skipped around it joyfully.

It was amazing how she was able to switch between being serious and silly. One moment being philosophical but later being full of joy and laughter, without a care in the world.

Charlotte laughed and caught her by the arm.

She looked at Nerissa and said, "Now back to bed. You have a long journey ahead of you tomorrow morning. Rainer is already asleep."

After few more persuasive arguments, Nerissa agreed that tomorrow's adventure would be exciting too, so she decided to listen to Charlotte and go to bed. They knew she did not need sleep; but *sleeping* enabled her mind to travel. That was the only way they could get her to bed.

Nerissa loved "dreaming" because, in an instant, she could visit any place she wanted.

Adara took Nerissa's hand, and they headed upstairs to the bedroom.

"Will you tuck me in?" Nerissa asked.

"Of course I will," Adara answered and kissed the top of Nerissa's head. *She is getting so tall; I can hardly recognize my little girl.*

"And tell me a story?" Nerissa added.

Adara laughed and nodded. "And tell you a story."

The night was calm and cool. Light breeze softly blew through the white, silk curtains in Nerissa's bedroom.

Gentle breeze dance between the trees...

Adara blinked few times, looked around, and realized she was standing in the doorway to the kitchen. Kyle, Ethan, and Charlotte were standing by the island in the middle, looking at her.

Adara did not remember how she got to the kitchen but realized that her memories had mixed with the memories of people surrounding her.

She smiled. *Time is a thief. But has no dominion over me; not anymore.*

Feeling embarrassed for unknowingly intruding on their memories and thoughts, she looked at them apologetically. After the Dragon's Blood poison opened all the channels in her body, she was in tune with everything around her. Thoughts, memories, sensations—they were all hers for the taking. She had not intended to intrude on them but somehow got lost in her own memories, which connected her to those she came in contact with earlier.

Adara was amazed at how strong her powers had gotten over the last several hours.

She looked at everyone and said, "So I guess Nerissa and Rainer's trip is continuing ahead as planned. I will miss seeing them around this house. I will miss them so."

Charlotte smiled. "Both Rainer and Nerissa are excited to go. The training will be a lot of fun for both of them." Then, seeing Adara's worried face, she added, "They will be well taken care of. Plus, you can visit them whenever you want. For you, they are just a thought away."

Adara glanced at the hallway leading to the bedrooms upstairs. "Yes, I know that. They will be with the best." Then she added, "I wonder how they will change when they return. Time is a thief."

Kyle went around the island and took Adara's hand. He kissed the inside of it ever so softly.

Adara's heart hurt so much. She felt terrible. Looking at him now, the guilt flooded her thoughts.

Kyle just pulled her close and hugged her until he felt her shoulders relaxing under his embrace.

Ethan looked at the island where Charlotte had placed different objects.

Charlotte put away her wine glass, cleared her throat, and declared, "House divided will not stand. Even more, it cannot lead." Then she looked at the three people in front of her. "Bonds created in magic can only be broken by magic. To release the hold, both sides need to let go. Hands that held love will always yearn to hold another; and until they do so, they will feel empty and incomplete." She looked at them. Her blue eyes showing magnitude of what was about to take place.

"Step forth."

Ethan, Adara, and Kyle approached the granite counter where Charlotte placed a wide, golden dish. It was filled with a green-colored liquid, smelling of various herbs. Inside the bowl was a single willow branch.

"Ethan and Adara, keeping it in the water, grab the willow branch with your left hand," Charlotte said, her voice clear and steady.

They did as instructed.

The instance they touched it, the images of tiny vines showed up on their arms that were holding the branch. It appeared that the pictures had been there all along, but surfaced and became visible the moment the skin made contact with the branch. The vines and leafs changed color; first starting faint, and later becoming dark and resembling black ink tattoos.

She continued, "Lift it above the water." When they did, Charlotte took two small glass vials and poured few drops on top the branch.

"Now break it in the middle," she instructed.

They tried, but the branch only bent without breaking.

"You need to want to break it. You need to want to break the bond and end your love," she said in a soft voice.

Adara turned her head and looked at Kyle.

Ethan looked at Adara and then at Kyle.

They bent it again. And suddenly, there was a loud crack when the willow branch snapped in two.

Such a small branch gave out a loud noise, as if the toughest and thickest tree broke in half.

As the sound carried across the room, Adara saw the images leaving her mind. Memories of Ethan kissing her. His embrace becoming a distant memory. His loving smile being covered by the veil.

All the hurt and heartbreak had left her. It turned into nothingness. The only thing that was clear as day was Kyle's face.

"Adara, now let Kyle take the broken end of the part you are holding. Now place it in the water," Charlotte commanded.

Kyle took the broken end of the branch.

The piece of willow bloomed and wrapped around his hand, climbing up on his arm.

After few moments, the images slowly started fading, and eventually disappeared, leaving a faint trace on Kyle's arm.

Shortly after, both Kyle and Adara's tattoos blended with their skin, almost seamlessly.

The warmth spread across Adara's chest. Each breath she took brought peace to her soul. She felt how the love for Kyle was filing the abyss in her heart.

It rushed in to close all the gaps.

It erased all scars on her soul.

It filled her with joy and hope.

She was complete. At last.

Ethan felt a sharp sting within him and dropped the branch. It rolled away from him, bouncing and spinning on the granite floor tiles.

Charlotte declared quietly, "Love hurts. Heartbreak hurts. But now, you are all free. No more ties."

The sorrow ended, Ethan and Adara's love became a distant memory and drifted away.

They were free. No more heartbreak. No regrets. No resentment.

They were free to love.

CHAPTER NINETEEN

The Beginning

THE LOUD NOISE startled Nerissa. She sat up on her bed, got up, and quickly ran to the door.

She was not afraid. But she was curious.

Tiptoeing towards Rainer's room and slowly opening the heavy wooden door, she made sure not to make any noise.

Her brother was sleeping.

Nerissa knew that she heard the noise coming from the hallway, so she did not go into Kayla's room, as it was in an opposite direction to the noise.

She wondered why no one else was in the hallway. Maybe the noise was only in her head.

Getting more curious by the minute, she stepped into the hallway again and went downstairs.

In the corridor leading to the kitchen, her bare foot stepped on something.

A small branch.

She bent down to pick it up, but as she grabbed it, she felt a sharp prick on the inside of her hand. Pointy end of the branch pierced her skin, and blood slowly pooled inside her palm.

Holding the stick, she walked towards the kitchen and saw Ethan standing next to the island, drinking from a wine glass.

He saw her standing in the doorway and put his drink away. "Hi there night owl. What are you doing up? I thought you liked sleeping," he said turning towards where she was standing.

Ethan saw her holding the branch and extended his arm to reach for it. Then he saw Nerissa looking at her palm.

Without taking her eyes away from the blood, Nerissa warned him, "Be careful. It's sharp."

"Only the broken end is sharp." He reached for it, but before she released it, he felt a sting on his finger.

"You can let go," he instructed her but then noticed that her hand was dripping with blood. He quickly reached for a towel to wrap around her hand.

She stood there, in her white nightgown, her dark hair loose around her shoulders and arms after her braid got untied. Her green eyes were fixed on her palm that was pooling with blood.

Mesmerized by the image before her, Nerissa whispered, "I have never seen my own blood. I didn't know I could get a cut."

Still staring at her palm, she said as if in a trance, "...and she will never let you go; her love for you will move the Mountains."

Ethan did not know how to react, and before he could say anything, she blinked few times, looked at him, and said, "Here you go," handing him the branch.

Ethan chuckled and asked, "What did you mean by that."

She did not answer.

Walking towards the sink, he placed the stick inside the golden bowl.

After plunging into the greenish liquid, it dissolved slowly.

As he was washing her blood away with the cold water, he looked at her palm and noticed that there was no sign of the cut anymore.

That did not surprise him.

The three children were nothing like the children born to their kind. They were not fragile. They were not like human children at all.

Ethan tilted his head towards Nerissa. Her hair was messy, and her green eyes were fixed on the golden bowl that was on the counter. At the first glance, she looked so innocent, but when looking at her eyes long enough, it was easy to sense the emanating power and her ageless soul.

There was nothing fragile about her.

Her appearance was only a façade.

Nerissa took a step towards him and hugged his chest. He gently and softly petted her head, surprised at her unexpected gesture.

"Let's get you to bed," he said.

They headed upstairs.

When on the second floor, they stopped by the window in the hallway.

The outside was softly lit by the lamps surrounding the stone terrace. They could see Adara and Kyle siting on one of the stone benches in the garden. They were there, embracing each other and gazing towards the moon that illuminated the lake in the distance.

Nerissa stated, "Now she is ready. She has what she needed."

Caught off guard, he looked at her.

She explained, "She always had love. But now she has the connection to Earth, on a different level. He can balance her and help her see things from a different perspective. He is someone who is on the other side. It's all good now." Nerissa looked at Ethan and slid her small, warm palm into his hand.

For Ethan, it was strange looking at Adara and Kyle sitting there close to each other. Usually it ripped Ethan apart, but not now. He felt no pain. No more resentment, nor anger. No more longing.

He was simply happy for them.

Nerissa's bedroom door was opened from when she left the room after hearing the loud noise that awoke her. Ethan went inside and saw pink and white covers lying partially on the floor.

He picked them up.

After Nerissa got in her bed, he tucked her in carefully.

"Safe travels, you amazing little creature," he said, messing up her hair. "Safe travels, in your sleep, tomorrow, and all days after that," he added getting up.

"We are going there to get ready. I want to get ready. And I will be ready soon. Really soon, you know," she assured him in a sleepy voice. He knew she was not tired. He wondered if she treated it as a game and was behaving like that just for fun—pretending she was like others, as part of her game.

"I'm sure you will," Ethan answered, smiling to himself. It was astonishing how she shifted between being a child and a grown up, almost without any warning.

Nerissa was drifting away but kept talking. "And we will practice fighting, we will read about all kinds of amazing things, and learn to use weapons, and... other things." She was almost asleep.

Ethan quietly left the room and closed the door.

He knew that the other children were sleeping, but he wanted to check on them. He had not seen them for such a long time.

Getting more tired, he quietly peeked into Rainer's room, and then continued towards the youngest of the three.

Walking up to Kayla's room, he stopped and pulled on the handle.

She was sleeping in her big bed, covered with a yellow-flower comforter. A dim night-light illuminated the area near her bed. Her now, strawberry-blond hair was long, and covered her shoulders, wrapping around the stuffed toy she was clinging to.

What a huge difference between Kayla and the other two.

Kayla was curled up into a ball on the same-size bed as Rainer, and Nerissa. She looked so tiny compared to her siblings.

Thinking about the unusual growth of the children, Ethan was reminded about how challenging it must have been to keep the mental veil over Kyle's family— shrouding Rainer and Nerissa's growth. Mind control ability came as a blessing in this situation.

Looking at Kayla's sweet innocent face, Ethan was reminded that the family had been worried about her because, although she was already two years old, she had not spoken a single word. She communicated with them telepathically. They spoke to her, but she answered them using her thoughts.

Tired, dragging his feet, he went back to the kitchen.

He poured himself a glass of wine and chuckled. He remembered how Nerissa told him to drink *their* wine if he wanted to get drunk.

That is what he was drinking now. It had been a long day.

Holding the wine glass, he went towards the front door of the mansion and sat on the steps.

The stone surface felt cold, yet comfortable. It relaxed him, sitting there and looking at the black sky sprinkled with countless tiny stars that twinkled brightly.

Ethan felt free, yet empty.

He missed something but did not know what it was. He recalled what Charlotte had said, *Hands that held love will always yearn to hold another; and until they do so, they will feel empty and incomplete.*

Upstairs, Nerissa was sound asleep, her thoughts traveling far from Water's Edge.

One of her hands was tucked under her neck, and the other stretched to the side. As the moonlight snuck through the uncovered window, it bathed her in the cool light. Nerissa moved slightly, and the shadows on her palm got caught in the moonlight. A faint line on the inside of her palm became visible—in the same place where the willow branch had pierced her skin not long ago.

❖

The next morning Kyle found Nerissa sitting on the sofa looking through the old map book.

"There you are; you little warrior." He smiled at her and rubbed the top of her head, slightly messing up her neatly groomed hair.

Petting her hair down, Nerissa looked at her father and confessed in a serious tone, "The battle is near. I need to hurry. We need everyone to be ready. I need to get ready now."

Kyle sat next to her on the big sofa.

"I know. You'll be ready. Don't worry. You will be well taken care of too," he said and kissed the top of her head.

Her hair was braided in a neat bun on the side, behind her ear. She looked so serious and stern.

Nerissa opened the book and pointed to a spot on the map. "There. That is where we will start. Rainer is already helping with the luggage. He wanted to show everyone how strong he's getting," she added giggling, her stern expression melting away.

Kyle thought about his son. Rainer was as tall as Nerissa, with the same green eyes. But where with Nerissa there was a sparkle of excitement and conviction, with Rainer, there was this strange melancholy, as if he was always thinking about something sad or carried some kind of heavy burden in his heart.

"Your mom and I will wait here for the two of you. You can come back whenever you want; or we can go visit you if you want. Do not rush; take your time," he said trying not to get emotional. To stop himself from losing it altogether, he thought about something else.

"Marcel will travel with you because he is more familiar with those parts of the world. He will keep you all safe," he explained, but he knew that neither Nerissa nor Rainer needed protection.

Nerissa's green eyes were glowing from within when she looked at her father. They both knew that it was their enemies who needed protection from her.

Nerissa stood up, put the book away, and hugged her father. Still holding him tight, she said, "I guess it's goodbye for now. I'll go say bye to mama."

She hesitated for a moment. "You know, when you see me next time, I'll be all grown up." She took a step back and looked down.

Kyle laughed and embraced her. "Then I better give you a huge hug before you're too big for that stuff." He lifted her up and spun her in the air.

Her giggles filled the room.

He slowed down and set her on the floor, where she was still giggling.

Nerissa's brilliant-green eyes beamed with happiness as she smiled joyfully.

Kyle watched her overjoyed expression and whispered, "Please do not ever lose that spark. Remember to leave room in your heart for those happy, silly, good moments. Do not grow up too quickly my love."

They walked through the hallway and, as they approached the door, right before stepping outside, Kyle stopped and said to her, "Nerissa... before you do things your way, please give people a chance to make the right choice by themselves."

He stood there waiting for her response.

She looked up at him and, after a moment of silence, promised, "I will do it for mama. When the time comes, I will give them a chance to switch sides... peacefully."

Relieved, Kyle smiled and gently patted her head. He reached out his hand towards her, and when she extended hers to him, he noticed something.

He asked her, "What is that on your palm?'

"Just a doodle I drew this morning," she answered and looked at her open hand. The line started in the middle of her palm and was twisting towards the fingers.

Embracing her shoulder, Kyle walked with her towards the door.

He stepped outside to help Rainer and Marcel with the luggage.

Nerissa stopped in the doorway, her dark, red tunic pressed against her body as the sudden gust of wind blew by her. She stared at the gravel road and the thick cover of trees in the distance. Another gust blow few strands of her hair across her face. Slowly, she moved them to the side.

She looked into the distance and whispered in a soft, childlike voice, which turned colder as she spoke, "Most of them. I will give most of them a chance. For others, there are no second chances." The last words she spoke were stone-cold and pierced the air like a swift knife. "And some... simply need to be punished; there is no mercy for them."

When she uttered those ice-cold words, her green eyes burned with anger and desire for revenge.

It would have been scary to hear this sweet-looking girl say what she did, but there was no one close enough to hear her.

Epilogue

"Did we do the right thing? Sending her to complete the mission?" the woman wondered.

"She may cause more trouble than we expected. She is too thirsty for life—too eager to experience," the short man said.

"She will do just fine," Margram answered.

"I fear that she is going to be too... driven. Too cold. She will need someone to ground her," the man suggested.

"Rainer is there," the woman said.

"No. That is not enough. She will soon outgrow his influence. She needs to feel love. Just look at her eyes. Can you hear her thoughts?"

"But if not Rainer, then who?"

"She already knows who," Margram declared, looking at Nerissa's eyes.

The woman cautioned, "That will be dangerous. It can quickly turn against everyone."

"No matter. She needs someone. If she has nothing to lose, she will become too dangerous and too unpredictable. We cannot allow that to happen," the man warned.

"But on the other hand, do we dare gamble and see what she's capable of. What will she do to protect something she does not want to lose?" Margram countered.

"We will have to watch her closely from now on."

To Be
Continued...

MERCY

"FROM THE STARS"

SERIES

BOOK TWO

A NOVEL BY C. M. STEPHENS